Broken

THERESA KAY

Broken
Skies

SKYSCAPE

Published by Skyscape, New York

www.apub.com

Amazon, the Amazon logo, and Skyscape are trademarks of Amazon.com, Inc., or its affiliates.

ISBN-13: 9781477820629
ISBN-10: 1477820620

Cover design by Nicole Spence at Cover Shot Creations
Library of Congress Control Number: 2014913351

Printed in the United States of America

To Elizabeth, who loved Jax from the very beginning and even during those times that I didn't. Your support and encouragement have been absolutely invaluable and I couldn't have done it without you.

And to the rest of my darling Rebel Writers: Caylie, Regan, Stormy, Kat, Deanna, Briggs, and Jocelyn. Step one complete! (And I couldn't have done it without you guys either, LOL.)

One

I drop to the floor at the sound of the knock, my breath hissing in through my teeth when I smack an elbow against the table on my way down. What is Emily doing here? She has to know that Jace went out with the hunting party this morning. Nosy sheep girl. I cradle my elbow and scurry across the floor, careful to stay below the level of the windows. I've got my long red hair pulled into a messy braid and I'm wearing my brother's clothes—not exactly acceptable attire around here for a girl and not easy to hide. If she sees me like this it will completely ruin my day.

"Jasmine?" Emily's voice calls from outside. Not after my brother then. She's after me.

I slide along the wall until I reach my bedroom and pull an over-sized dress out of my closet, sliding it over my head and smoothing it down. She calls my name again and I roll my eyes. "Jax," I mutter to myself. "My name is Jax."

My fingers twist my braid into a loose bun and I secure it with two pins from my dresser before I finally answer the door, a smile plastered on my face. "Hello, Emily. What can I do for you?"

Emily startles and takes a step back, but her smile never falters. "Good morning, Jasmine. I was wondering if you'd like—"

"Jax," I say. "And my brother's not here."

Her brown eyes flick down to my crossed arms and she sighs, shaking her head slightly. "I'm not looking for your brother . . . Jax. I was looking for you. I was hoping you'd join us for the sewing circle today. There are quite a few things I'd like to discuss with you."

I barely manage to conceal my snort. Emily flinches. I guess I didn't manage to conceal my expression. "Um . . . I can't. I have to take this . . ." My eyes travel around the room, darting from one item to the next. I grab a small knife sitting on the table. ". . . Knife to Jace. He's out hunting and it's his favorite."

She has to know I'm lying, because I'm sure she's fully aware that I'm not allowed outside the gates without an escort, but she's too nice to call me on it.

"Well, you're welcome anytime," Emily says, still smiling. She brushes a few strands of dark brown hair, escapees from her super-tight bun, behind her ear. "We'd very much like to get to know you."

I smile and nod at her. What am I supposed to say to that? *No, thanks, I'd rather pull my fingernails off than sit around and chat about being Promised while sewing a dress I have no intention of wearing?* They don't need to get to know me. I'm not going to be around long enough to make a life here. "Well, uh, maybe next time?"

"Sounds great," says Emily. Her hand lands on my shoulder before I can move away. She drops it almost the same second it touches me, but I have to close my eyes to keep my breath under control. *In. Out. One. Two.* When I open my eyes again, her face is twisted with concern.

"Jasmine . . . Jax . . . I'm so sorry . . . I"

"No biggie." I force my shoulders to shrug. "Just . . . I'll see you later, okay?"

Her smile returns, weaker now, but still warm. "Sure."

When she turns and walks back down the path, I let out a sigh and rest my back against the door, willing my muscles to relax again. Five minutes later, after ditching the dress, pulling on my boots, and wrapping a large cloak around myself, I'm out the door.

It's only a few blocks to the east gate and I've gotten pretty good at small smiles and jaunty waves, but there's still quite a bit of civilization I have to make it through, and there's always the risk of getting caught. I've been caught before and still avoided punishment. You'd be surprised how well the mentally unstable card plays around here in getting me out of things. Of course, my brother is the best hunter in town and he's also best friends with the son of our "illustrious" leader, so that might have something to do with it, too. Better not to get discovered sneaking out, though—I'd prefer to avoid the scrutiny.

People already look at me funny, no need to add to their opinions of me. They say I'm unsociable, but mostly I just have nothing in common with the girls—sitting around and being obedient, just waiting to be Promised and start popping out kids—and I have even less in common with the boys who grew up under Dane's watchful eye and think I'm less just because I'm female.

No matter what I do, I'll never fit in here. And thank goodness for that. I would never want to be one of those silly sheep girls who inhabit this place. Dresses, buns, silence, and subservience. That's what's expected from the females around here. I have a little wiggle room as I've still got two months until I hit eighteen. I guess I'm supposed to suddenly turn docile and compliant when it's time for me to be Promised, but that's not going to happen. I don't plan to be Promised at all.

I didn't ask to come here, to live within the walls of this stupid town. The largest and relatively the safest human settlement left within hundreds of miles or not, I'd much prefer to be back out at our cabin than here. Jace and I were doing just fine on our own after Dad disappeared four years ago. We hunted, grew food, and traded for anything we couldn't make ourselves. It was perfect, and quiet, and private.

Somewhere along the way Bridgelake's leader, Dane Jacobs, heard about our situation and set about offering his "help." On our third or fourth trading trip, the man ambushed us, smiling like he was approaching a cornered animal he didn't want to spook. An overbearing, broad, brown-haired man, he frowned at my jeans and, after a simple hello to me, talked mostly to Jace. My brother got a kick out of that.

Dane offered us a place to stay and went on and on about how we shouldn't be out there on our own. Admittedly, he almost had us, but then he started going on about how a lady should not be wearing pants and certainly shouldn't be hunting. In Bridgelake, he claimed, they would make a proper obedient woman out of me and find a good husband for me.

Jace snickered when my jaw dropped.

"I don't need a husband," I said through clenched teeth. "We will be going now." I spun on my heel, grabbed Jace's sleeve, and pulled him away from the idiot.

Most of the way home, Jace laughed and muttered about me wearing a dress and how he pitied any man who ended up with me as a wife. He didn't stop until I punched him in the arm, leaving a bruise that didn't fade for two weeks. We didn't go back to trade for almost three months and Dane kept his opinions to himself.

Then, a year ago, a couple of men found their way out to our isolated cabin when I was home alone. When Jace got home a few hours later, the men were dead and I was huddled in the corner, covered in blood.

After that, Jace insisted that we move behind the protective walls of the settlement, and since I wasn't speaking at the time, I didn't argue.

I'm arguing now. Jace doesn't know it yet, but we're leaving soon, very soon. I've put up with the restrictions here because it made Jace feel better after what happened, but the only thing worse than being a sheep is being a broodmare. We will not be sticking around long enough for Dane to marry me off and breed me.

My steps slow as I approach the gate. The folds of fabric disguise my curves and as long as I don't call attention to myself, I can slip past the two gate guards without much effort. It's not like I haven't done it before with no trouble. Put enough swagger in my step and no one pays much attention.

"Where are you going, Jax?" Flint's voice stops me in my tracks. Dammit! It would be just my luck that my brother's best friend is on guard duty this morning. There's no way he won't recognize me.

Flint's gun is still slung across his chest, his arms are crossed rather than making a move to grab me, and the other guard is busy examining a trader's cart a good ten feet away. A decent start, at least. I have a chance at convincing Flint to let me by.

I turn my face and force the corners of my mouth up. There may even be a bit of eyelash fluttering going on. He just rolls his dark-blue eyes at me, obviously not impressed—or maybe I just look like I have something stuck in my eye. Sometimes it would be nice to make use of some feminine wiles. I sigh and drop my shoulders. "Out."

"You're going to have to do better than that. You know I'm not supposed to let you out without an escort."

"Please. I can't breathe in here." I step forward, stare up into his face, and lower my voice. "Do you know Emily wanted me to come to sewing circle this morning? Can you even imagine?"

Flint's mouth rounds up into a smile and he coughs to cover his chuckle. "No, Jax. I can't possibly imagine you doing anything remotely feminine."

I narrow my eyes. I'm no girly girl, but I know an insult when I hear it.

"Relax. I understand," says Flint. "Just make sure you come back with Jace and don't tell anyone I let you by."

The smile on my face now is genuine. Reaching up, I ruffle his blond hair with my fingers and he smiles back at me. "Thanks. I owe you one." I nudge him with my shoulder as I pass.

"Let Jace know I'll meet up with him later, okay?"

"Sure will," I call out over my shoulder.

Success! I wait until I'm out of sight of the gate before stuffing my cloak into my backpack and breaking into a jog.

§

Even though it's mid-September, summer's heat has lingered and by the time I make the short hike out to the lake, wisps of hair stick to my face with sweat. I hadn't really planned on a swim, but the idea of jumping into the cool water sticks in my mind and my feet speed their pace, picking through the underbrush until I reach the gently sloped shoreline.

The lake is isolated and not something I've shared with anyone but my brother, but I still check to make sure no one else is around before I start stripping off my boots, followed quickly by the faded jeans. My underwear and tank top stay in place, but I throw my bra into the air with a whoop. Damn uncomfortable thing. It doesn't fall far from the rest of my clothes.

My arms and feet propel me out to the center of the lake. I hold my breath and sink into the water until my head is covered. With my eyes closed and the water pressing in around me I can shut out the rest of the world and just be. No rules. No expectations. No voices in my head. It is a wonderful feeling.

I stay under until my lungs are screaming for air, popping up at the last possible second and taking a gasping breath. This breath is cleaner and fuller than any I can take behind the walls of Bridge-lake and it leaves me feeling more alive than I've felt in ages. It's been much too long since I've left the house and relaxed under the open sky. I wasn't exaggerating when I told Flint I couldn't breathe in there. I'm not meant to be caged; some part of me just doesn't handle it well.

I turn to float on my back, red tendrils of hair swirling around me. Puffy white clouds dance across the sky and a hawk glides on the breeze. A feeling of contentment settles in my stomach and the edges of my mouth turn up into a soft smile as I study the bird, a near perfect match for the metal pendant that rests against my chest, the one and only thing I have of my mother's. The hawk shifts into a dive and disappears, but I continue looking up and begin picking out shapes in the clouds. A horse. A rabbit. I tilt my head to the side. There's one that I can't quite figure out . . . A hand grabs my ankle and pulls me under the water.

For a moment the darkness under the water is more a tomb than my refuge and my heartbeat picks up, pounding in my ears and sending a jolt of icy terror through my body. But then the hand squeezes my ankle and another comes up to tickle the bottom of my foot and a warm sense of safety washes over me.

Kicking the hands away, I pull my head above the water, sputtering. "Dammit, Jace!"

My brother's head appears, his hazel eyes, the mirror image of my own, sparkling with humor. "I wish I could have seen your face. Was that a scream I heard? Did I scare you?" He laughs and pushes shaggy red hair the same shade as mine out of his face.

I scowl and send a splash of water toward him. "Not funny."

"Aw, come on, Jax," he says, grinning and sending a splash my way. "Even you have to admit that was pretty good. I mean, I swam halfway across the lake underwater. You didn't even know I was there. You should at least be impressed with my stealth skills."

I fight a smile. I rarely let my guard down, so it actually is pretty impressive that he was able to sneak up on me.

I swim closer to him. "I guess your stealth skills are pretty good . . . but not as good as mine!" I kick up in the water until I can grasp his head and push him under. Soon after, his hand finds my leg and I go under, too.

We spend a long time goofing off, dunking and splashing each other, before we exit the lake. I turn my back to Jace, remove my tank top, and wring it out before pulling it back on. He just stands there letting the water drip from his boxers and down his legs. Once we find a patch of grass under a tree to sit on, I squeeze the water out of my hair and braid it until it falls in a damp line down my back. With my bare legs extended in front of me, I lean back against the tree, my shoulder butting against my brother's.

"Make any friends today?" Jace asks.

"No." I narrow my eyes at him. "I can't stand those girls."

"You haven't even given them a chance. I know Emily's been—"

"Emily, huh? She spent an awful lot of time batting her eyelashes at you last time she stopped by. Anything you want to tell me about?"

Redness in his cheeks gives away his feelings more than words ever could. "No," Jace says, frowning. "I'd just like to see you branch out, socialize . . . get better . . ." He glances at me and winces, his next words coming out in a rush. "It's gotta be a lot more fun than sitting around the house and hiding from everyone. No offense, sis."

I snort. "A lot more fun for you, maybe." I settle my back against the tree. "Every time they try to pull me into the fold, I'm worried one of those sheep girls is going to ambush me and force me into a dress so I can be Promised to the first guy willing to take me."

"Well, it might improve your temper."

I punch him in the arm.

Jace leans against the tree next to me. "There's nothing wrong with being sociable, Jax. It can't be just us forever."

"I'm happy with just us." I cross my arms over my chest. "Plus, it's not about me being *sociable*. It's about conforming and being some perfect little obedient robot. Oh, and Dane's desire to marry me off. The only way I'll ever be Promised is if they lobotomize me. I am not one of those girls."

"Lobotomize?" Jace raises his eyebrows. "You've got to be reasonable here. I'm sure one of the guys would be more than happy to take you on, bad attitude and all. I mean, look at me, I'm gorgeous and you're my slightly less attractive twin." He grins when I nudge him with my shoulder. "What about Flint? He's nice enough."

"Oh yes, I'm sure Dane would be willing to part with his precious son." I roll my eyes. "Besides, it's not going to happen."

"It's not up to him." He won't meet my eyes. "Flint is my friend and he makes his own choices. He likes you. He'd take good care of you. It wouldn't be that awful, right?"

It's my turn to blush. "Whatever. I don't want to talk about it anymore." Tomorrow. That's when I'll tell him about my plan. We can't stay in Bridgelake much longer.

I close my eyes and let the sun warm my skin, enjoying the quiet companionship. Jace's hand finds mine and I drift off to sleep.

TWO

The distant screech of a hawk and a tremble in the ground startle me awake. The sun is much lower in the sky and I must have slept for a few hours. I blink a few times to clear my eyes and stretch my arms over my head. Jace is still fast asleep beside me, softly snoring. I poke him with my finger, but he only hunches his shoulders and slumps farther down. That boy can sleep through almost anything.

My mouth drops open and my breath catches in my throat when a silver ship comes into view over the crest of the trees. Obviously E'rikon, but what the hell are they doing way out here? For that matter, what are they doing outside of their city? I don't know much about the aliens, but I do know they don't belong out here. I scramble for my jeans and pull them on, slam my feet into my boots, and run into the woods the ship has just passed over.

I'm running so fast I almost run right into the meadow where the ship has landed. I stumble over my feet, stopping myself, and shimmy up a tree. I should turn around, wake Jace and get out of there, but ever since the aliens showed up, I've always wanted to see one up close.

There are a lot of rumors flying around about them—most probably untrue—but everyone agrees that they look remarkably like us and that they aren't looking for a fight, even though a few groups tried to engage them when they first showed up about ten years ago. They pretty much ignore us, actually. Thank goodness, because although there don't appear to be that many aliens, there aren't many of us left, either.

The war was bad enough, with fighting on every continent, but it was the biological weapons that did it. Each country had vaccines and cures for their own, but no one ever stopped to think about what would happen if the bugs mutated, combined, or whatever it was that happened to create something that killed over 90 percent of the world's population.

It's been thirty years since the Collapse and I'm almost glad that I'm too young to know what it was like before. Sounds to me like people were stupid and selfish. Not much different than now, but on a much larger scale.

Of course, now has its own dangers. Like breeders, traveling bands of men who will pay a good price for a woman—or girl—of childbearing years. For some reason the plague was especially virulent in females and we're a valuable commodity now, along with any children we're able to bear. That's the one good thing about Dane— he sends his soldiers out to keep breeders out of this area. Though, he's got his own breeding program with the whole Promising thing, so I guess he's just the lesser of two evils.

Hopefully, these particular aliens aren't here to become a third evil.

My stomach churns as three male aliens exit the ship. They do look remarkably humanlike in their proportions and their stature. All three are older, maybe around fifty if they were human, with various shades of wildly colored hair, at least by human standards. My hair is pretty bright, too, but nothing like this.

One has close-cut silver hair with a slight gold tinge. And I'm not talking about a blond gone gray. His hair has the metallic shine of metal. The other two have slightly more normal-looking hair, one with a bluish tint to his brown locks and the other with a more yellow hue. If it weren't for the hair and the fact that I'd seen them disembark from an E'rikon ship, I could have easily mistaken them for human.

Their clothes, form-fitting pants and some kind of fancy high-collared jacket covered in gold markings, are a boring gray. Knee-high boots in the same shade cover their feet and they all wear a silver cuff on their right wrists. A uniform of some sort?

I'm about to climb down, fade into the trees, and head back, my curiosity sated, when a fourth alien leaps down from the ship. He's young, maybe close to my age, with angular lines making up his clean-shaven face. He's wearing darker clothing than the others and his jacket is plain. The pressed charcoal fabric hugs his frame, broad in the shoulders and tapering at the waist. He stands straight with his shoulders back, as if at attention, and scans the forest around him. The only thing even slightly mussed about him is his hair. It stands up in short curled tufts scattered over his head and framing his face, the shine of gold standing out among the bright green tips. He is beautiful.

The tallest alien, the one with the gold-and-silver hair, pushes the green-haired youth forward. I can't make out their words, but the steady set of green hair's shoulders isn't enough to hide his shaking hands. His steps are steady and the other three follow behind him, almost as if they're stalking prey. The boy stops and the tall one pushes him again, but this time the boy doesn't move forward. Instead he turns and faces the group behind him.

They appear to be arguing, one of them gesturing toward the ship and then throwing his hands up in the air. I lean out over the branch, hoping to hear their conversation, and the branch I'm sitting on cracks. I scramble back toward the trunk and push my face into the rough bark, closing my eyes. *They didn't hear. They didn't hear.* I crack my eyes open and the three aliens have stilled and are looking into the woods—in my direction.

I gulp down the acid in my throat. The only weapon I have is a small knife in my boot. I could throw it, but that would only take out one . . . maybe. As far as I know, they aren't very susceptible to human weapons. Any information I have at all is, at best, third- or fourth-hand, and that's all from observation, not interaction. But they've never attacked us, never really had anything to do with us. These aliens aren't a threat to me, right? I should climb down, calmly approach them, and let them know I'm not a threat, either. But something keeps me in that tree, gripping the trunk with white knuckles.

A whistle comes from the woods to the right of me and the sound of someone crashing through the underbrush reaches my ears. I see a form approaching the meadow. It's Jace. I open my mouth to call out to him, to warn him, but he looks directly at me and shakes his head, putting one finger over his mouth. He knows I'm there and he's trying to draw their attention. Of the two of us, Jace is the more diplomatic one and in a normal interaction he could probably talk his way out of almost anything. But something about these three . . . I don't know.

Wait a second. Three? Where did the green-haired alien boy go? My eyes dart around the clearing, but he's nowhere. Maybe he ran off while the others were distracted.

The aliens move closer to the edge of the meadow where Jace is about to appear. They are silent, the one gesturing before stopping the others with a raised hand when they move forward. As if they're waiting in ambush. Why would they be doing that?

Jace does an exaggerated trip into the meadow, catching himself and then straightening to greet the aliens. "Hello," he says.

The alien that stopped the others from moving into the woods steps forward. "Hello, human," he says. "What are you doing in these woods?"

"Hunting," says Jace, holding up a rabbit. "Gotta eat something."

The alien looks at the rabbit with distaste, much the same look he gives my brother. "Are there any other humans in the area?"

"No," says Jace. He's too busy making eye contact with the speaking alien to notice the glance that passes between the other two.

"Wonderful," says the alien. He smiles, but it doesn't reach his eyes. Raising a hand, he motions the others closer. They fan out on either side of the third, forming a semicircle with Jace in the center.

Jace narrows his eyes. "What's going on here, *alien*?"

The alien says nothing, but the smile drops from his face as Jace takes a step backward. "Stay."

"I'm not a dog," says Jace.

The alien ignores his comment. "Do you have any weapons?"

Jace turns his head, looking at the other two aliens, and takes another step backward. "Yeah," he says. "I've got this!" Jace swings the rabbit forward by its ears, sending it straight into the alien's face, and takes off into the woods before the other two have time to grab him. I let out the breath I didn't even know I had been holding. Jace knows these woods almost better than I do. The aliens don't stand a chance of catching him.

After a moment of hesitation, the three aliens take off into the woods—a lot quicker than I expected them to. Jace led them off so I could get away, so why am I still sitting here staring into the clearing? I shake my head and climb out of the tree. My knees bend at the impact of jumping the last few feet, and when I straighten up again, the younger alien is standing in front of me. Why did he sneak off and why isn't he with his buddies?

This close I can see his eyes more clearly. Black pupils ringed with a sliver of gold and blending into an emerald green on the outer edges, much like his hair. I've never seen anything like it. Now I could never mistake those eyes for human.

It takes a moment before I realize I'm gaping at him and move to back away. My foot hits a rock and I stumble, barely catching myself before I fall. I wince, but he hasn't made a move to pursue me, so I dash farther into the woods. In only three steps, I crash against a hard chest and bounce backward, this time landing on my butt on a cushion of pine needles.

Looking up, I'm face-to-face with the alien. *Damn. He moves fast.* I don't have time to think anything else before he springs forward and grabs my wrist, pulling me to my feet. He takes a step away once I am standing and glares at me.

"Where are you going?" he asks.

I say the first thing that comes to my mind. "Away from you." He almost laughs. I don't know why he would find that so funny. It's the truth. I narrow my eyes and return his glare, putting my hands on my hips. "What do you think you're doing in my meadow?"

"Your meadow?" He raises an eyebrow.

"Yes. Now take your friends and leave." The less he says, the more my hands sweat. I hope he can't tell how nervous I actually am.

This time he chuckles. He mutters the word *friends* under his breath and shakes his head to himself. "They are no friends of mine, little girl."

Any fear I felt is replaced by a fast-striking anger. "I'm not a little girl." I move to turn around and walk away, but he grabs my arm again and I freeze in place. His fingers dig into my bicep and ice-cold fear seems to spring from his grip, slowly working its way through my body. I have to remember to breathe. *In. Out. In. Out.*

The blood leaves my face and my head spins. My eyes involuntarily widen and as I work on controlling my breath and swallowing the lump climbing up my throat, the alien cocks his head to the side with a curious look on his face. Then his eyes widen and in another second, I hear it, too. There's someone coming this way—a group of someones, by the sound of it. The alien puts one finger to his lips, moves his hand to my shoulder, and shoves me down to the ground.

We have just enough time to slide down behind a bush before the three older aliens crash through the brush only feet from our location. The last one is dragging a struggling Jace by one arm, the other arm hanging limp at my brother's side. Jace stumbles, crashing into a tree with his shoulder, and cries out in pain. I try to catch his eye to let him know I'm there, but he just trips along behind the alien, not even pausing to look around.

When they reach the clearing, the lead alien faces Jace and shoves him hard. Jace staggers back a step and then falls to his knees.

"Now let's try this again, human," he says, leering down at my brother. "Do you think you can cooperate this time?"

"I don't have much of a choice, now do I?"

The alien backhands Jace across the side of his face. "I don't tolerate disrespect from vermin."

Jace's head rocks to the side and it's as if someone has taken all the air from my lungs. I inch toward the clearing.

The alien tilts his head and narrows his eyes down at Jace. "What . . . ?"

Jace doesn't get up, but the alien pulls him to his feet by his shirt and tosses him to the other two aliens. "It seems we may have already found what we are looking for. Take him."

"No!" I can't stop it. The shout comes echoing out of my mouth and into the clearing. The aliens tense, instantly on alert.

Jace looks almost directly at me. "Jax, run!"

I scramble backward on my hands, then spring to my feet and take off into the woods with tears running down my face. I don't hear the aliens pursuing me, not that I would. After my experience with the younger alien, I know that if they want to catch me, they will. I keep running anyway. The world slows down around me and my feet drag. My brain barely registers the surge of—something—behind me before I'm knocked forward into the dirt and blackness overtakes my vision.

Three

My eyelids stick to each other, but I pry them open anyway. Two green orbs float over my head. "Pretty," I murmur before my eyes shoot open and I scramble backward, away from the alien boy standing over me.

I back up until the top of my head connects with a tree—ouch—and I use the tree trunk to pull myself up. On my way up, I reach into my boot and pull my knife from its sheath, waving it in front of me while the forest keeps spinning around me. "Get away from me!" He holds his hands up in a position that I guess is supposed to put me at ease. It doesn't work. If anything, his movement causes my heart rate to increase and my breaths to come faster. "Stop it."

"I am not doing anything," he snaps. "Put the knife down. I just saved your life, you know." He takes a step forward. Wrong move.

I fly at him, swinging my knife in an upward arc, aiming for his chest, his stomach, anything. He moves away quickly enough to avoid what should have been a fatal strike, but when he puts his left arm up to block my blade, it cuts through his forearm and he winces in pain. I'm a flurry of movement, striking here and there, just hoping to land one hit. The alien stops trying to block my swipes and starts trying to fight me instead. Unarmed, he's really no match for me.

Then again, maybe he is. He manages to grab my wrist during one of my more reckless movements and he twists it until I drop the knife. He pulls me toward him until my chest is against his and holds me tightly against him. There are words coming out of his mouth, but they just don't register.

Must get away. I can't move. I must move. I beat at his chest with my fists, screaming whimpers flowing out of my mouth. "Stop it. Stop it. Stop it."

Something must get through to him, because he releases me. The knife sits near my feet and I go for it, but I end up being held from behind with his arms wrapped around my chest. My head flies back and I hear a satisfying crunch and his arms drop. I pick up the knife again, but my hand is shaking too hard to use it. *Fingers, get a grip!* A giggle works its way past the terror in my throat. The shakes travel up my arms and down to my legs and I collapse onto the ground, laughing.

"Blazes, you must have hit your head harder than I thought," says Alien Boy, one hand over his nose. "Calm down. I am not going to hurt you." He reaches one hand forward—to put it on my shoulder? To put it around my neck? I jerk backward, moving out of his reach.

"Don't touch me!"

He drops his hand and backs away. I move backward too until my spine bumps against a tree trunk. I close my eyes and concentrate on slowing my breathing. *In. Out. In. Out.*

When I open my eyes again, his gaze meets mine. The slim ring of gold around his pupils is such a vivid contrast to the brilliant green that I almost want to fall into them. Is that some alien thing? Some power in his eyes? I shift my gaze away.

He has removed his jacket and wrapped it around his arm, revealing a tight gray short-sleeved shirt. The fabric shimmers in the light and I start to reach out to touch it, but quickly pull my hand away before he notices. I can't, however, draw my eyes away from the lean muscles of his chest showcased by the undershirt. He catches me looking and I fight the blush trying to form on my cheeks.

Maybe his eyes aren't the problem here. I raise my eyes to meet his. He stares steadily back at me, not lowering his gaze and not flinching away. A quiet anger simmers in those green-gold depths, and I can tell he's trying to hide the pain he's in.

He speaks first. "Can we move past this now?" His voice drops. "I am not dead yet and I would like to stay that way."

"I didn't assume you would be," I say. "*I* wasn't trying to kill *you*."

He laughs and shakes his head.

The dismissal grates on me. "What I meant was you were the one trying to kill me. I only defended myself. Nice to know you guys are able to be injured after all. Thanks for the intel."

The muscles in his jaw clench. "Defending yourself from what? I was only trying to talk to you." His glare grows colder. "Of course, I should have known better than to reason with a human. Savages."

I scoff, standing up and moving toward him. "If we're such savages, then what the hell did your friends take my brother for?" The alien's eyes widen, but he quickly hides his surprise, setting his face back into the stoic glare from before. "What? You don't have an answer to that?" My voice rises, worry for Jace beginning to strangle my words. "Just came on down to harass the humans? Is that it? Couldn't you leave well enough alone?"

"It was not my intention to harass you." The calmly delivered words meant to placate me do the opposite and I can feel heat building in my face. These aliens—*this* alien—just thinks he can come down here and do whatever he wants? This is my world; they don't belong here and they certainly have no right to my brother.

"Intention or not, you don't belong here. This is my forest, my meadow, my lake, my home," I yell. "You can't just come here and take . . . Why here?" My voice breaks on the last two words and the choking burn of tears fills my throat, making me even angrier. Worry, adrenaline, and anger collide, bringing me to a seat on the ground. "What the hell am I supposed to do now, Alien Boy?"

"Lir," he says, shifting his eyes from me to his hands.

"Leer? I'm supposed to ogle you?"

His breath huffs out in something like a laugh. "No, that is my name. Lir."

"Oh." The single syllable pops my anger like a balloon. He might not be human, but he is humanlike, and besides asking me questions and generally being rude, he really hasn't taken any action to harm me. And I attacked him. "Sorry," I mumble.

He raises an eyebrow. "What exactly are you apologizing for? Attacking me or calling me names?" The situation is so ridiculous, I can't help but laugh. It's more of a nervous laughter, but it seems to release the tension and even Lir chuckles.

"My name's Jax. And I'm sorry for attacking you . . . and calling you names, I guess." My shoulders relax and I take a deep breath. "Why are you even here?" I ask, hoping he's willing to help me. "I mean, why did you even get off the ship?"

"We landed for repairs." Lir shakes his head when I open my mouth to ask what was wrong. I guess that's more information than he's willing to give.

"Why—"

"That is all you need to know," Lir shoots back.

My faces heats and I look down at my hands. My next words are quieter. "Why did they take my brother?"

"I do not know." He sounds truthful, but I jerk my head up to look at him. There's nothing but openness in his face. I don't think he's lying.

"Are they going to come back for you"—I look into his eyes, biting my lower lip—"and bring Jace back?"

"I do not believe so."

I look away, clenching my hands in my lap. "I have to get him back. I'm not just going to sit here and . . . I'm going to get him back." I stand up before Lir can respond.

He thinks for a moment, watching me. "Look, I understand that you want him back. But have you got this idea in your head that you can just walk up to the city and demand his return? It does not work that way. As a rule, we do not like humans and they are not allowed into our city."

I think for a moment. "But they'll let you in, right?" I lean closer. "I'll get you to the city if you get me inside it."

Lir gapes at me. "You cannot be serious. Why would I need you?"

I almost laugh at his arrogance. "How long have I been out?" When he doesn't answer, I look up and study the angle of the sun. "Around an hour?" Lir nods. "If you thought you could have handled it, you would have just left me here. Why is it that you stuck around?"

His chest rises and falls while he studies my face. What is he looking for? His eyes dart away when he finally answers. "The pulse knocked out my *kitu*."

"Pulse? *Kitu*?"

"The energy force that knocked you over. It is a weapon. The *kitu* . . ." Lir holds up his arm and points to the cuff on his wrist. "It is . . . important."

"So, without your fancy bracelet you're pretty helpless," I say. "You have no supplies. You don't know where you are and you're in human territory. I don't know what they tell you in that city of yours, but humans don't much like you guys, either. Without me you'll be lost in the wilderness with no supplies and no weapons. If you manage to escape the predators and avoid starving to death or dying of thirst and stumble into someone else that could help you . . . they'd more than likely kill you. I'll keep you alive."

"You are human. What guarantee do I have that you will keep your word?"

I roll my eyes. "I want my brother back. I don't care about anything else. Once you've gotten me into the city, you can just be on your way, or whatever."

Lir tilts his head to one side and furrows his brow. "You do not expect me to assist you in getting your brother? Only in getting into the city?"

"Right." I smile. "Once I'm in, I can take care of myself."

Lir doesn't look very sure. He simply shrugs. "Fine, then. We have an agreement." He lowers his chin in a nod and then gestures at the wound on his arm. "I need to do something about this. How far is your residence?"

"Not far. Follow me."

§

We don't speak as we walk; I prefer to keep my terror-filled thoughts of Jace's absence to myself and Lir because . . . because he's an alien, I guess. They don't seem big on small talk. My mind is lost in the latest horrible scenario of Jace's fate that it has come up with when Lir finally speaks.

"Jax, does your residence have security of some sort?"

"Yeah." I slow my steps and turn to face him, walking backward. "We don't have any sort of fancy force field thingy to keep aliens out, though, so no worries."

"Thingy? Tech that is more advanced than anything you humans came up with or probably even could come up with and you call it a thingy?" He shakes his head with his eyes upward and smiles. "That is not why I was asking."

"And . . ."

With an amused sparkle in his eye, he looks at me and smirks. "Are all humans this petulant or just you?"

I narrow my eyes. "Are all aliens this arrogant or just you?" Lir laughs. I don't. "No, really, are they? Because your whole prim and proper 'humans are vermin' attitude is beginning to get on my nerves."

"Look, we got off to a bad start—again." He holds his hands up by his chest in surrender. "I only asked about the security because I am not going to fit in, and that might make it difficult for me to gain entrance."

He's right. Doesn't mean I have to admit it, though. "I'll get you by the guards," I say. I swing my pack off my shoulder and pull out my cloak. "Here. Put this on. Make sure you cover your hair."

Lir catches the cloak before it hits him in the head. Okay, so maybe I was aiming a bit high. I don't have to be nice to him just because I'm stuck with him. Shaking it out, he wraps it around his shoulders and pulls the hood up. "Better?"

The hood shades his face, and with his oddly colored hair covered, Lir could almost be just another human. My eyes linger over his face, the brightness of his eyes standing out even under the hood. Those might be an issue, but as long as he keeps his head down and no one looks too closely, we shouldn't have any problems. Flint did tell me to be sure I came back with an escort; this is just not the one anyone will expect.

Anyway, I'm not planning on hanging around Bridgelake long enough for anyone to take notice of my guest. Or is he my prisoner?

I lean forward and grab one corner of the cloak, pulling it closed in front of his chest. "Keep your head down and don't talk," I say. With a jerk, I pull my hand away, suddenly aware that I'd let it linger too long on his chest. *What the hell is wrong with me?*

Lir falls in behind me. He's at least a few inches taller than Jace, but he slumps his shoulders and hunches down. Maybe I can pull this off. I stride ahead and walk through the gate, nodding at the guards. The one on my right, Steven, squints his eyes a bit and purses his lips. He knows I'm not supposed to be out there, but he's not going to say anything, either.

My breath flows out of my mouth in a slow stream once we're past the gate. I hadn't even realized I'd been holding it. It's just a little farther to the house. We're going to make it.

Then again, maybe not. Flint's voice calls out behind us, "Hey, guys, wait up." He has the worst timing today.

"Just keep walking, straight ahead, the house on the left with blue curtains," I say under my breath. Lir's steps speed up at my whispered instructions. I wait until he's a few feet ahead of me before turning back to Flint.

"Hey, Flint." I smile, going for the innocent look. "Jace had a bad day today, not feeling well or something, so he's headed in to lie down."

Flint's brow furrows and his eyes follow Lir's retreating form. "He was just fine earlier. We were supposed to . . . meet up to go over some stuff."

I shrug. "Maybe tomorrow? I'll let him know you were looking for him."

"Yeah, sure," Flint says. His gaze narrows and lands on my face. "Is something wrong?"

"No." I shake my head. "Nothing at all. Just have to get home. We'll catch up with you later, or tomorrow, or something. Sound good?"

Flint nods slowly, his eyes not leaving mine. "You know you can come to me if something is wrong, right?"

I'm smiling so big my jaw is cramping. "Of course I know that." I spin on my heel and practically run to my door, calling out a strangled good-bye to Flint over my shoulder.

Lir's waiting on the small porch when I reach the house. He starts to speak, but I wave him off and open the door.

Following me silently into the cabin, Lir settles into a chair and watches me pull down a first-aid kit and wet a clean towel. I rustle through the cabinets for some food, loading up my arms with a loaf of bread and some cheese. Everything goes to the table with me and I push the medical supplies and some food across to Lir. His eyes follow each movement.

"What?" I ask.

"Uh, nothing," says Lir, "I was just . . . Thank you. For the food. And the help."

"I couldn't very well leave you lying on the ground."

"Well, you could have—"

"And never get my brother back? Nope. It was the only choice I had. Don't think I'm doing any of this for you." My eyes narrow as he picks at his food. "I expect you to pull your weight, so don't think you can just sit back and let me serve you all the time."

One eyebrow quirks up. "Is that what this was?" Lir motions to the food and first-aid kit on the table. "You serving me?"

I roll my eyes and stuff another chunk of bread in my mouth. He laughs. He actually laughs at me, full-out, mouth open, eyes twinkling. I squash the answering smile trying to creep across my face and force myself to look away. It's no good getting too friendly. He is the enemy, after all.

A drop of green liquid traces its way down Lir's forearm from underneath his makeshift bandage and drips to the table. Blood? I think I'd heard somewhere that the aliens bled green. The amount of information we actually have on Earth's—invaders? Visitors? Settlers?—is pretty lacking, but I guess that little tidbit must have been correct.

"You're bleeding on the table."

Lir's shoulders jerk. "Oh, sorry." He pulls the first-aid kit closer. "I suppose I should go ahead and take care of this then." He carefully unwinds his jacket from the wound, a hiss escaping his mouth when the cut is fully revealed.

The slice is a good eight inches long, nearly from wrist to elbow. It's still bleeding sluggishly, too. Green blood. Interesting. Despite their near-human appearance, how many other oddities do these creatures have that set them apart from us?

"It's a clean cut," I say. Lir's head shoots up at my words and he sends me a dirty look. "You might need to sew it up, though."

The eyebrow goes up again. Damn eyebrow. "You are a helpful one, aren't you?" He smirks and scoots his chair closer to mine, pulling the white box along the table until he's next to me. "I am left-handed and it is not exactly in a convenient spot. Not to mention, you are the one who caused it. I think *you* might need to sew it up."

"Me?" The word comes out in a croak.

"Well, I cannot exactly wander around leaking blood, now can I?" He tilts his head to the side. "Not if you want my help, anyway."

Closing my eyes, I take a deep breath and will my hands to be steady. I can do this. "Okay," I say quietly.

Lir leans closer and sets his arm down across the table in front of me. It's just an arm, nothing special. Warm skin with a dusting of pale gold hair. Nothing scary. It's going to sit there and I'm going to sew it up. I've sewn up wounds for Jace before. No big deal.

Except I've never been as . . . aware . . . of Jace as I am of Lir. Jace is Jace, my brother, no one who could hurt me, but Lir is different. An unknown. He's been pleasant enough, but that could change in an instant. I slide the med kit across the table and take out some gauze, suture thread, and the small curved needle.

Lir shifts when my fingers brush against his arm and I flinch, jerking my hand back.

"I'm not going to bite, you know," he says.

He's facing away from me—*Is he queasy?*—so he must not have seen my expression. His head turns and I bring my eyes back down to his arm. No good to have him thinking I'm scared.

I settle my left hand on his wrist and use my right to wipe at the cut with disinfectant-soaked gauze. He inhales sharply and stiffens, and I almost snatch my hand away again, but he relaxes once I've finished cleaning his wound and so do I. Well, mostly. My breathing is pretty steady, at least. This is a little harder than I thought it would be.

I fumble when I go to grab the needle. It slips from my fingers and slides off the table. Before it can hit the floor, Lir's hand darts out to catch it and he holds it out to me, his fingertips brushing against my palm when I take it from him. A chill passes over me in a mist of unease, more from the intense expression on his face as he studies me than the touch. He tilts his head to the side and I quickly look away, concentrating instead on trying to get my shaky hands to thread the needle.

After my fourth or maybe fifth attempt, Lir shakes his head. "One would think you humans would be a little more advanced than a needle and thread."

There's just enough derision in his tone for my rising temper to push out my nervousness. "We are. I mean, I could parade you down to the med center. They've got stuff there that will fix you right up. I don't know how keen they'd be on letting you out, though." He doesn't respond so I continue, "I'm horribly sorry that you have to be stuck with these *primitive* medical techniques. Would you rather I leave it be?"

He holds his arm out and looks away. "Just get on with it." His jaw tenses as he clenches his teeth and waits for me to start stitching.

§

I shoot to my feet as soon as the last stitch is in place. I've managed to hold my hands steady this long and now the only thing I want is to get out of this room and take a few real breaths.

"I think you're capable of wrapping it up. I'm going to find you something to wear. Since you can't wear that." I motion to the now disheveled uniform. "Dead giveaway."

Striding across the kitchen, I go into Jace's room and shut the door behind me. It takes a moment before I feel comfortable enough to continue with my task. If I'm this thrown by sitting next to the alien for a few minutes, how am I ever going to survive traveling with him? It doesn't matter. I have to make it work.

I open Jace's dresser and pick through the clothes, searching for something that will fit Alien Boy. My heart lurches just a bit as I shuffle through the haphazard pile of shirts. Jace was always the messy one. *Is.* I mean, Jace *is* the messy one. I pull out a green T-shirt and drop it on the bed, then I find a pair of faded jeans with a hole in the knee—Jace won't miss those—and put them on the bed with the shirt.

I manage not to jump out of my skin when Lir just walks into the room. Don't aliens know how to knock?

"Change," I say, sending him a dirty look, and then stride back through the doorway.

Flopping into the chair in the den, I begin making a mental list of supplies we'll need for the trip. As I'm tallying the supplies

I have on hand and what we may need to trade for, a loud thump draws my eye to Jace's doorway, where Lir is standing with his back to me—shirtless.

My hand shoots up to cover the sound of my gasp. I'd heard of the green blood, but I'd never heard of anything like this. Golden scales with green tips extend from the hairline on the back of his neck in a line along his spine and flare out over his hips, disappearing into the top of the dark gray uniform pants. The line of scales, the trail down his back only a few inches wide, is brilliantly colored, almost like jewels. I've never seen anything like it and I want to know what they feel like. Are they soft, like a snake's sun-warmed skin, or hard and jagged like the colored rocks they resemble?

I'm up and almost halfway across the room before I realize what I'm doing and stop in my tracks. Mentally cursing myself, I step back, jostling the table behind me when my hip hits it. Lir looks back at me over his shoulder and I can feel flames licking at my cheeks.

He raises his eyebrow and simply stares at me while I stammer out something about needing to get to the kitchen. "You know, for supplies," I say. "Food. To pack . . ."

I can almost see the truth hit him as he takes in my red face and almost incoherent phrases. He begins to smile. He knows I was watching him and I'm mortified. "I've just never . . . I didn't know . . . the scales . . ." He only looks at me expectantly and my horrible mouth won't shut up. "They're beautiful." If my face could get any redder, it just did.

"I think this is the first time I have seen you speechless," Lir says with laughing eyes. "Had I only known, I would have removed my shirt sooner."

His teasing tone is lost on me as my stomach drops and ice-cold terror begins to seep up from my toes with every beat of my now pounding heart. I'm alone in the cabin with a half-naked man.

Someone I don't know. Without Jace. Something must show on my face, because Lir's smile falters and another expression crosses his face. Concern? I scramble backward two steps before whirling around and heading out the front door.

I can't run away like every one of my instincts is screaming at me to do. I can't even really afford to be out here on the porch. What if someone sees? Then they'll ask questions and . . . *Breathe.* I sit down on the steps and put my head between my knees. Deep breaths. In and out. In and out.

That's where Lir finds me a few minutes later, my eyes closed, pulling deep noisy breaths in through my nose.

"Jax . . ." At his voice I startle and look up. He inches toward me with his hand out, but must change his mind about touching me when he drops it to his side. "Are you all right?"

"Peachy." I hop to my feet. "Gotta go pack. I'd really like to get going as soon as possible, and we're wasting time. You need to get back in the house before someone sees you. So do I, so come on." I spin around and head back toward the door.

He stops my retreat by grabbing my arm, but releases it just as quickly when my whole body tenses. He backs up with his hands raised. "Fine. You go pack." I can feel his eyes on me when he follows me back into the cabin and I wonder if he's still looking at me with that searching expression.

Four

Lir's eyes track the circular pattern of my pacing from his spot on the couch. Kitchen. Den. Hallway. Kitchen. Den. Hallway. This house has never felt so small. Adding the two bedrooms to my rotation would make it bigger, but the buzzing agitation in my head will only get worse if I go back into Jace's room. Because he's not there and he's not going to be there until I go get him . . . until I go into the woods by myself with an alien and get to the city . . . where there will be more aliens, probably lots of them . . . Are they all as attractive as Lir?

Crap. There is something seriously wrong with me. And he's smiling like he finds this amusing.

This isn't going to work. But this has to work. I'm going to go off alone with this boy who is not my brother and I'm going to deal with it. Who cares if my fingers still itch to find out what the scales feel like? Who cares that he keeps looking at me like he's not quite sure what to make of me . . . and I don't even mind his eyes on me? What else can I possibly do? If I can't get a handle on myself . . . this isn't going to work. Gah. Even my thoughts are circular now.

Priorities would be . . . breathing, *calming down*, and . . . "Stop looking at me!"

He jolts and averts his eyes. "Sorry?"

Now that I'm no longer under his gaze, the creeping freeze of anxiety slows and then stops. A few more circuits and I'm almost back to normal—well, normal for me, anyway.

Packing for this trip might be an issue. I can pull together some clothes and a couple bedrolls, but the pantry is rather empty—we were supposed to go to the market today. Although we get plenty of fresh meat, with both Jace and me hunting, it's not the most portable stuff. Plus, Jace's haul from today was left lying on the ground in the clearing.

Even though we'll be in the woods and I'll probably be able to hunt and gather plants, it might not be enough to feed both of us. Lir seems pretty helpless . . . or does he just want me to think that?

I narrow my eyes and study him. "Are you going to be useful or are you just going to sit there?"

"What would you like me to do?" He swings his arms out to the side with his palms up. "I am happy to assist you."

I shake my head. "No, I didn't mean right now. I meant when we're out there. Do you hunt? Do you know plants? How far can you hike in a day? How strong are you? Are there any . . . differences about you I should know about?"

"Why do you need to know?" he asks, suspicion lacing his words.

Maybe not helpless, but he sure is difficult. He was pretty quick back there in the clearing and strong enough to subdue me. I'll just assume he can hold his own physically and I'll have to teach him some of the other stuff.

"Never mind." I roll my eyes and spin around, retreating to my room.

After quickly throwing together two packs, I make a list of things I need to run to the market to trade for. By the time it's complete, Lir is settled back on the couch, his eyelids drooping. The injury must have taken more out of him than I thought.

"You stay here and rest. I'll go to the market and get some more supplies."

"And I was so looking forward to seeing your primitive bartering center," says Lir. One side of his mouth slides up. "I am sure I can see it another time."

I roll my eyes, not responding to his insult, and stomp out the door. My feet hit the dirt at the bottom of the steps before a thought makes me pause. Now that his wound has been cared for and he's eaten, what's to stop the alien from just sneaking off and leaving me here? Is he really even sleepy? Could he be faking? I have no reason to trust him. Back up the stairs.

I tilt my head in the doorway. "Don't run off. There are bears." Lir's chuckle follows me back out and my cheeks heat. That must have sounded incredibly stupid. Hopefully it will still deter him from trying to get out of our deal.

The market, located just inside the south gate, is made up of some permanent shops, but it's mostly traders from outside that Dane allows to enter. Once they're cleared, the traders are permitted to set up stalls just inside the gates. Some of the more . . . unsavory . . . ones set up shop *outside* the gates sometimes, but I stay away from them.

It feels like people are staring at me, their eyes crawling over me like little bugs. Well, they always stare a little bit, but this time they aren't even bothering to hide it. What? So I've never gone to the market without Jace. Do these sheep really have nothing better to do than worry about me?

I stare at the ground. Who knows what they'd do if I actually spoke to them. I've barely made it past the main stretch of shops and into the rows of trader stalls when someone calls my name from a stall to the left with animal pelts lining its display.

I have no use for the pelts—Jace brings plenty of those home—but there's still something at the stall that interests me.

My eyes dart to Matt, all long limbs and shaggy brown hair, and then to the kestrel perched on his arm. His birds bring down the small animals whose furs are set out. He strokes the kestrel's chest with one finger. "She's nearly fully trained now, Jax. Do you want to hold her?"

I don't really have time for it, but I've been eyeing that bird since the first time he brought it out and I'm sure he knows it. I shake my head. "Maybe another time," I say.

He smiles, one side of his mouth twisting up farther than the other due to the puckered scar running from his jawline nearly to his temple. "I've been training a hawk too, a Harris, just like your necklace." My hand goes up to grab the pendant. How much attention has he been paying to me? "If you'd like . . ." His voice trails off. He huffs out a breath and meets my eyes. "If you'd like you could have her."

Whoa. His words may be offering me a bird, but his face seems to be offering me something else. I take another step back. I'm sure if I were looking to be Promised, Matt would be a good candidate, young and, despite the scar, attractive, but that is just not in my plans.

A creeping discomfort works its way through my body. He's not standing too close and I doubt he's a threat to me, but the shyly hopeful look on his face throws me off. It's best for both of us if I get that idea out of his head right now.

"I don't think that's a good idea . . . I'm going on a trip and I won't be around for a while." I cringe. I did not mean to say that. "You know, for training the bird and all. It's just . . . a bad time."

"All right, I understand." Matt's shoulders droop, but he recovers quickly. "Next time then?"

"Yeah, definitely," I say, returning his smile. "I've gotta run, but I'll see you around."

A few discreet trades and I've got some dried rabbit meat, a few ration bars, some cheese, and an extra loaf of bread. It will have to do. The longer I'm here and the more stuff I get, the more people are watching me.

The last stall I pass has a selection of knives displayed. I hadn't thought much about weapons, but it couldn't hurt to have a couple extra. Knives are good—they're easy to use and there's no risk of them locking up the way some of the more techie stuff out there, like jolt guns, does.

I study the selection and run my fingers over a few. A longer one catches my eye and I pick it up, testing the weight and grip. This one will work. When I look up to ask the seller how much, my eyes land on an old-fashioned rifle hanging on the back edge of the stall. That would be even better.

I wave the seller over and he slithers across to me. "What do you want for it?" I hold up the knife and use it to point at the rifle.

"The knife?" His eyes dart from me to the gun.

"And the rifle."

The seller looks at something to my right and pales. "Not for sale."

My body goes rigid when someone steps up behind me, not touching me but close enough to send my heart racing.

"Now, Jax, you know guns are reserved for guards and hunters only, neither of which you are." The voice is familiar. Flint may be Dane's son, but Daniel is his lackey. His breath on the back of my neck sends warning signals tingling through my limbs. *Fight. Run.* No, *breathe.*

My chest expands with a deep breath and I step away from Daniel, turning to face him. "Back off."

Daniel smiles, but it doesn't wash away the cruelty in his eyes. He takes one step back with his hands up and his smile morphs into a mocking grin. "Sorry, forgot you were a bit touchy."

The heat of anger starts trickling in to chase away the icy fear and my limbs and tongue unfreeze. "Jace is a hunter. The rifle is for him. Early birthday present." My words are still choppy and short, but the more deep, even breaths I take, the easier it gets. "I am allowed to buy a gift for my brother, right? You know, the *hunter*?"

"Sure," says Daniel. "You would be, except everyone knows your brother doesn't use guns. He's too fond of those throwing knives of his. Why don't you just pick him out a set of pretty little knives and leave the guns to the real men?" He steps forward again and I instinctively take a step back, running into the edge of the counter. "I'm sure there's something here he'd like . . . how about this one?" Daniel reaches around my left side and his arm brushes against the side of my breast.

My right hand comes up, clenching the knife from the table, my knuckles white. I jam the point up into the soft spot underneath Daniel's chin, pushing hard enough to get his attention, but not drawing blood. Yet. Air hisses in and out of my nostrils as I struggle to control my quaking limbs and my urge to just ram the knife in a little farther and be done with it. Not a good idea. I am not a killer. Well, I am, but Daniel's just being an asshole, not really trying to hurt me. Right?

The knife bobs with Daniel's throat as he swallows, bringing me back from my internal argument. "I. Said. Back. Off!" The volume rises with each word I squeeze past my gritted teeth.

Daniel jumps back. The movement flicks the switch in my head to fight and I lunge forward, lowering the knife and moving to shove it up underneath his ribs.

"Jax! Stop!" A hand comes down on my wrist and I spin, bringing the knife from my boot up with my left hand as I turn. Flint's wide-eyed face is enough to break me out of my frenzy and I force my left hand to release the knife before completing the arc into Flint's stomach. My hand still lands there though, too much momentum to stop completely. I relax my right arm and Flint releases it.

"Sorry," I mumble. I retrieve the knife I dropped and return the other to sit next to the rest of the seller's wares.

"She's crazy!" I cringe at Daniel's words. "Something needs to be done about her. Dane's let this go on too long. Loony bitch just attacked me for no reason."

"You provoked her," Matt says from somewhere off to the side. "I saw it."

"Stay out of this, Bird Boy," Daniel practically hisses. "Go back to your birds."

"Did you?" asks Flint. "Provoke her, I mean."

"No!" Daniel flings his arms up. "I was just explaining to her that guns were for hunters and guards only and then trying to help her find a more appropriate birthday present for her brother."

"Why were you trying to buy a gun, Jax?" *Crap. Crap. Crap.* Flint knows Jace almost as well as I do and my present excuse is not going to get by him. He studies my face, waiting for an answer, but, too worked up to think of a new excuse, I just look away. "Never mind. Daniel, go find something productive to do. Jax, come with me."

I cross my arms over my chest. "I don't need a babysitter."

He ignores my protest and moves to grab my arm.

I smack his hand away. "You don't want to do that right now."

"Fine, then. Go home." He points a finger at my nose and narrows his eyes. "I'm going to take care of Daniel, but you, me, and Jace are going to sit down and have a talk later."

Does he think I'm some disobedient child to be ordered around? I scowl at him.

Flint runs his hand through his hair. "Sorry. I didn't mean for it to come out like that . . . just tell Jace I'll be over in a couple hours."

"Will do." *Just not right now. Or anytime soon.* Forcing my mouth into a reassuring smile, I give him a mock salute and then walk off.

Once out of his sight, I quicken my steps, close my eyes, and let out a long, slow breath. I should have stopped walking for my little stress release, because, since I can't see where I'm going with my eyes closed, I collide with Emily and land on my butt in the dirt.

"Oh, goodness, I'm sorry," she says. She puts out a hand to help me up but quickly retracts it as I get back to my feet on my own.

I brush the dirt off the back of my pants. "It's okay. I wasn't watching where I was going."

"Did you hear about the alien ship that was spotted east of town? One of the hunters thinks it may have even landed for a while." My stomach drops. "Wasn't Jace out hunting today?"

"Uh, yeah, he was." My mind searches for the right words, the ones that will get rid of her and get me back on my way. "But he came home early today. Wasn't feeling well."

"Oh, no," says Emily. "Is there anything I can do?"

"Nope, there's nothing at all you can do for Jace right now." Bad choice of words.

Emily's brow furrows. "Is everything okay?"

Why is everyone asking me that today? Am I that obvious? I'm saved—if you can call it that—from answering by a commotion up the street. Three soldiers are jogging in our direction. They brush right by us and Emily steps closer.

"Jax, are you okay? You've gone a bit pale . . ." She places a gentle hand on my shoulder. For once, it's not the touch of her hand that sends my stomach dropping to the ground, it's the direction the soldiers are heading—east, toward my house. Of course, I don't know for sure that's where they're going, but . . .

"Crap."

Emily looks from my face to the soldiers. "What's going on? Let me help you."

I shake my head. "I think the only person who can help me now is about to be taken into custody."

"Jace?"

"Nope." I take off toward my house at a run. Emily calls out behind me, but I ignore her, my mind set on figuring out my next step. I need that alien in one piece in order to get my brother back, and I will do whatever it takes to keep him that way.

Five

Please be wrong. Please be wrong. The chant repeats in my head with each pounding of my feet as I run back to my house. I dart in between houses, through yards, and around people. Maybe I can beat them there?

No such luck. By the time I near my house, I can already see the soldiers milling about. My feet skid with my sudden stop and I take a detour behind the row of houses across from mine. I travel through backyards until I am directly across from my front door, which is wide-open and flanked by two soldiers.

Great. Just great. How the hell am I supposed to get around them? My luck doesn't improve. Daniel exits between the soldiers, his hand around Lir's upper arm, just as Flint rounds the corner and jogs closer.

"I told you that girl was crazy," says Daniel, shaking Lir's injured arm roughly. "I knew a trip over here would be . . . what'd you call it? *Productive.* She's brought one of those things in here. And where's her brother? That twit is probably in on it. They're working together to—"

"Shut it, Daniel." Flint's words are quiet, but the tendons in his neck strain against the collar of his uniform as he clenches his teeth and his hands are in fists at his side. "I will take it to my father and we will find out what's going on. I'm sure Jax has an explanation . . . leave Jace out of it."

Daniel steps closer to Flint, sneering. "What is it with you and that idiot and his nutso sister? Not even you can protect them from this. You know the rules. No outsiders without permission and this erk's about as outsider as you can get. Why, I bet Dane'll even let me be the one to pull the trigger if I ask nicely."

Lir chooses that moment to break out of Daniel's grip and start running, heading right toward my hiding spot. The alien may be quick, but he's no match for the five soldiers who have him surrounded, especially injured and with his hands bound in front of him. One of the soldiers easily trips him, sending Lir to land face-first on the ground. He struggles to his knees, but Daniel moves forward, stepping onto Lir's back, slamming him to the ground. Before I can move, Daniel brings the butt of his gun down onto the back of Lir's head.

Daniel stands, raising the barrel of his gun to point at Lir. "Let's just go ahead and take care of this problem now."

"No!" I step out from behind the house, raising my hands slowly. "I need him."

Daniel turns, bringing his gun around to point at me. "So I was right. You're a traitor on top of being crazy." He grins. "Dane's going love this."

Flint steps forward, pushing Daniel's gun toward the ground as he does. "Knock it off, Daniel." His eyes meet mine. "What the hell is going on, Jax?"

I focus on Flint, ignoring everyone else. He will understand. He has to. "Flint, they took him. They took Jace."

"Who?" Flint's eyes widen and his gaze travels back to Lir. "The erks? What the hell?"

"I've got a plan. I'm getting him back. But I need his help."

Flint's eyes narrow "You're trusting the erk? Why? Do you really think it's helping you?"

"*He* is helping me." I cross my arms over my chest. "Something you're not right now. He and I have a deal. I get him to the city and he gets me inside so I can get Jace. Just let us go."

Flint shakes his head. "I can't do that. I'm going to have to bring it in . . . There are other things . . . never mind." He grasps my arm and pulls me forward. "Come on."

"No." I plant my feet and refuse to move.

"I don't have time for this, Jax." He runs one hand through his hair, causing the blond spikes to stick up even more. "We'll get Jace. I'm not letting you go there alone."

"But you don't understand—"

"No." Flint leans in closer, his voice strained. "You don't understand. I can't let you go to that city. Jace would never forgive me. You and I will figure this out, but you have to come with me and I have to turn the alien in. There have been attacks . . ."

"Attacks?" Something in his voice tells me that this is serious.

"The erks," Flint says. "They've been wiping human settlements off the map. Bombs. Guns. Some things we don't even know what they are. Whatever that thing told you, whatever promises he made you, they're lies." When I don't say anything, he continues, "I don't know how you came across it, but I can guess—it was a single ship doing a flyover? They're scouting us out."

"Scouting us out . . ." As much as I don't want them to, Flint's words make sense. The single ship. The aliens' heated conversation and their reference to looking for something. Even Lir never really said what they were doing out there. "And Jace? Why would they take him?"

"I don't know." He averts his eyes and shifts us back toward the other men. "But I bet *it* does. The erk was using you to get back to his kind. Who knows what it would have done when it got you there? Maybe even taken you, too."

I shake my head and back away, the burn of tears stinging in my eyes. Lir has been nothing but nice. We had a deal. He's my only option. There's no way he . . . or is there? Has he even been honest with me? My eyes reach Lir as Flint grabs my arm again. Maybe he thinks I'm being hurt—more likely he's just worried about losing his leverage—but Lir jumps up and moves toward me, much faster than before. Has he been faking his weakness?

It's not fast enough, though. One of the men catches up with him and hits him twice on the back of the head with the butt of his gun and Lir goes down to his knees. His eye bore into me, begging me to do something, but my feet are frozen. What if Flint is right? I turn my head away, unable to watch anymore, even though I can still hear the sounds of fists striking flesh. I blink quickly to prevent the tears from falling and lean into Flint.

"Let's go," I say. One way or another, I'm going to figure out what's real and I'm going to get my brother back.

We stop outside the large building where Dane's office is and Flint motions Daniel forward. "Take Scott and Michael and put the erk in one of the cells."

"Sure thing," says Daniel. "Come on, guys, let's put this thing where it belongs."

Two of the soldiers step forward, Lir's limp form draped between them. He hasn't woken since the last time they hit him. The splash of green blood on his collar draws my eyes up to the still-dripping wound on his temple. Shouldn't he have stopped bleeding by now? Should I even care?

I pull my gaze away and shake my head. Flint wouldn't lie to me, especially over something that involved Jace's safety. Besides, this rescue mission will be a whole lot easier with some soldiers behind me. Forget the alien. Forget that he may or may not have saved my life in the woods. Forget that compassion in his eyes on the porch and the feel of his skin under my fingers. *Really* forget that last one.

After filling my lungs with a deep breath, I follow Flint up the stairs, without looking back.

"Enter," Dane's voice booms after Flint's knock and we walk into his office.

Flint nods at his father. "Sir, there's been a breach. An . . . unauthorized outsider was found within the perimeter."

Dane's eyes travel from Flint to me and back again. "And why is she here?"

"The intruder is an erk . . . an E'rikon. They took her brother, sir."

Dane tilts back in his chair and intertwines his fingers in front of his chest. "And?"

"She witnessed the event. One was left behind." I move forward, but Flint stops me from saying anything by tightening his grip on my arm. "And it offered to help her in retrieving Jace."

"It's been secured?"

"Yes, sir. Daniel and two others are escorting it to the holding cells right now."

"Am I to take it that the reports I've been getting about a landing are true?"

Flint nods. "Yes, sir."

"The reported landing occurred east of town," says Dane. His eyes swing to me, narrowing. "What were you doing outside, Jasmine?"

Flint's fingers dig into my bicep, but his face remains still. His message is clear: I need to watch my words. "Jace left one of his knives at home and I was bringing it to him." It's a weak excuse, but at least it is one Emily could confirm if anyone asked.

"Your brother went out with the hunting party this morning." Dane leans forward, the leather of his chair creaking softly. "You're not permitted outside the gates without an escort. Who let you by?"

Flint lets go of my arm and steps forward, angling his body slightly in front of me. "I did, sir."

"Leave us, Jasmine. I need to speak with my son alone."

"There's no time . . . uh, sir," I say. "We need to go get my brother now. The longer they have him—"

"No!" Dane's fist slams down onto his desk, the vibration toppling a cup. "You need to do what you're told. There will be no rescue mission, Jasmine. If your brother is stupid enough to let himself be captured, then he suffers the consequences. I have a town to protect and I can't spare any of my men to go traipsing off after your wayward brother."

Heat fills my body and I clench my fists, driving my fingernails into my palms. Losing my temper is not going to work here. "Send me. I will do it on my own."

Dane laughs. He actually laughs, like my brother's situation is some sort of joke to him. Then his eyes harden and his lips curl over his next words. "You are not permitted to leave."

So much for not losing my temper. "I will leave if I want to!" I can't help yelling, but Dane doesn't even react to the volume of my words.

"You know the rules. You know what you agreed to when you accepted my protection." His voice is even.

"No, I know what you coerced my terrified brother into agreeing to for me when I was catatonic," I say through gritted teeth. "I didn't agree to anything."

"I don't need your agreement, Jasmine." Dane smiles. "Do you need to be locked up to ensure your cooperation?"

I open my mouth, a scathing retort resting on my tongue. *Are all humans this petulant . . .* Do I really think I'm going to argue

Dane into agreeing with me? If I get locked up, there will be no one to rescue my brother. I force my shoulders to drop and look down. "No, sir," I say softly. "I'll behave."

"Good. Now leave us." A patronizing smile slithers across his face.

I shuffle out of the room, keeping my head down except for a glance at Flint as I walk through the door. His face is pale and his body tense. He and Jace are friends, but is that enough for him to stand up to his father? Either way, I'm not waiting around for someone else to do something. Whether Lir is using me or not, he's really my only ally right now.

Step one, get Lir. Step two, rescue Jace. Sounds simple enough, right? Stupidly so. How in the hell am I going to get to Lir, much less get both of us past the gates without being noticed?

I walk back toward my house, head down, potential scenarios swirling through my head to be examined and then discarded. I could just leave without him. It's not like I've never gotten past the gate guards before, but what would happen once I reached the E'rikon city? There's that barrier and I won't be able to cross it without him, at least that's what he said. He doesn't have any reason to lie, though . . . right?

If only I knew who to trust. If there were only one person in this stupid town who . . .

"Jax!" The whispered exclamation pulls me from my thoughts. Emily steps out from between the houses on my left. "What is going on?"

Great. Just what I need. "Nothing, Emily. Don't worry about it."

She rolls her eyes, purses her lips, and exhales. Her obvious exasperation stops my forward motion. I've never seen Emily any less than perfectly composed and cheery. "Look, Jax, I know what you think of me . . . of us, but there's a lot you don't know." When her gaze meets mine, there's something new in her eyes, a hardness I don't recognize. "I don't know what's going on, but I might be able to help." When I don't respond, she continues, "Come with me. I'm not asking you to trust me blindly, but at least let me try to help you."

My muddled brain manages to direct my head to nod. I'm stuck anyway—might as well see what assistance she has to offer.

§

Emily leads me toward the girls' dormitories, where single girls with no adult male relatives are required to stay until being Promised. Thankfully, I never ended up there. When we arrived here, Jace made it clear that he refused to be separated from me and he fought for us to be assigned one of the smaller houses near the gate, even though we weren't of age at the time. Maybe if I had been placed with the other girls I might be different now, better? More likely, I would never have recovered without my connection to Jace pulling me back into myself. Without him there to chase away the nightmares . . . I would never have slept.

When we reach the front doors, Emily smiles at the man standing guard. "Hello, Seth. I'm just bringing Jasmine in so she can join our sewing circle today."

While I try to contain my laughter and twist my face into a vapid smile, Emily bats her eyelashes at him. Seth returns her smile and waves us through without pause. Feminine wiles really do come in handy.

Once we're out of earshot, I pause. "We're not really sewing, right?"

Emily laughs and shakes her head. "No, I'm not expecting you to sew. I know better than that."

I follow her up the stairs until we reach the third floor. She leads me into one of the rooms off a large common area, shutting the door behind us.

"Now tell me." She sits on the bed and folds her hands in her lap.

I pace back and forth in the small space, putting the right words together before I speak. *Keep it simple. Don't give away too much.* "The aliens took my brother. There's one locked up in the holding cells. I need him to get into the city to rescue my brother."

Emily's eyes have widened and she blinks quickly. "Wow. I can't say that's what I expected you to say."

I shrug. "Can you help or not?"

She crosses her legs and leans forward, resting her chin in her hand. "I know I can get you past the gate. With all the hubbub surrounding the festival tonight, that will be no problem." She raises her eyes. "Getting your alien friend out of lockup might require a bit more planning."

"Festival?"

"Really? Do you pay attention to nothing around you? The fall festival is tonight," she says. "You know, food, dancing . . . the fall Promising ceremony."

"Oh, yeah, that." I smile sheepishly. "I definitely don't pay any attention to that." Emily giggles and raises her hand as if to touch my arm, but quickly lowers it again. "So why are you doing this? I haven't exactly been very nice to you."

"I know how you feel about this town and its restrictions . . . Did you ever stop to think that others might share those feelings? Do you know how I ended up an orphan, how I ended up stuck in these dorms with guards by the door and people watching my every move?"

I shake my head, moving to sit down on the bed. Emily's body tenses for a moment and she shoots me a look I can't interpret.

"My mother was Promised to one of Dane's cronies. He was twenty years her senior and not a nice man. Five years later, she fell in love with a trader, my father. He managed to smuggle her out of town and they lived on the run for nearly two years." Emily takes a deep breath and stares out the window. "Dane had some of his soldiers hunt them down. They killed my father and dragged my mother back to Bridgelake. She was eight months pregnant.

"Her Promised husband welcomed her back . . . with closed fists. She had me and we lived there with him until I was ten. He'd always hit her, but the first—and only—time he went after me, she killed him. Dane had her executed. And there I was, no male relatives and too young to be Promised." She turns to face me, her eyes shiny with tears. "My father was killed for having the gall to go up against Dane. My mother, for disobedience. Do you really think he's not going to continue taking his revenge out on me?"

My mouth opens, but no words come out. I break away from her gaze. "I'm sorry. I didn't know," I say.

"It's okay." Her head down, she twists her hands in her lap.

"Why didn't you just say all this to start with? What's with all the sewing circle stuff?"

She raises her eyebrows. "They are always watching. Not everyone, but most of the soldiers and at least half the others. Dane rules this town and those that aren't bowing down to him are terrified of him. I could tell you weren't exactly itching to be indoctrinated into Dane worship, but your brother is best friends with his son. You're pretty chummy with him, too."

I shrug when she glances at me. "I've known Flint forever. He and my brother were friends before we even moved here. He's almost like another brother to me." When her brow furrows, I rush to explain further. "Doesn't mean I agree with everything he does. And I certainly don't agree with the way Dane runs things."

Emily nods. "I couldn't take the risk of revealing myself without feeling you out first. It was the only excuse I could think of." Her mouth turns up at the corners and she shakes her head. "Who knew you'd be so against anything sewing related."

Our laughter fills the room and warmth seeps into me. Jace is my brother and I love him, but there's something different about laughing with another girl. Despite our differences, Emily and I share some common ground and the fragile threads of friendship forming between us give me hope. That, plus she talked about my brother in the present tense, and she's willing to help me when no one else would.

"So, where do we start?"

"The festival begins in an hour," Emily says. "First we'll work on you learning to have a conversation without looking like you're about to vomit. I can distract the guards, but you'll have to play your part, too. Then we get dressed."

"Dressed?"

She motions toward my clothes and I smack myself in the forehead with my palm. No wonder people were staring at me. I'm still wearing the pants from earlier.

§

Twenty minutes later, Emily no longer falls over laughing at my attempts to flip my hair and bat my eyelashes. She still giggles a little, though. It will have to do. Emily turns her attention to my clothing.

"I don't suppose I can just wear what I have on?" I ask.

Emily laughs. "Everyone's going to be dressed up. You need to blend in, be more girly. I think you're going to have to borrow some of my clothes." My face twists into a grimace and she laughs again. "A dress won't kill you. Besides, you don't have to wear it all evening, just until you can get to your own clothes." She swings her feet over the side of her bed.

It takes her a moment to select a dress from the closet, but when she does my quick intake of breath causes her eyebrows to raise. "You like it?"

I hate to admit it, but I do. She's selected a dark green dress made in a soft, flowing fabric. It's not a work dress and certainly not a dress made for anything practical, but it's beautiful. Long enough to brush the middle of my calves, fitted in the top and flaring at the waist. I slide into it and marvel at the feel of the fabric swishing around my legs.

Emily smiles warmly. "It looks beautiful on you," she says when I study myself in her mirror. "It was always much too long for me."

She walks up behind me and puts a hand on my shoulder. I inwardly cringe at the touch, but don't let it show on my face. Emily is being astoundingly nice to me and I don't want to insult her. I am finding it easier to be around her. My breaths stay even and my limbs stay relaxed, so that's progress, I guess. "Thank you," I say.

"May I do your hair?"

I nod, too stunned to do anything else, and she leads me to a chair in the corner.

It's a strange sensation for someone else to brush my hair. Since my mother died when I was born and I lived out in the woods with only my father and Jace, I've never had any female companionship. Jace would laugh if I asked him to brush my hair.

I find myself actually enjoying the sensation of Emily's quick fingers braiding and twisting my hair and I relax into the soft touches with my eyes closed. She steps back to admire her work in the mirror and I open my eyes. She's left a few wispy tendrils down to frame my face and used tiny braids to pull the rest of it back and create an intricate twist on the crown of my head. I've never seen anything like it. "Wow."

Emily claps her hands. I'm beginning to get the impression that she's rather pleased with herself. "Oh, Jax, I always knew you were gorgeous. Your hair is the perfect shade of red to set off this dress."

My face heats with a blush and I turn away from the mirror. "So what exactly are we going to do?"

"Dane keeps a spare set of keys to the holding cells in his office." She waves off my questioning look and continues, "He will be officiating the Promising ceremony tonight and that's going to be when you go in. We'll meet up once you have the keys. The entrance will be guarded, but I'm known for delivering food to prisoners and we can make it seem like you're just keeping me company or something. Depending on who's on duty, one or both of the guards will look the other way."

"How do you know all this?"

"Yours won't be the first prisoner to have a little help escaping the holding cells."

"Thank you, Emily," I say. "For all of this. For everything."

"You're welcome." Her eyes bore into me and she swallows. "Just promise me, once you've gotten Jace, you'll come back here. There aren't many people strong enough to go against Dane, but I think you and your brother are. There's something special about you two. Even Dane knew it. He hadn't let any young male outsiders inside in years—until he let your brother in. He hasn't forced you to work and didn't force you into the dormitory. He wanted you here, so he's let the rules slide for you. I don't know what that means, but . . ." She reaches over and grabs my hand. I don't even flinch. "I think with your help we could change things here."

There's so much more here than I had ever noticed. Have I really been in this much of a fog to miss the undercurrents in Bridgelake?

What else have I missed? I want to know more, but there's no time. Once I have Jace back safe and sound, then I can focus on learning more about how I can help Emily. Wait. To join her cause I'd have to stick around, and that's not in the plan.

I study Emily's face, this girl who's had so much tragedy in her life and still pushed through my walls to try to befriend me, who is helping me now even though the consequences could be awful for her.

My earlier conversation with Jace plays in my head. *It can't be just us forever.* He's right. "I promise, Emily. I'll get Jace and then do whatever I can to help."

Six

Although Emily's plan is good, some of the details could have used a little more thought. The dress, clearly my least favorite part, works like a charm. In it I'm just another decorative sheep girl waiting for the festival, and I'm able to walk down the streets without really being noticed. I practice my fake smile and my hair flip when I see a couple soldiers and they just wave me on, no recognition in their eyes. So getting to the building that holds Dane's office is a breeze. It's how I'm going to get into his office that's a problem.

It's full dark now, but the front door of the building is lit up and two guards flank the door. No matter how nice my dress is or how much I bat my eyelashes, I'm not going to get past them. Based on what Emily told me, though, Dane's office is toward the back and it has a window.

I slink around the back of the building. Wonderful. Emily's information would have been really helpful if that window weren't about six feet off the ground—just slightly out of my reach. The brick won't give me enough handholds to climb it and even jumping still leaves the windowsill beyond the grip of my fingers.

Good thing I know how to climb a tree. One of the outreaching branches of the poplar tree growing near the corner of the building looks like it might be perfect for this task. Cursing the stupid dress, I wrap my legs around the trunk and use my arms to pull myself up until I can grab the lowest branch. My inner thighs are scraped all to hell, but I make it up until I'm resting at the branch I saw from below.

It's still a bit of a leap from the branch to the windowsill, but at least the window's open. The branch creaks under me as I shimmy farther out from the trunk and I send out a silent plea that the branch will hold. The fall wouldn't kill me, but it wouldn't be very pleasant, either. I rise into a crouch, my thigh muscles straining to hold my balance.

When I push off, there's a loud crack and my leap starts a few inches lower than it should have as the branch falls. I make it across, my shoulders protesting as I hang down against the outer wall and my fingers scrabbling for purchase on the windowsill. My biceps shake and my knuckles whiten around the ledge. Slowly raising my body, I collapse into the room, lying on my back for a moment while my breath comes back to me.

I stand, rolling my shoulders and clenching and unclenching my fingers a few times. Shaking my limbs gently loosens my muscles and gets me back on track.

Moonlight filters in through the window, giving me just enough light to work with. I start with Dane's desk. There's nothing on top of it, but it has plenty of drawers. The first one opens with a slight click. At least it's unlocked. Of course, that drawer is not the one with the keys. The next drawer down is also unlocked and so is the third. No keys in any of them. The wide drawer in the center, however, resists my attempts to open it. Great. I need a key to find the keys. Maybe he keeps it nearby.

My fingers trace the underside of the drawer. *Come on. Just one bit of luck this evening would be nice.* A rough edge brushes against my index finger. It's tape, and my fingers quickly determine that it's holding a small key to the bottom of the drawer. *Yes!* I crouch down, twist my body so I'm facing the ceiling, and crawl under the desk, picking at the tape with my fingernail.

The door swings open and the overhead light turns on, freezing me in place. How far does the front of the desk come down? Am I visible from the other side? Turning my head to check, any movement really, would only draw attention to myself if the desk does not extend all the way to the floor. I know this, but I still have to fight the urge to look.

My rocketing heartbeat is loud in my ears and my raised arms are starting to shake. *Don't move. Just breathe.*

"Nothing here, Daniel," a voice calls out from the doorway. "The noise you heard was probably just that branch falling."

There's no response from Daniel, or at least none I can hear, and the light goes off. The bar of light shining on the wall from the hallway narrows and then disappears as the door closes. A loud breath flows past my lips in one long whoosh. Daniel's not one of the guards at the cells—that's good news. Though if I get caught here . . . he's the last person I want to run into besides Dane himself.

After a few more swipes with my fingernail, the edge of the tape lifts and I'm able to grasp it and pull it off, the key following. I scramble out from under the desk. My hands are shaky, so I miss on the first attempt to fit the key into the lock, but it slides in easily the second time. Another sigh of relief eases past my lips.

The drawer is nearly empty and I can tell at first glance that what I need isn't in there. Still. No. Key ring. What is the point of the locked drawer if all it has in it is more useless paper? Dammit. I start to close the drawer, but something shifts in the back and I stop. The drawer doesn't open all the way, so the far corners are hidden from view. Reaching my hand inside, my fingers brush against cold metal. I grab the object and pull it forward out of the drawer.

It's . . . I have no idea. Vaguely round in shape and almost entirely smooth, the palm-sized object is not anything I've ever seen. It must have some use, maybe even be something important, for it to be locked in the drawer. I pull it out, set it on the desk, and reach back in.

Another brush of metal against my fingers, but this object is a little more identifiable. It's a bracelet—no, a cuff. Similar in style to what Lir called a *kitu*, but with intricate engravings. It goes to the top of the desk as well.

The papers might be helpful, too, so I pull on one of the stacks. Turns out it's one piece of paper folded multiple times. The edges are yellow with age and it's heavily creased. Placing it on the desk, I carefully unfold it. A map. Not just any map, but one from before the Collapse. I trace the lines connecting all the cities, streets, roads, highways . . . The scope of it all amazes me. To think, there used to be so many people, so many cities, so much civilization.

My father taught me enough about before that I know this is a map of what used to be Virginia and I easily find what is now Bridgelake on it. Even better, I can navigate the lines and miles over to the nearest large city, the one taken by the E'rikon. A grin breaks across my face. This I *know* will come in handy.

My thumb pauses over a large red *X*, not something on the original map, but something written on it. I draw my eyes away from the route to Jace and study the rest of the map as well. There are four more *X*s spread out across it, each one with numbers written next to it: 2,345 . . . 1,506 . . . 3,124 . . . 3,003 . . . And then there's a large red circle around an area about three hundred miles to our west. Inside it are the words *Population 11,537*.

Population of what? It can't possibly mean people. Bridgelake is the largest remaining human settlement and there are only around ten thousand people here. And the *X*s? Could they be population numbers, too? Flint's earlier words come back to me. The alien

I nod my head slowly.

That's enough to encourage her and she continues to babble. "I'm really excited, to tell you the truth." She actually bounces in her seat a little. "I'm just hoping that he's selected someone young enough to give me children. I've always wanted a baby." A dreamy smile pulls her lips up. "A little girl . . ."

Dane's voice pulls her out of her wistfulness and she jumps to her feet. "That's me," she says. "Good luck!"

The hand Dane links with hers is thin-skinned and liver spotted, the man easily thirty years older. Her pained smile stays in place, but her eyes gloss over with the sheen of unshed tears. Poor thing. What did that girl do to deserve that matchup? Maybe, like Emily's situation, it was punishment for something her parents did. Or is it some sort of reward for the old guy? There's just so much I don't know about this place, so much I never bothered to learn. I almost feel guilty for that.

My name rings through the air next. This cannot possibly be happening. My eyes go out to the crowd again, begging, pleading for Flint to appear, to jump onto the stage and . . . do something, anything. I don't stand and step forward like the others, choosing to stay in my seat and blindly hope for something to intervene. Dane crosses the stage and leans down until he's face-to-face with me.

"Get up, Jasmine," he says. "You're embarrassing me. Don't make me call your name again. I can make things rather unpleasant for you if you test me."

I rise onto numb feet and my legs carry me to the front of the stage with jerky, robot-like movements. Flint steps up onto the stage and my entire body relaxes into the sigh of relief that breezes out of me. Finally. But something isn't right. His expression isn't triumphant or angry or anything but resigned. He reaches out and takes my hand.

I move to pull my hand away, but Flint simply shakes his head. My gaze goes out to the onlookers, waiting for the rest of the rescue team or whatever Flint has planned. Eyes drill into me, curious ones, pleasant ones, and maybe even a few hostile ones. I have no anchor here and my mind is flailing for something, anything to hold onto. Nothing is happening.

Zoned out, I only catch the end of what Dane is saying, ". . . the last one of the night and the most important one of all." I shake myself and concentrate on his words. "My son, Flint Jacobs, and Jasmine Mitchell."

What? Flint and me what? My eyes dart around looking for answers.

Flint pulls me closer to him and plasters a smile on, nodding out at the crowd. "Smile," he hisses into my ear.

"What? Why?" *What the hell is going on?*

"It's the only way I could protect you. Just go with it. You at least need to try to look happy about it." Flint's breath tickles my neck and I shiver.

"Happy about what?"

"Our Promising."

Hold on. My body stiffens and I blink rapidly. Did he just say that we were Promised? "What are you talking about?"

"I promised Jace I'd protect you if anything happened to him. This is me keeping that promise," he says against my neck. "It's not so bad. Dad could have given you to that old guy." A fleeting sensation of his dry lips pressing against mine sends my mind spinning out of control.

I hold myself together, though, barely. *Stand. Smile. Wave. Walk.* Flint leads me back down the steps. Once we're through the crowd and out of sight, huddled in a dark corner behind the library, I turn on my heel and send my fist toward his nose. He must've been expecting it. He dodges.

"What. The. Hell." I punctuate each of my words with a punch to his arm. Those he doesn't try to avoid. Good. I need to hit something.

"It was the only way." He winces as another punch lands on his arm.

"It was a stupid way!" I yell. "Of all the idiotic, lame-brained ideas in all the world, it was the worst!"

Flint catches my next jab at his arm. "It was what your brother wanted." His words are soft, but his eyes blaze with anger. "Stop hitting me."

I swing my other hand at him. "You're not my brother. You don't get to order me around."

Flint's shoulders tense and he closes his eyes for a moment before sighing. "I know that," he says. "I just—there's a lot we need to do."

"You're right," I say. "We need to plan how we're going to get Jace back." I cross my arms over my chest, daring him to argue.

"Jax . . ." Flint sighs and runs his hand through his hair. "I don't know if we can."

I step forward until I'm right in front of him, our toes nearly touching. "No. Maybe you can't, but I can and I will. With or without your help."

The muscles in his jaw clench and I can see the pain in his eyes. "You don't understand."

"No! You don't understand. I will not leave my brother there. I will not. I will not." I turn to storm away, but Flint's hand catches my arm. Before he even has a chance to say anything else, I bring my right fist around, landing it directly on his temple. The hook shot knocks his head to the side violently. His eyes roll back and he crumples to the ground.

Well, that's one way to occupy him while I break Lir out and go get Jace, but damn, my knuckles sting.

Seven

The one good thing that came from the stupid ceremony is that everyone is gathered over by the square, entirely the opposite direction from where I need to go. Already late, I walk quickly, the moon lighting my way. A breeze flows down the street and raises goose bumps on my arms and legs. I rub my hands up and down on my arms to try to dispel the chill.

Before the Collapse, Bridgelake was just another small college town. It didn't really have much of a police station or a jail, but it did have a science building with a basement full of metal-lined lab rooms. I guess that was where they kept lab animals or something. Those rooms became the holding cells. There are only about ten cells and most of them are empty at any given time. Breaking the law here will get you swiftly kicked out, so it's not like people sit around there for long. The cells are more for containing people until Dane can do some sort of public exile ceremony. But I don't think exile is what he has planned for Lir. Not the way Daniel was talking about it.

Probably the only thing keeping Dane from taking care of Lir already is the festival. Can't keep his loyal public waiting, although many of them might enjoy the spectacle of a public execution. I shiver, but it's not from the chill creeping into the air. What would Dane have done if one of the groups of soldiers had found Lir in the woods? What would have happened if I hadn't been there when Jace was taken? My brother would have disappeared and I would never have known what happened to him—just like our father.

Dwelling on that isn't going to help me now. I shake my head and speed up.

"Jax." Emily's whispered call comes from my left.

"Yeah." I slide into the space between two buildings, where she's waiting.

"What the hell took you so long?" Her hands fly up in exasperation. "Did you run into trouble? I've been getting worried."

A chuckle escapes my lips. "Well, if you call running into Dane, getting Promised to Flint, and then knocking him out *trouble* . . . then, yeah, I ran into trouble."

Her arms drop to her sides and she gapes at me. "What?"

"If you call—"

"I heard you," she says. "I don't even know what to say to that." Emily shakes her head and then her eyes find mine. "Did you at least get the keys first?"

That brings a laugh bursting out of my mouth. "Not one to get distracted by the little things, are you?"

One side of her mouth twists up. "Seems like you took care of it."

"Are the packs in place?" I ask.

While I was getting the keys, Emily was supposed to grab the packs at my house and put them by the west gate for Lir and me to grab on our way out. They aren't even half as full as I'd like them to be since my market trip was interrupted, but we'll have to make do. Dane is bound to realize pretty quickly that I'm gone and he'd assume I'd head straight to the city. They'd start looking by the east gate, so I'm going in the opposite direction. We'll have to make an extra stop for the satchel now, too.

"Of course, Jax. You're not the only one that knows how to sneak around here." Emily threads her arm through mine and we step out onto the street. "Let's do this, then."

Two guards stand silhouetted by the doorway and they tense up as we draw closer. Neither of them is anyone I know, but that's not saying much. "What's your business here, ladies?"

Emily smiles. "Hello, Brian. Hello, Seth." Emily knows the guards—that's either really good or really bad.

"Hello, Emily," says Seth, a grin lighting his face. So good thing, then? My stomach twists at the hungry look in his eye, but Emily ignores it.

"We've come to deliver food to the prisoner." The guards eye the covered dish resting on Emily's palm as she shifts on her feet.

"Aren't you just the good Samaritan," Brian says, leering at Emily. "Has this been approved?"

Emily opens her mouth to reply, but Seth breaks in. "Emily's always taking pity on the prisoners. Just let them go down and get it over with." He points his finger at Emily with a stern look on his face. "Just slide the food in through the bottom like normal, Em. Stay away from the door. It's subdued, but it might still be dangerous." He reaches out and brushes his hand down Emily's arm. "Then maybe you can keep us company for a while?"

Emily giggles. "I'd like that. You too, right, Jax?"

He's not touching me, keep it together. I fight the desire to close my eyes and count my breaths. "Yeah." It's the best I can do, the only word that is small enough to make it up my shrinking throat. Emily adjusts her arm and gives my elbow a gentle squeeze. Some of the tension leaves my limbs. It's only a part to play. I won't actually be coming back up here with them.

Brian waves us by and I let out a long, slow breath. Then a hand grabs my arm and I freeze.

"You're Jace's sister, right?" asks Brian.

I nod. Emily, slightly ahead of me, looks back. Her eyes anchor me enough that I relax a little. "Yeah, I am."

"I hear you're pretty good with a knife."

"I guess so."

"You the one that cut its arm?"

Sewed it up, too, but I don't think that's what he wants to hear. "Yeah."

Brian tilts his head back, a new respect in his eyes. "Great shot. I think that's the first I've ever heard of someone getting the drop on one of them. You must have weakened it enough so it could be taken."

I did? Obviously the aliens are fast, but someone before me had to have fought with one, injured one, something. If they're that strong, how in the world will I get Jace out?

Brian rubs a hand through his hair and meets my eyes. "You girls just let us know if you have any trouble down there, okay?"

I nod and pull my arm away from his grip. Once Emily and I are out of sight, I stop and lean against the wall. "I just need a moment." Emily stays silent and I focus on taking one big breath and letting it pass slowly through my lips. "Sorry, I just . . ."

"It's okay. Take all the time you need." She squeezes my arm. "It's actually a good thing Seth was on duty this evening. I don't really know Brian, but Seth is one of the good guys." When my eyes widen and my eyebrows raise, she continues. "You can't always think the worst of everyone."

She's right. When I replay the interaction in my head, it's clear to me that Emily likes Seth. Her blushing. Her giggling. Maybe he even genuinely cares about her. Even Brian grabbing my arm was nothing like what Daniel did earlier. Between getting knocked out in the forest, getting Promised, and my swelling knuckles, it's been a long day and my fight-or-flight instincts are on overdrive. I'm no good to Jace like this. I'm no good to anyone like this. I've got to pull myself together.

Emily and I descend the stairs into the darkened lower level. Upkeep down here has obviously not been much of a priority. The paint is peeling on the wall, and although it doesn't smell really bad, there's a persistent musty odor in the air, like a wet animal. The farther down we go though, the worse it gets. When we finally reach the basement level, my lip curls and my nose scrunches.

What had been only mildewy before has morphed into the stale stench of mold and age. Old equipment clutters the narrow hallway and the lights flicker and buzz, giving the whole place an eerie feeling. I can only hope that Jace isn't being kept in a place like this. A shudder travels from my shoulders down my back and I swallow while trying to avoid inhaling through my nose. It doesn't work very well and I gag, a burning starting up in the back of my throat.

"Here." Emily hands me a small piece of cloth and I use it to cover my mouth and nose.

I smile gratefully. The cloth doesn't block out the stench entirely, but it keeps the worst of it at bay for now.

We peer into the window at the top of each door until we find one cell with a shadowed form lying in the corner.

Emily glances at me. "Keys?"

I pull the key ring out and toss it to her. She locates the correct key and fits it into the lock. The lock releases quietly, but the door hinges squeal when she pushes it open.

Emily looks from me to the interior of the cell, a questioning look on her face. I nod. I should be the one to go in and talk to him. Lir might not exactly consider me a friendly face at this point, but at least I'm someone he knows.

"Just wait out here for me," I say, slipping into the cell through the small opening.

The smell isn't as bad inside the cell. Metal walls reflect the light from the buzzing overhead fixture. There's a small cot against the wall, but nothing else besides a ratty blanket. Lir is slumped in the far right corner, head bowed down over his chest, the flickering light creating shifting shadows across his face. He doesn't even look up when I enter the cell. Ropes bind his hands and I can't tell if he's even had water. Probably not, if Emily hasn't been down here today. Seth might be one of the good guys, as Emily said, but it doesn't seem like he's too concerned about their prisoner. Seeing Lir huddled on the cold concrete floor, injured and alone, sends a shot of guilt into my gut. It's my fault he's here.

"Lir," I say softly. "Wake up."

His head slowly rises until his eyes meet mine. "I am not sleeping. The accommodations leave a little to be desired." A bruise mars his cheek, expanding outward and swelling his eye nearly shut. I gasp and reach forward to put a hand on his cheek, but he flinches away from me. "What is it that you want, Jax? Come to weasel more information out of me? I must admit you guys had a pretty good setup there. How did you know we were coming?"

"What are you talking about?" I ask. He doesn't sound like the cheerily sarcastic guy I met earlier. Though perhaps this is who he really is.

A snide laugh passes his lips. "Cut the innocent act. Obviously you have had this planned for some time. Even planned for me to take pity on you, is that it? The shaky hands, the big terrified eyes . . . I must say, you almost had me." He pitches his voice up into a mocking falsetto. "Oh, dear, I've injured you. Come with me and I'll help you. By the way . . . what are your weaknesses? How do I get into the city?" His face is cold and hard. "And when it did not work, you had your friends come to lock me up . . . and now what? You are trying a new tactic?"

I back away and rise to my feet. "What?"

"The dress is a nice touch, too." His eyes run up and down my body. "Can't beat it out of me, so you'll seduce it out of me, huh?" My face flushes, a mixture of embarrassment and anger.

Lir is on his feet before I can blink, throwing his bound arms over my head so I'm in between them. He pushes me back until my shoulders hit the door, slamming it shut, and he holds me there. "Well, come on, then. Though I must admit your previous attempts have been rather amateurish." He leans down to whisper into my ear. "This is what you wanted, isn't it, pretty girl?"

The phrase echoes in my brain, ricocheting around in my head—*pretty girl . . . pretty girl . . . pretty girl.* My whole consciousness focuses on those two words. Breathing becomes secondary, and my heartbeat sounds in my ears, marking the rhythm of the words. A keening noise escapes my lips and the door vibrates against my back when Emily starts pounding on it from outside. Stone and ice shoot through my veins, stiffening my limbs, but almost as quickly a fiery heat flows through me and I'm kicking and I'm flailing and I'm biting. I'm a blur of motion, pushing back, snarling like an animal.

When I come back to myself, my cheek rests against scratchy fabric and a hand is stroking my hair back from my face.

"Jax," a voice says in my ear. "It's okay. You're safe. Relax." It's Emily and my still rapid breaths slow. Color bleeds back in around me and the room comes into focus. My head is cradled in Emily's lap and she continues gently running her fingers over my head. "Better now?"

I nod and shift into a more upright position, a slight residual dizziness keeping me on the floor for now. The on-edge feeling that's haunted me since this afternoon is gone. Great cure for creeping anxiety—a panic attack. If only I'd thought of that sooner. At least I feel a bit more like myself now.

The door is wide open, but Lir sits in the corner watching me sit up. "Jax, I—" He reaches a hand out and cringes when I shy away from it. "I did not mean to . . . I didn't know. They said . . ." Emerald eyes meet mine. "I am sorry."

Lir shifts closer to me, bringing his bruised and battered face back into the meager light. There's fresh blood dribbling from the side of his lip. From something I did, no doubt. He wipes his mouth with the back of his hand, sending a streak of green blood up his cheek.

I flinch. "Sorry for the . . . new blood there. Friends?"

Lir eyes me for a moment, a mixture of confusion and guilt on his face, and then chuckles awkwardly. "With friends like you, who needs enemies, right?"

"Well, you wouldn't be the only friend I hit today."

There goes that eyebrow of his, amusement flooding into his eyes. "I hope I'm the only one you hit twice today, at least."

"I've already apologized for the first one." Forehead to palm, I shake my head. "It's just been a bad day."

"You're telling me," Lir says, raising his bound hands. "And you're not even the one tied up."

I rise to my feet, pulling out the small knife strapped to my thigh. It's a good thing I didn't lose the thing when I was crawling through Dane's window. Normally my knife would be secure in my boot, but I'm stuck in Emily's flimsy sandals—my boots are waiting for me in one of the packs. I start sawing at the ropes around Lir's wrists.

"Are you sure releasing it is still a good idea?" asks Emily. She glares at Lir with narrowed eyes. "I'm worried about you, Jax. You're going to travel to the city alone? With only that alien to help? After that . . ." She flutters her hands and pulls her lower lip into her mouth. "I know you have some sort of agreement . . . but there's got to be another way. I don't trust it, not after what it just did. It's dangerous."

Lir speaks up, sarcasm biting at his words. "I am sure you are familiar enough with the distinction between male and female to realize that I am a *he* and not an *it*, correct?" Lir returns her glare. "I did not ask to be here. Who are you to question my trustworthiness? If anyone here has a reason to doubt motives, it is me. Since arriving, I have been attacked, beaten, knocked out, and tied up." His voice gets softer. "The altercation was a misunderstanding on my part and I have already apologized." My knife finally gets through the rope and Lir rubs at his wrists and flexes his fingers. "I gave Jax my word. I will do everything in my power to get her to the city safely."

"How do I know your word is good, alien?" Emily asks haughtily.

Lir rolls his eyes. "What is it with you humans and your affection for labels instead of names? My name is Lir. Please address me by it."

"Okay, then, *Lir*, how do I know your word is good?"

"Does it matter what you know? Can Jax not speak for herself? She obviously trusts me at least that far. You should, too."

"Jax doesn't know any better!" Exasperation laces Emily's words.

"What?" *I'm not perfect and I make mistakes, but* . . . "What does that mean, Emily?"

Her eyebrows draw together and she puts a hand on my shoulder. "You're just . . . your decisions aren't always very reliable."

I shake her hand away. "Well, this is my decision. Like it or not, this is the only way to get Jace back." The warm friendship I'd been beginning to feel for her recedes a little. Emily is just like the rest of them, thinking I'm some fragile child. "So will your friends upstairs look the other way or not? We've got to get out of here."

"I didn't mean it like that . . . I'm sorry. I just don't want you to get hurt," says Emily.

"Stuff happens, no matter what you do. If anyone knows that, it's me. I can't sit here behind these walls while my brother is out there. Lir, alien or not, is the only way in I have. I know how to look out for myself." Bringing my hands up, I place them on her shoulders and stare into her face. "If you can't trust him, trust me. I can do this."

Emily looks away and nods. "Okay."

Emily isn't quite sure where Brian's loyalties lie, and even if I were sure of the two guards' loyalties, they don't seem very fond of aliens. Getting Lir up the stairs and out the door is going to be more complicated than we thought. We throw a couple ideas back and forth, but nothing really seems feasible. Emily's ideas mostly consist of getting more people to help, but that makes me uneasy—Lir too, though he doesn't actually say it. The more people involved, the more potential for us to be caught.

"We've been down here too long," says Emily. "Either way, they're going to start getting suspicious, if they aren't already. We could try again in the morning."

"Sounds great," says Lir, "except they plan to execute me in the morning."

"Execute you?" It's the first time Emily has looked even a little concerned for Lir's safety and not just my own. "Without a trial? For what?"

Anger and maybe even a touch of fear flashes across his face. "For being an alien. You are not the most accepting lot."

"Why are you surprised at this?" I ask. Seems I'm not the only naive one around here. "After everything you've seen, did you really think they'd let him go? You know how things work around here."

"I do . . . but . . . he hasn't done anything."

"Nothing except be nonnative to this planet," Lir says. "Would not be the first instance of the human superiority complex. You have destroyed your planet and much of your race and yet you believe we are the enemy."

"Aren't you? You came to our planet—"

"The planet you did not bother to take care of."

"Our city—"

"That you were no longer able to manage. There is plenty of space here now. Why can you not share?" Lir stands face-to-face with Emily, glaring, his words edged with anger.

Emily doesn't back down. "Why couldn't you stay on your own planet? Why are you here?"

Lir breaks her gaze and his eyes shift to the side. "We have our reasons."

I throw my hands up. "Why the hell are you guys arguing? None of this is helpful. Emily, they're here and they have Jace, that's all that matters." I turn to Lir and poke him in the chest with one finger. "And you . . . drop it. Seems like you have your own complex. Stop lumping all humans together. Most of us weren't even alive during the Collapse and had no part in any of it." Lir smirks and Emily looks at me in surprise. "What?"

Emily's eyes flick from my face down to my hand—which is once again lingering too long on Lir's chest. It's one thing for me to allow others to touch me, a completely different thing for me to touch someone else. Yet once again, I've unconsciously touched Lir. What is wrong with me? Even after . . . I pull my hand back quickly, like it burns. Maybe it actually does, a little, because my face heats up.

I direct my gaze to the wall. "Can we just get on with it? We're wasting time." The steam of my irritation flows out and my shoulders droop. "Who knows what they're doing to Jace."

Eight

It ends up that Emily calls the guards down to "help us with the unruly prisoner," Lir knocks them out, and I tie them up. Simple enough, really, once the two of them stopped arguing and we worked it out. Emily is staying behind. She's tied up, too, better to sell the story that the alien escaped with me as a hostage. That way no one will get in any real trouble, except me—hopefully.

Lir and I slip up the stairs and into the open air. As soon as he's outside, Lir takes a big breath and lets it out slowly. "Smells much better out here," he says.

There's really nothing for me to say to that. I'm glad he's enjoying his freedom, but we don't have time to waste.

I grab his shirt and pull him in the direction of the packs and the west gate. The moon rests behind a cloud and there's little light to navigate with, but we manage. He follows close behind me, darting in between buildings and hiding in doorways. We try to avoid the main street, but are forced to travel the last few blocks on it after making a quick detour to grab the satchel. There aren't many people—in fact, we've only seen six and they were guards on patrol. The festival must still be going on.

An open grassy area stretches between the edge of the last building and the gate. Unfortunately, it's also well lit by two lampposts on either side of the gate. I scan the surroundings.

No guards in sight. Where are they? There's always someone on duty. There—a shape to the left of the gate pulls my attention. Only one guard tonight, and he's sitting against the wall, looking in the opposite direction.

The packs are waiting behind a bush along the wall to the right, about twenty feet from the gate and thirty feet from the guard. He might look like he's not paying much attention, but I'm not going to risk both of us getting caught. I glide to the right, my back pressed against the building. Once I am directly across from where the packs are supposed to be, I take a cautious step forward. Lir steps up behind me and I shake my head, pointing at him and then back at the building. He nods and fades back into the shadows.

Quick and careful steps bring me to the bush and I sit down beside it, out of the sight line of the guard farther down. The rustle of the branches makes me cringe, but I have no choice—I've got to get the packs. Not only for the food and water they contain, but I damn sure can't waltz around in the woods in a dress. I can't wait to get back into a pair of pants. But my wardrobe will have to wait, at least until we're well away from here.

The guard is just sitting there, not even scanning the area. What is going on? I'm pretty sure Dane wouldn't put up with that level of incompetence. Something isn't right and a twinge of anxiety creeps down my back. Lir slides up to the wall beside me, startling me into nearly screaming. As it is, I jump and then turn to glare at him.

"What are you doing? I told you to wait." The whisper hisses past my teeth.

"That guy is not going anywhere." He points toward the guard.

I follow his finger and really study the guard leaning against the wall. He's not moving, and now that I think about it, he hasn't moved since I first observed him. Is he sleeping? I shoulder one of the packs and skirt around the bush and press close to the wall on the other side. Slow side steps take me closer to the gate and the guard. Lir mimics my actions behind me, joining me in scooting closer.

The caution isn't necessary. Ten feet closer and I can already tell the guard is dead, his head tilted at an unnatural angle. I should be relieved. I'm not. Instead my muscles tense up and my eyes move around my surroundings in short, quick movements. Whoever did this might still be here and they aren't someone I want to run into. Even more concerning is that the body is going to draw attention to this gate, the one I so carefully planned to take to throw them off our trail.

There's no time to slink along the wall to the next gate—the festival will be wrapping up soon and people will be headed back to their homes for the night. There really isn't even time for me to be standing here thinking. No other choice, then. I'll find another way to throw them off. Grabbing Lir's arm, I run the last few feet to the gate and slip through.

§

We've been making fast progress away from Bridgelake for what feels like forever, but in reality is probably only a couple hours or so. There should be plenty of time for us to make our escape. Emily said the guards don't switch over until morning, so our escape won't be discovered until then. Our westerly direction, away from the city, should help keep them off our tail as long as the dead guard doesn't give us away. That is, if Dane actually cares about retrieving me. It's not like he was very concerned about Jace.

The weight of the day's events is catching up to me and my steps are slowing. We walk in silence, the sound of the forest and the occasional twig breaking underfoot surrounding us. I mumble an apology when a small branch swings back after I push by and hits Lir. He mumbles something in return. Small talk is not my specialty and it doesn't appear to be his, either. The lingering quiet between us unnerves me, sending doubts flooding into my mind.

What have I gotten myself into? Now that I really have time to stop and think, or at least concentrate on thinking, I realize I have no idea what I'm doing, not really. The combination of hope and adrenaline that has been keeping me going is fading, leaving me with nothing but a very vague goal to work toward. Yes, I'm going to get Jace back, but how?

The increased anxiety speeds my steps until Lir falls behind. My feet beat out a steady cadence. *Step. Breath. Step. Breath.* What if I should have waited for Flint? *Step.* What if the alien is dangerous? *Breath.* What if I'm too late? *Step.* What happened to the dead guard? *Breath.* What if Jace is dead? What if—

"Jax?" He's beside me now, his voice breaking me out of the endless stream of *what if*s floating through my brain. "Are we stopping here?"

Huh? I realize I've stopped walking and I'm practically hyperventilating. The buzz of anxiety is back, filling my body and throbbing in time with my rapid breathing.

Lir's brow furrows. "Are you all right?" His hand extends toward me and mine flies up to meet it, grasping his wrist and squeezing.

I can feel his wrist bones grating together under my grip. "Don't touch me." My hand releases and he yanks his arm away.

"Got it. No touching." Wariness enters his eyes and he takes a step backward.

"Don't look at me like that."

And his hands go up in front of him. "Like what?"

"Like I'm crazy." And there goes the eyebrow. "And stop with the eyebrow thing!"

Lir blinks his eyes twice and then a short burst of air escapes from his chest. "Eyebrow thing?" His lips fight to turn up at the edges.

I scowl, but the wavering edges of his mouth start my lips to mimicking the motion. I lose the battle first. A smile spreads across my face and my anxiety releases into a laugh. "Yeah. The eyebrow thing. You know, like this?" My pointer finger goes to his brow and lifts his left eyebrow up. "Just the one."

The muscles in his forehead move under my finger and the green tips of one curl brush against my knuckle. If I move my hand his eyebrow would stay up. Lir doesn't say anything; he just trails his eyes down my arm and up to my finger until his gaze is twisted up. Crap. I'm touching him again . . . right after I told him not to touch me. What is wrong with me?

I was right—the eyebrow stays up when I pull my hand away and drop it to my side. The tingling buzz recedes along with the previously unnoticed tension in my limbs. "Sorry," I say. "I'm just a little on edge."

"Really? I hadn't noticed," Lir says dryly, rubbing at his wrist. "I would hate to see you a lot on edge." His eyes widen at his own statement and he starts stammering. "I mean . . . just . . . I wasn't referring to . . ."

"It's okay." I sink down, my backpack pressing against a tree trunk, until my butt lands in the dirt. "I think I just need a moment. There's too much noise in my head right now."

Lir sits down across from me, pulling his knees into his chest and wrapping his arms around them. I mirror the movement. The edges of the dress flap against my thighs. Oh, yeah, I'm wearing a dress. So not only did I touch him, now I'm flashing him. My face heats and I slide my legs to the side, pulling the dress down around my knees.

I shrug out of one shoulder strap and swing the backpack around. First things first, I need to change. A light jacket. Two soft

T-shirts. A small bundle of food. Canteen. Sleeping bag. My knife and hilt. Pants? *Please tell me there are pants in here.* My fingers brush across a rough texture that can only be denim. Thank goodness.

I pull the jeans out and shimmy them up underneath the dress. Next come socks and some nice sturdy boots. I'm almost as excited to get rid of the stupid sandals as I am to get out of the dress. A shirt goes over my head and I strip off the sleeves of the dress, pulling it down and stepping out of it before sliding my arms into the shirt-sleeves. Lir jumps a little when I toss the now crumpled dress past his head and into the woods. It probably would have been better for me to stuff it in the pack, to cover our tracks and all, but it's too late now. I lean back against the tree and close my eyes, finally a little more comfortable.

"So what is your plan exactly?" His words are quiet, near a whisper.

So far, I don't really have much of a plan, but that probably wouldn't be the best thing to admit to right now. I open my eyes and squint at him. He's staring at the ground. It's the first time since Lir stepped off that ship that his wall of confidence really cracks. For just a moment, a flash of vulnerability, maybe even fear, passes across his face. What must it be like for him, stranded out here, alone and hurt with only me to depend on? He looks so incredibly lost in that moment—and young.

"How old are you?" I ask.

The wall slams back down. "In your years? Nineteen." His head comes up and he narrows his eyes. "Why?"

"Just curious." I roll my shoulders and straighten my legs out in front of me. "I'm seventeen—well, almost eighteen now. My brother, too. We're twins." His head tilts to the side, his shoulders lower and one leg extends forward. Silence fills the gap between us again. I want to know him, to know something, anything to ease my fears about Jace. "What about you, any siblings?"

"One," he says. I just stare, waiting for the rest. Lir avoids my gaze and his voice softens. "A sister, Stella. She's seven."

"I've always wanted a sister. Do you guys get along?"

"Yes." Again, I wait for more words, but he doesn't continue.

Elaborate swirls appear in the dirt as I trace my finger through it. There's a burn behind my eyes and I have to swallow twice before I can get my next question past my lips. "Do you think they're hurting him?" My eyes dart up to meet Lir's emerald gaze and one of my hands curls in on itself, my nails pressing into my palm.

"I don't know." At least he's honest. Though I might have preferred empty assurances.

There are so many other questions begging to squeeze out of my mouth. *Why did they do it? What do they want with him? Who did it? And is Jace even alive?* Lir doesn't have the answers to these questions, though, and even if he did, I might not like them. I can't afford to get sidetracked.

I look away and rub my eyes with the back of my hand. *Get it together, Jax. No tears.* "I don't have one. A plan. Not really, anyway." I laugh nervously. "Just get my brother back or die trying." Grabbing the strap of the satchel, I pull it into my lap. "I've got a map. I know where to go." Lir scoots across the ground until he's next to me. The map rustles on my lap as I unfold it and point out our route to him. He leans closer, following my finger with his eyes, until I can feel the heat of his chest against my back. "Bridgelake is here, your city is here." My finger jabs at each location. "We're about here."

"We're moving west? That is the wrong direction."

"Yes. Well, it's away from the city, anyway," I say. "It's to throw them off if they try to follow us. We'll head west and then cut north here, near one of the red circles, then back east here. This road should take us almost all the way there."

Lir nods. "How much farther should we travel tonight?"

It's hours until morning and the longer I sit here, the heavier my eyes get. My joints are starting to ache, especially my shoulders. Hanging from a window ledge was not friendly to my arms. "Maybe we should rest for a bit now and then head out at first light?" I don't really mean for it to be a question.

Lir shrugs, his shoulder brushing my arm with the movement. "Sounds good to me."

I fight a sigh of relief when he moves away until he's across from me again and opens his pack. Puffs of dirt drift up when he rolls out his sleeping bag. He slides inside and closes his eyes.

Lir's breathing has evened and his body relaxed into sleep before I even move to get my sleeping bag. At least he trusts me a little, if only enough to fall asleep in my presence. I envy his ease as I toss and turn for at least an hour before falling into a restless sleep.

My dreams are filled with blood and knives, a bright white light and Jace's screams. And then they're not. Images of towering buildings and silver ships creep into my head, followed closely by bright green eyes and a single upraised eyebrow.

Nine

Sunlight filters through the leaves and onto my face, waking me up. I push the sleeping bag down and stand. My shoulders are still stiff, but I do a couple stretches and they loosen up. Clenching my fist a few times loosens up my sore knuckles. Flint has a hard head.

The woods are quiet and I look over, expecting Lir to still be sleeping. He's not there. "Lir?" I call out, but there's no response.

He left? I thought we'd gotten somewhere last night, at least a tentative truce, a mutual reliance on each other, but I guess not. One of these days I will learn my lesson about being kind to people who don't deserve it. Hopefully it's the same day I learn the lesson about how to figure out who *does* deserve it.

Stupid alien. No, stupid me for taking him at his word. I broke him out of jail and this is how he repays me? By ditching me when we've barely gotten started? My plan, crappy as it is, will not work without Lir's help to get me into the city. I've got to find him. Unused to the forest and somewhat injured, he couldn't have gotten very far.

I pull on my boots and I'm into the trees in minutes. I scan the area, looking for the signs of his passage. A broken branch points me in the right direction and it isn't long before I find a footprint.

I creep through the woods, carefully placing my feet so not to disturb the quiet. I'm not good with people, but I know the woods and how to move through the forest in near silence. A few minutes later, I hear a curse and scramble up a tree to get a better view. About twenty feet from my perch is Lir, sitting on a fallen log. His face is pale and sweaty. He runs his hands through his hair and stands up, turning in a circle and looking panicked. He curses again and kicks the log.

My hands catch my giggle, but not quickly enough. He freezes, moving only his eyes around, searching out the source of the noise.

"Jax?" He scans the area around him. "Is that you?" When I don't respond, he starts walking in my direction. "Who's out there?"

I wait until he is practically underneath me before dropping out of the tree and landing on the ground behind him. He spins around, his eyes wide.

"Where were you going, Lir?"

Redness floods his face. "I needed to relieve myself," he says to his shoes. "I got lost."

I want to believe him, but should I? "You must have snuck away awfully quietly."

"I did not want to wake you." He's still talking to his shoes, but he looks up and smiles sheepishly at me.

Whether he's telling the truth or not, he must realize now that I was right when I told him he'd need me, that he can't make it back on his own. "I'm sure you would have eventually wandered around in a circle and found your way back," I say.

"I suppose so," he says. "But thank you for finding me anyway."

We head back to our makeshift campsite and pack up. Rather, Lir tries to just stuff everything back in the pack and I roll my eyes and end up packing for both of us. *You can't just shove stuff in. It has to be folded and fit together, otherwise it just won't work.* He offers to carry the satchel as well as his pack, but I refuse. I'm holding on to the map. Lack of survival skills or not, he might still have a sense of direction.

Once everything is put away and my knife is back in its hilt in my boot, we set off; I gauge direction by the angle of the sun and Lir follows along behind me.

Hours and miles later, I'm wiping my forehead with the back of my hand. The sun is high in the sky and even in the shade of the woods, it's hot. I pause, waiting for Lir to catch up. His pace has been steady, but he's obviously not used to hiking. He's only about ten feet behind me now, but the distance has gotten bigger as the day has gone on. He hasn't complained, just kept walking even though I've made a point of sending branches zinging back to hit him and not warning him about spiderwebs. That'll teach him to try and sneak off. Or maybe I'm just being mean. Then again, maybe I was wrong to distrust him this morning.

What do they do in that city anyway? Doesn't look like exercising is on their agenda. Or maybe it has something to do with the malfunctioning cuff. "What exactly does it do?" I ask out loud.

"Huh?" Lir stops beside me. His breath is coming a bit faster than normal and his hair has curled up even more with sweat and humidity, making the green in it more vivid.

"The *kitu*. What does it do?" I ask. Jace is always telling me that I need to work on my people skills, that people can't always follow what I'm saying when I only verbalize half of what I'm thinking. It's never bothered me. Why would it? The only person I see on a regular basis is Jace. I guess I've always taken for granted the fact that he usually knows exactly what I'm talking about. Maybe it's a twin thing.

Lir narrows his eyes and edges back slightly. "Why do you want to know?"

The sharpness of the words startles me until I realize he must think I'm trying to interrogate him or something. I shrug. "I don't really know much about you guys and, well, I'm curious. Kind of an annoying trait of mine, actually. If I hadn't been so set on getting a glimpse of an alien, Jace wouldn't have gotten taken."

"Why are you so interested? Most humans . . . are not very fond of us."

I snort. "That's true. Humans resent you for coming to our planet and then ignoring us, not even offering to help with our problems. I'm sure you guys have problems of your own, though." I glance at him and he nods. "Most even blame you for the Collapse, but I don't know how you could be to blame for something that happened decades before you arrived . . . and I'm not most people."

Lir smiles. "I am beginning to see that." He motions for me to follow him and sits down on a log. I perch next to him. He stares at me with his brow furrowed before starting to talk. "The *kitu* is mostly a communication device. It allows us to link to each other and interact, but it can also boost my strength, allow me to move faster for a brief period of time, enhance my vision . . ." He stops and then shrugs. "I am not sure how they work."

"So they're like a physiological crutch?" Lir tilts his head to the side and gives me a strange look. I continue to be sure I've gotten it right. "It must link into your biomechanical and chemical functions or something. Either you have specialized functions that have developed to help you control the link or somehow the cuff must link directly into your biology. Perhaps even altering your basic makeup to allow you to use it."

"That sounds about right," says Lir, both eyebrows up in surprise. "How do you know so much about biology?"

"My dad taught me. He was a scientist, you know . . . before." I push back the wisps of hair that have escaped my braid and stand up.

"Your dad sounds like an intelligent man."

"He was." I look away and sigh before straightening my shoulders and changing the subject. "I don't think we should try to travel too much farther today. It will be dark before long and I'd like to try to set a few snares," I say, smiling. "Fresh rabbit is so much better than dried."

Lir's eyes sparkle when he returns my smile. "I'm sure you could make a great meal out of anything."

After that, Lir keeps pace with me, though that might have more to do with me actually being nicer to him than anything else. I point out various features of the forest and explain some of my navigation methods. He seems particularly interested when I start going over the edible plants and how to find water. It gives me a small thrill to have him focused so intently on me and I end up smiling and joking more than I normally would. That worries me.

Lir laughs more, too. I like the sound and that downright terrifies me. I shouldn't be getting attached. I shouldn't be enjoying his company. Even so, the air feels clearer now, like we've moved past a simple truce and into some sort of friendship.

§

The night brings with it a drop in the temperature and a new sense of hopelessness to me. We huddle close to the small fire I built, a rabbit roasting on a stick across it. Every time the fire sizzles, my stomach rumbles. We ate only a little bread and some berries I found for lunch. The food I packed is already running low. I set five snares, but only caught one small rabbit. It will have to do.

The flames reflect off Lir's eyes, lighting up the golden ring around his pupils so it almost drowns out the bright green of the irises. He was impressed that I actually caught anything with my "primitive hunting techniques," as he called my snares. When I pulled out a lighter for the fire, he half gasped. He must have expected me to rub sticks together or something. I rolled my eyes. Cleaning the rabbit—something I've done since I was eight—made him go pale and look away. He's not looking away now, though. His stomach's growling nearly as loud as mine as he watches the meat crisp.

The silence between us tonight is different, somehow softer. We're both dirty and tired, but I'm clearly in better shape than Lir. His injuries from the soldiers remain. Although it's not swollen shut, his left eye is shadowed in bruises. His lip is split and there's still blood on the side of his face from his beating. At least his knife wound hasn't reopened. My stitches have held it well, but the edges of the wound that I can see are red around the black thread.

I need to find us somewhere to get cleaned up tomorrow. Water alone might not hold off infection, but it couldn't hurt to clean his wounds and bandage his arm with something other than the dirty piece of fabric he has wrapped around it.

So many things could go wrong out here. What would I do if he got sick? Does his body even work like mine? So far his injuries haven't healed at superspeed or done anything else out of the ordinary, but would I even know if something were wrong? More importantly, would Lir tell me if something were really wrong?

Too many questions. Too many worries. I run a hand down my face and my stomach speaks up again, a loud noise in the quiet night. There's an answering noise across the fire and I grin. He's hungry and he's been eating and drinking, so he can't be too bad off. Lir looks up and smiles at me, one side of his mouth turning up and a sparkle in his eye. My original assessment of him really was spot-on. He's beautiful.

During the day he looked at home in the woods, the green in his features blending with the forest. Now, the firelight brings out the gold, and even dirty and exhausted, he shines. Too caught up in everything else, I hadn't noticed it last night. He has an inner light that is nowhere near human and I think it should bother me or maybe scare me, this otherworldly illumination. But all I want to do is move to him and bask in it. I'm drawn to him in a way I don't understand. That's what frightens me.

And now I'm staring. The eyebrow goes up and heat floods into my face. I busy my mind and my hands with pulling the rabbit away from the fire. I divide the meat and pass a little more than half to Lir without meeting his eyes.

It's hot, really too hot to eat yet, but my stomach doesn't care. The grease burns my fingers as I shovel the meat into my mouth. It's gone much too soon and I'm not even close to full. Even with the mishap in the market, I should have found a way to bring more food. We're going to have to live off the land when the food in the pack runs out and we won't be in the forest forever. I didn't really think about how long this trek would take, how much physical exertion would eat into our supplies—hell, I didn't even really think about exactly how much two people would need to eat. Just another example of my poor planning.

I'm going to end up getting both of us killed. All three of us, really, if I'm not in time to rescue Jace from who knows what. My eyes sting and my stomach rumbles, quieter now but still audible.

"Here, Jax." Lir leans across the fire with some rabbit in his hand. "I'm full." He's lying. I know he is, but I take the food anyway.

"Thanks," I mumble.

Still short of sated, I wipe my greasy fingers on my jeans and pull out my sleeping bag. I spread it next to the fire and snuggle down into it. Fall weather would choose to finally arrive when I'm stuck out in the woods. Everything seems to be working against me, even the temperature.

The rustle of leaves to my right signals Lir settling into his sleeping bag. His breathing evens out quickly. Looks like another night of easy sleep for him while I'm left lying here staring up at the stars, the scenarios of all the things I should have done differently playing on repeat in my mind.

The bright twinkling lights look so close, but they're really millions of miles away from me. Jace feels just as far away as those stars. Only the second night that Jace hasn't been here to hold my hand while I fall asleep to chase the nightmares away, and I'm already losing it. The burn in my eyes overflows into tears that trickle silently over my cheeks and down to the ground.

"Would it help if I told you I was scared, too?" Lir's voice is soft, just barely carrying over the fire to my ears. Not asleep, then.

I don't answer. I can't, not without giving in to the tears, without admitting how weak I am. If he had any idea how broken I am . . . he has followed the Bridgelake nutcase into the woods, trusted her to know what to do. I'd be scared if I were him, too.

There's a puff of air across my face when Lir's sleeping bag flops down next to me. What is he doing?

"Is this acceptable? Me over here instead of over there?"

I just nod, still not trusting my voice.

He settles down to the ground beside me. There's still a few feet between us, enough for me to be comfortable but not so much that I want to scoot closer. "It will all work out," Lir whispers before making himself comfortable and falling asleep. For real this time—I check before closing my own eyes and counting my breaths to help me drift off.

Without Jace, the nightmares come back again. Hot breath. Long red hair twisted around a fist. The knife. The blood. The images retreat, though, rather than lasting all night long, and are replaced with new ones. Firelight. A long red braid trailing down my back. My smile. My laugh. A feeling of amusement at my narrowed eyes and my hands on my hips.

Ten

I crack one eye open. It's not quite dawn, but it isn't far off. The dreams weren't so bad last night and I actually feel rested, something I normally can only achieve with Jace's presence to ground me. It isn't until I go to sit up that I realize Lir's fingers are wrapped around mine. Did I reach out for him in my nightmares or was he trying to comfort me?

Yanking my hand away is what I should do, but the press of his palm against mine is too tempting. The touch of another's hand, such a simple thing, anchors me and helps to clear my head. Sure, people other than Jace have touched me in the past year, but they stick to my arms or shoulders and I have to brace myself in case I start to lose it. It's that way even with Flint, who's like a second brother to me, and he's the only person besides my actual brother who I will voluntarily touch. Until now, that is. Just lying here and being able to revel in the feeling of someone holding my hand without reminding myself to breathe or listening to my pulse thunder in my ears . . . I can almost feel normal and whole.

With that thought, I finally snatch my hand away. Lir's hold tightens briefly as my fingers leave his, but he doesn't wake. His touch is a luxury I could get used to much too easily, and it's bad enough that I need Jace to get a good night's rest. I can't afford to become dependent on someone else, especially someone I'll never see again once this mission is over—someone who already has some sort of unexplainable draw for me.

I don't get up, though. Instead, I roll onto my side and run my eyes over his face. He looks so peaceful that I just lie there and trace his features with my gaze. The bruise around his eye is already fading to yellow and I know enough to realize that means the E'rikon must heal faster than we do. At this rate he'll be back to normal in only another day or two. I guess I don't have to worry about his arm as much as I thought I did. It'll heal up just like the rest of him.

His hair just barely brushes the tips of his ears before curling upward and this close I can see that the hair is actually gold at the root, only turning green after about an inch of growth. It's not a dye job. Not even the strongest dye would be able to cover that metallic gold color, so his hair must grow like that. Gold blending into green, like his eyes . . . and the scales on his back.

I push myself up on one elbow and lean forward. Without the high-collared jacket he was wearing before, the scales are clearly visible. I was too busy studying the ones on his back before to notice that the scales also flare out at the top and edge into his hairline and behind his ears. They're fainter the farther up they go and almost entirely gold by the time they disappear under his hair. Could it be this gold . . . base . . . that gives him that subtle glow? Would all of them look a little shiny up close or just the ones with the metallic colors?

Lying back down on my side, I move closer and examine his forehead. His skin does have a very faint gold sheen to it. So it was probably this that reflected the firelight last night and made him appear to be illuminated. Good to know I'm not entirely crazy.

When I bring my eyes back down, Lir's awake, his eyes little more than an inch away from mine. He blinks slowly once and my body startles into action, pulling my face back. I scramble out of the sleeping bag and turn away without a word, a hot flush of embarrassment building a fire behind my cheeks.

"Jax?"

I don't turn around. "I was just, uh, checking your injuries. Looks like they're healing nicely. We should probably still try to find someplace to clean your arm today, though." Holding my breath, I set my shoulders. *Please don't say anything. Please don't say anything.*

"Sounds like a plan," he says slowly. Rustling signals his exit from his sleeping bag. "Should we pack up or eat first?"

"Pack," I reply immediately. It's as if he knows I need something to do with my hands to distract me from what just happened.

By the time we both have our stuff folded or rolled neatly into our packs, I'm calm enough to meet his eyes without getting flustered. I pull out the map and estimate our location before we set off.

The hike today is a little more difficult, the trees closer together and the incline steeper. What the route lacks in ease, it makes up for with isolation. We're quite a ways from any large settlements and those humans that chose to live on their own normally stick to the abandoned towns rather than deal with the wilderness. At least, I hope so. After Lir's reception in Bridgelake, I'd prefer not to run into anyone else, human or alien.

Despite the rough terrain, I set a fast pace and Lir lags behind early on. I make sure to keep him within sight, but I'm well in the lead. It's midday before I slow my steps and sit down up against a tree. Lir joins me a few minutes later.

"Perhaps after our rest you could slow down a bit so I am not constantly in fear of losing you?" A bead of sweat trails down his neck and he's slightly out of breath. He must have sped up when he saw me stop. "All either of us needs is to get injured because we're rushing."

He's right. I've been punishing myself for my fascination with his touch and his skin this morning and I didn't even take into account that it made Lir suffer, too. It's not his fault that I wish I'd gotten a chance to run my finger along his cheek to see if his skin *felt* any different.

I close my eyes and bite my lip. "Sorry. I didn't really think about it."

"I realize that this is . . . uncomfortable for you, but you are going to have to trust me and—"

"Just like you trust me? What happened to the guy who thought I was going to seduce information out of him?"

He cringes. "That was . . . a mistake, and one that I've already apologized for. Today you have pushed yourself to the brink of collapse just to get out of speaking to me. I am not someone you need to fear. If I desired to harm you, haven't I had plenty of opportunity?" One finger under my chin, he pushes my face up. Instinctively I close my eyes and prepare for the creeping chill of fear . . . but there's nothing but a warm calm flowing through my limbs. I slowly open my eyes and he smiles. "I will not hurt you. If you're curious, please just ask. I much preferred our conversations from yesterday to the drudging silence this morning."

"Okay."

Lir stands and reaches a hand out to me. I eye it for a moment before accepting it and allowing him to pull me to my feet. Trust has to start somewhere, I guess.

§

It's still cold once the sun goes down, but our campsite doesn't feel quite as dreary. We stumbled across a stream, and although the water was a bit chilly, I'd certainly underestimated the effect feeling clean could have on morale. Even better, the stream fed into a small pond that had a bunch of watercress growing in it and my snares managed to snag three rabbits. Dinner is actually going to fill our stomachs and there will even be leftovers for tomorrow.

I teach Lir about the different sizes of firewood, show him how to build the fire and even let him start it. When I offer to show him how to clean a rabbit, though, he declines, saying, "I do not believe that is a skill I will ever need."

"What do you guys normally eat? Obviously not fresh game, but what else is there?"

He lets the silence draw out for a while before answering. "As you know, we stay within the city and are restricted by that . . . limitation. We primarily eat vegetable matter that is grown hydroponically. Meat isn't something we cultivate so much as synthesize. We require very little of the synthesized compound, as it is highly concentrated."

"I bet it tastes like crap, too."

A laugh bursts from him mouth and he nods. "Very true."

"So if you have everything you need in the city, what were you doing out here?" He opens his mouth, shuts it again, and presses his lips together, obviously uncomfortable. "You don't have to tell me if you don't want to."

"It's not that I do not want to, more that it is complicated and there are things . . . that have changed and—"

He hasn't pressed me on my issues; I won't press him on his. "Don't worry about it." I take a bite of a rabbit leg. "So tell me about the scales."

His brow furrows. "What about them?"

"Like, do they mean you're reptilian or something? Cold-blooded?"

"Reptilian?" Another laugh escapes from him. "The scales are more ornamental than anything. The colors are determined by our family line, so anyone can tell just by looking at me that I'm of Vestra and Linaud descent. Well, any E'rikon could tell, at least."

"Does that mean everyone with the same color is related?"

"To a point, yes." A wrinkle forms between his brows and he thinks for moment before continuing. "But there are degrees of color and even differences in the shades that we would recognize that a human would not. For example, one of the males from the clearing whose coloring you probably saw as silver actually has a distant relation to the Linaud line."

"His hair did have a gold tint to it," I say.

Lir eyes widen in surprise. "Interesting. I was always told most of the more subtle color variations were not visible on the human spectrum."

I shrug. "I just have good eyes. Jace does, too. He's the best hunter in Bridgelake because he's fast and has near perfect aim."

"Impressive."

"My dad always called me his little redtail." He looks at me blankly. "It's a type of hawk. Hawks have great vision . . ."

One of his hands comes up and rubs a strand of my hair between two fingers. "And you are red."

My eyes are so transfixed by his hand in my hair that I miss what he says next. "What?"

"I said, it's a beautiful color. If you were E'rikon, you would be of the Reva line."

"Oh." He's still staring at my hair and running his fingers across it. When he turns his eyes back to my face, the intensity there freezes me in place. My mouth goes dry and I'm struggling to swallow, not from fear, but something else. Heat gathers in my stomach and races down my arms to my tingling fingertips. Lips parted, I raise one hand and reach toward Lir's cheek. A green branch pops in the fire and my hand jerks. What am I doing? I avert my eyes and twist my hands together in my lap.

Releasing my hair with one brisk shake of his head, Lir stands and walks over to the packs. "Are you ready to get some rest?" I nod and manage to stammer out a yes. He pulls both sleeping bags out and lays them side by side. "Last night . . . I thought . . . but if you'd rather . . ." He gestures from one side of the fire to the other. "I can . . ." Under almost any other circumstances, I'd laugh at how flustered he is.

"No, it's fine." I slide into my sleeping bag beside him and lie on my back with my arms crossed over my chest.

Slipping into his own sleeping bag, he settles in next to me. "May I ask . . . the nightmares, are they—"

"I don't want to talk about it."

He simply nods and closes his eyes. I can't help but notice the hand he leaves extended out between us. I *can* help my urge to grab it, and I dig my fingertips into my biceps instead. Soon after, he has drifted off and I'm left staring up at the stars through the tree branches.

Unwilling to subject myself to the dreams if I don't have to and maybe even a little because I just crave the comfort and connection his touch brings, my hand finds his as I surrender to sleep.

This night is not so bad. The flash of a knife. Ice and fire in my veins, and then I'm flying. Swooping, drifting, diving, a hawk on the wind with wings outstretched. Peaceful blue sky with white puffy clouds. I'm looking down on myself with my red, red hair and a smile on my face.

Eleven

The next three days pass in much the same way—easy conversation during the day when I can laugh and joke, and then my slowly escalating nightly freak-out once the sky darkens. The shifts have become more rapid and unpredictable and the back-and-forth is exhausting for me. I can't even imagine how it must make Lir feel. He doesn't complain and he doesn't push me, though, so our friendship continues on, a careful balance of acceptance and shared experiences. There have been no repeats of . . . whatever almost happened between us the night he touched my hair.

The nightmares still come every night, not that I expected them to stop. But they're shorter, and more often than not, the truly scary parts get run out of my head by other things. For some reason, there's a lot of me in my dreams. It's odd, really. Of course, I've always been in my dreams, but from a first-person perspective. Now I'm like an observer. And from the outside looking in I hardly recognize myself. I stand tall and my hazel eyes aren't quite as haunted. The sunlight brings out shades of burnished copper in my hair. I smile and laugh and talk with my hands. If only I could be that version of me . . .

Dinner last night was less than meager. I haven't caught any fresh meat for the past two days. I've been pushing the pace and we just haven't remained in one place long enough for snares to be truly effective. We saved the last rabbit from a few nights ago for breakfast this morning and after that . . . I'm not sure what we'll do for protein.

My mouth tastes horrible and it's been two days since the last time we found a small creek to get cleaned up in. I've already cycled through the clothes I've packed and what I'm wearing is stiff with dirt and sweat. I feel gross. What I wouldn't give for a stream, a lake, some water I can swim in and dip my head under. Exhaustion and hunger are just beginning to take their toll on both of us, forming a sea of tension that is slowly rising to a boil.

I push my sleeping bag down and crawl out. Lir's stuff is already packed up and he's not here. Since the morning he woke to find me studying his skin, he's started getting up early. I've gotten used to his early rising and morning walks, so I don't worry anymore. He's also better about not getting lost now.

I leave most of my stuff where it is, taking only the satchel with me, and walk into the trees. After taking care of other needs, I wrap my legs around the trunk of a tall tree and climb up until I can see the path ahead of us. This has been my routine since the third day, when we spent hours going around a ravine that we could have avoided if I'd scouted our route better. There's nothing I can see that will require a change of course today. I pull the map out and try to work out where we are. We're heading north now and it looks like we should soon run into the secondary road that can take us over the mountain and toward the city.

Rustling noises come from the campsite as I return. "It looks like we might hit the road today, means easier walking, at least. I hope—" I stop, my feet skidding across the ground. It's not Lir moving around the campsite. A large black bear has ripped open Lir's pack, strewing items everywhere. It's already been through my things. Openmouthed, I take in the destroyed backpacks, ripped clothing, and shredded sleeping bags.

For a moment, I'm frozen, not able to do anything but watch the big, hairy brute rummage around with its snout. What are you supposed to do when you run into a bear? I back away slowly, pulling my knife from my boot as I go. At least I'll be ready if it decides to come after me. Not that my small knife, sharp as it is, will have this huge effect on it, but at least it makes me feel a little more in control.

Once the bear is out of sight, I circle around the campsite, hoping to catch Lir before he stumbles upon the thing. He *really* wouldn't know what to do. I take sideways half steps, crouching slightly and keeping the knife in front of me. A loud noise brings me spinning around, blade at the ready.

Lir steps out from behind a tree with his hands up, eyes wide and on the knife. "What's going on? You know I was not going any-where. I was—" Ripping fabric and a sound somewhere between a snort and a growl silence him.

"Bear," I say. "We need to go, now." I don't even wait for him to follow before I start hiking through the woods, quickly but quietly, away from the campsite.

"But what about our supplies?"

I look back over my shoulder. "Would you like to fight the bear for them?" His eyebrow is just itching to creep up. "It's all ruined anyway."

"Oh." With a furtive glance toward the campsite, he follows.

Twenty tense minutes later, I stop and sit on a rock, my head in my hands. Our difficult situation just got worse. The only weapon I have is this one knife. No sleeping bags. No clean clothes. No food. And dammit, even our canteens are gone. My heart beats against my chest and my breath comes quickly. Heat starts at my toes and flows up my body until a frustrated scream flies out of my mouth. I'm up and slamming my fist into the nearest tree before I can stop myself.

Well, that was a brilliant idea. Now I'm angry, frustrated, and in pain. I wiggle my fingers and shake my hand in the air, blinking back tears.

"Feel better?" he asks. The eyebrow is up in full force and a smirk is twisting his lips.

"No!" I can't help the volume and he flinches. "No," I say again, quietly. "My hand hurts."

"Let me see." Lir reaches out and takes hold of my throbbing fingers. He pauses when my body stiffens, but then I relax and he pulls my hand closer, examining my battered knuckles. "I think it will be okay. You did not break the skin, at least."

Did I step forward or did he? His gaze moves from my hand to my face and he smiles. An entirely different kind of heat travels from my fingers to the rest of me, rising to my face. The green of his eyes draws me closer and I lean forward. The satchel swings forward across my body and clanks against Lir's legs.

The satchel? I've still got it! I jump back and grab the sides of it, holding it up. "We've still got this. We've still got the map."

Lir clears his throat and takes a step back, rubbing his hand over the back of his head. "That's great, Jax."

I fumble with the buckle and pull up the flap, suddenly desperate to have the map in my hands, a physical reminder that we haven't lost everything. "At least we know where we're going and . . ." My searching fingers find the small metal orb from Dane's office, another thing we still have, though I have no idea if it's even useful. I pull it out triumphantly. "And then there's . . ." My voice falters as I take in his expression.

Lir's face goes pale and a choked noise escapes his throat. Tension vibrates the air around him as he stares at the object in my hand. When he finally brings his eyes up to me, my stomach drops. The light in his gaze is gone, his eyes cold, hard, and empty. There's no smile, no smirk, nothing even remotely friendly on his face. Instead, there's an emotion twisting his features that I've never seen on him before: fury.

"What are you doing with that?" His hands are fisted at his sides, knuckles white. "Was this all some sort of trick? Let you into the city so you can destroy us like you destroyed yourselves?" His eyes bore into me and I step back.

"I don't know what you're talking about. I found it . . . it was—"

"You are lying!" One hand shoots out and grabs my wrist. "Why else would you have hidden it from me?"

My pulse starts to race. "I didn't!"

He steps closer, backing me up to a tree. Too close. Friend or not friend? Anger or fear? Indecision freezes me and I'm stuck there with him leaning into me, a subtle tremble starting in my fingertips. I squeeze my eyes shut and count my breaths. *One. Two. Breathe . . .* It's not helping, so I open my eyes, hoping he can see that I'm telling the truth.

"How many others have fallen for this? What happened to the supply ship? Where are the rest? How was it done?" I frantically shake my head, but he just keeps going, question after question. The movement wiggles my hair loose from my braid and it falls down around my face. It catches Lir's attention and understanding breaks across his face.

He drops my wrist and takes a step back. "It was not you." A soft shake of his head. "Blazes. I cannot believe I did not figure it out before. It was your brother. The hair . . . it's why they took him."

"What?"

"Your brother is a thief and a murderer."

§

There's a new suspicion in Lir's eyes as he stoically recites the story. About six months ago, an E'rikon supply ship vanished without a trace somewhere in the vicinity of Bridgelake. The last communication from the crew showed a red-haired human standing over a fallen alien, his face splashed with green blood. And it wasn't the first of their ships to disappear. The details are vague and Lir's holding back. He won't tell me what the cargo was, just that they've been trying to retrieve it. Obviously the metal object I pulled from Dane's desk was part of it, but there's something bigger going on, too. Something he doesn't want me to know about. Just like that, he doesn't trust me anymore.

It explains a lot—why the aliens were there, why they landed, and even why they took Jace. But rather than being relieved at finally having some answers, I'm all the more terrified for my brother. It was one thing to think they took him mistakenly or just because. It's completely different now that I know their real purpose—interrogation.

Lir claims they would have never taken him if they weren't sure of his identity, but it just doesn't sound like my brother. Could he really have done it? How would he have become a killer without me noticing? I can't just accept it, not until I hear it from Jace. I let Lir examine the object and explain where and when I found it, but I keep the *kitu* I found to myself. If he can have secrets, then so can I.

The camaraderie we have developed over the past few days disappears. I don't like him assuming the worst of my brother, and Lir . . . he just retreats into himself. No words, no jokes, just hiking in silence with rumbling stomachs. In the beginning, I would have welcomed this quiet and near solitude, but I've gotten used to the easy conversation calming me. With nothing else to distract me, my worries play over and over in my head with every step.

Night comes and there's nothing to cook over the fire, only some blackberries I scrounged up. It's hard and cold on the ground and the descent of darkness only amps up my anxiety. I rock back and forth and close my eyes, but it doesn't help and there's silence on the other side of the fire. Even when I get up and start pacing, there's no reassurance from Lir. Not a word. He just rolls over and goes to sleep.

The nightmares don't let me sleep. Every time I close my eyes all I see is red and hands and pain.

I'm up before the sun, scavenging around the campsite and plotting our route for the day. I use the knife to scrape off some pine bark to take the edge off our hunger and we start walking.

Today's no better than yesterday. Hungry, dirty, and stiff, we trek along without speaking. I refuse to believe the worst of my brother and Lir won't talk about it. He won't listen to my pleas for more information and he snaps at me when I ask him to explain how they know for sure it was my brother. Either way, I'm not Jace and had nothing to do with it. The alien shouldn't be taking it out on me.

Finally, after another cold night on the rocky ground spent battling with my dreams, I can't take it anymore. "It wasn't me," I say.

"What are you talking about?"

"I didn't do it." I stop walking and wait for Lir to catch up to me.

"I am aware of that." He sighs and pushes ahead of me without stopping.

And that's our conversation for the day. I fight against tears and a hurt I don't quite understand.

Up in a tree the next morning, I see the first town we have to pass through. It's deserted like most of them nowadays, but I'd much rather stick to the woods. The forest only gets sparser on this leg of the journey, though. At least there might be food somewhere in there. Cans keep for a while, and before the Collapse there were lots of other things with shelf lives longer than I've been alive. Even better, there might be a camping store or something. I'm sick and tired of sleeping on the ground.

"We're headed into what used to be civilization today," I say. He just looks at me and nods. "Might find some food. Sleeping bags. A soft place to sleep." Still just nodding. "If we spend some extra time there, we could probably find enough supplies to last us."

"Whatever you think is best."

How can I possibly decide what is best? The words bubble up past my lips before I can stop them. "Is it just going to continue this way? I don't know what you want me to say, and it's exhausting."

"I want you to believe me."

"I do believe you." I throw my hands up and pace in front of him. "Someone stole your ship and—"

"Not someone," says Lir. "Your brother. And it is not the ship I am angry about. A good friend of mine was on that crew."

"I'm sorry about your friend, but you've got to understand I can't just accept that my brother—"

"It was him."

"You won't even explain to me how you know this. You don't explain anything to me." My steps falter and I cross my arms over my chest.

"I do not have to explain anything to you. I only have to get you to the city. That is what I am going to do." He brings his eyes up to meet mine, the stupid, emotionless tone of his voice ringing in my ears. "And nothing more."

Tears burn at the back of my eyes. I'm torn apart with worry for Jace. I have to leave the safety of the forest. I'm hungry. I'm dirty. I haven't had a good night's rest in three or four days. Not only is my hopelessness coming to a head, it has been joined by loneliness. My only ally has turned his back on me, and as much as I hate to admit it, I miss him. Well, at least the boy who was my friend. This snappy, uncaring, and downright cold boy before me is nothing like the one I got to know before. I even miss that frustrating eyebrow.

I take a deep breath and open my mouth, but it's useless to argue. Instead of the angry words festering in my throat, I simply say, "Fine." I keep my eyes on the ground. "I think it's best if you wait here and I go into the town. I'll find some supplies and we'll just spend another night here." I don't wait for him to respond before storming off. Maybe I just need some time alone, when the weight of my brother's crimes doesn't hang between us.

Twelve

I work my way through a subdivision and head in the general direction of the big building I saw from above. The Collapse happened quickly enough, wiped enough people out, that looting wasn't really a huge problem. Yes, a few cars litter the street and there's some destruction, but mostly the town is quiet. Nature is creeping her way back in, with overgrown yards, roots pushing up sidewalks, and branches growing through power lines. I have to change directions and backtrack a few times, but eventually I reach what looks like a grocery store. It's a lot bigger than I thought, but definitely a good find. I just hope it has what I need.

It's a strain to force the doors open. Their tracks are rusted and the grating sound they make when I am able to get them to move is loud. At least it seems like no one else has been in here recently. I slip through the opening I create, just barely squeezing through. Windowless, the store is nearly pitch-black, the only light coming in through the dingy glass of the doors. I flick the lighter and cup the flame with my hand to prevent it from going out. First thing to do is find a better source of light.

Alone time hasn't really helped as much as I'd hoped. My eyes aren't threatening tears anymore, but the back of my throat burns from holding them back. Why do I even care what he thinks of Jace? Because I care what he thinks of me. Even more aggravating. I'm not some delicate girl who needs people's approval to function—in fact, I'd much rather not worry about other people at all. Yet here I am worried that my alien friend is mad at me, that he won't forgive me for something my brother did. And just a little part of me that had butterflies when Lir gave me his undivided attention is crushed.

Whatever. Once I get Jace back, I'll never see Lir again anyway. My stomach twists at the thought, but I press on. There are much more important things for me to worry about, like food and supplies.

It's not just a grocery store. Clothes racks line the front and there are many other sections. As much as I'd love some clean clothes, the metal edge of the lighter is starting to burn my hand, so I make my way to the back corner.

Automotive stuff. Not very helpful either right now. I turn and walk down the back of the store. Toys. Electronics. Sports. Camping equipment. Now that's what I need.

The first camping aisle I go down has seen better days. Hasn't everything, though? Cookware, camp stoves, and a variety of utensils. The items are out of order and scattered on the shelves. At some point they were picked through, but carefully, by someone who knew what they wanted. Strange.

Farther down, I find lanterns and flashlights. Batteries will be hit-or-miss. It's been too long since the Collapse to rely on them even if the packages are still sealed. But butane should work just fine. I spot a butane lantern, grab it off the shelf, and scan the row of fuel canisters for one that will fit. The second canister fits and I fiddle with the settings until a bright light fills the area.

Even though I picked one of the smaller ones, the lantern is still heavy and awkward. I take it to the next row over and leave it sitting on the floor. It puts off just enough light that I can see either end of the aisle. Backpacks and sleeping bags! I grin and start shuffling through the packs. Once I've selected two, I do the same to the sleeping bags. This town must have really been out of the way for all this stuff to be here. I know Dane sends people out to gather supplies. Even Jace and I raided a few nearby towns when we lived on our own, but we often didn't find anything useful. This is great!

I shove a few more fuel canisters and two candle lanterns into one pack and then take the other in search of food. Anything even remotely cooler looking, I avoid. There won't be anything useful in there, but there are at least five aisles lined with plastic packages and cans.

I pull a can of beans off the shelf in front of me. The can isn't dented and it hasn't expanded. Probably safe. Thank goodness it has a pull tab, because my stomach practically twists into a knot at the thought of some real food.

My fingers dig into the can and I get one bite carefully into my mouth before I give up on manners and just start shoving it all in. I don't stop until the can is empty. A smile on my face, I slide to the floor and laugh. Who knew beans could taste so good.

For the first time in days, I relax. I'm still filthy, but at least I'm not really hungry. There's more than enough stuff in this store to get us the rest of the way to the city, and even farther if need be. Who cares if Lir is mad at me?

I'll get my brother and then I'll never see the alien again. Not if I can help it. All I need is my brother. Hell, I wanted an excuse to get out of Bridgelake anyway. Now I don't even have to worry about telling Jace I want to leave. We never have to go back again.

But I promised Emily. And Jace won't leave Flint behind.

I do care what Lir thinks of Jace, however, because I care what he thinks about me . . . And what if it's true? My brother has always been there, protecting me, teasing me, supporting me. What if I don't know him at all?

Six months ago I wasn't even able to leave the house and it's not like he would have said, *Oh, by the way, sis, I killed a few erks today.* As far as I know, he's never thought one way or another about the E'rikon, but even Flint was calling Lir names and it only makes sense that Jace would share his friend's mind-set. And Dane? Always sending my brother off on one important errand or another . . . maybe one of them was the retrieval of whatever it is that has brought the E'rikon out of their city and landed my brother in their hands.

What did you do, *Jace?* As the truth of Lir's accusations sink in, tears form wet tracks down my cheeks and drip off my chin. I don't even bother to wipe them away.

He's next to me before I can even rise to my feet. He puts his hand out and pulls me to my feet, pulls me into his arms. I bury my face in his chest, sobs shaking my shoulders and wetting his shirt.

"I'm sorry. I'm sorry. I'm sorry." Over and over again. They're the only words I can find.

"Me too." Lir holds me steady and rubs one hand over my back. "Me too."

We both tense at the sound of a gun cocking. I pull my head up and I can just see them over Lir's shoulder. Three men, two of them with guns pointed directly at us.

Lir leans forward and whispers into my ear. "Stay calm. I won't let anything happen to you." He pulls away from me and turns toward the men as he steps in front of me. "We mean you no harm."

The man in front, the one without a gun pointed at us, snickers. "You wouldn't get a chance to. Stu there is a crack shot." He jerks his head toward the man on the right. "And Dale's not half-bad, either."

"I would appreciate it if you'd lower your guns. We're unarmed." Lir holds his hands in front of him to demonstrate.

"I'm sure you would, boy. Why don't you bring that girl out front here?"

Lir's throat bobs as he swallows. He keeps his hands out, but motions me forward with one of them. "Come on around, Jax."

My hands shake, but I do as he asks, stepping forward with short slow steps until I'm beside him. I take deep breaths through my mouth and fight the urge to wipe my sweaty palms on my jeans, the beat of my heart like a drum in my ears.

"Pretty little thing, isn't she," says Stu. He steps closer to me and I get a whiff of unwashed male and smoke. My throat closes. "You got any weapons, girl?"

"No." I'm lying. My knife is in my boot, but I'm not telling him that.

"I told you we are unarmed." Lir's voice loosens my limbs slightly, his presence the only thing keeping me from losing it completely.

"You been stealing from us. How you gonna pay for all that?" asks the apparent leader of the bunch.

"I wasn't aware this store belonged to anyone." Lir pulls me closer until I'm pressed up against his side. He steps back. "We'll just leave you to it and be going."

"Nah." He shakes his head. "I think that breeder camp north of here would pay pretty good for a pretty young thing like that. We'll be keeping her. So you've got a decision to make. Would you like to live or die today, boy?"

Breeder camp? I can't keep my eyes open anymore. Words and images bounce around my head. *In. Out.* I can't breathe. The trembling starts at my toes and travels up my body until I have to clench my teeth to keep them from chattering.

Lir's hand gently squeezes my arm. "She's leaving with me." He takes another step backward, pulling me along with him. Another slow step back and I can open my eyes again.

The men still haven't moved forward, but their guns are still pointed at us. Mostly at Lir, actually. I'd left the lantern at the end of the aisle and each step takes us closer to its light. It can't be this easy, of course not.

We're so close the lantern is heating my back when there's a sharp inhale from one of the men.

"Once the guns are off you, I want you to run," says Lir. Off me? Where's he going?

"Good Lord. It's one of them." The leader's shout echoes through the store. *The lantern just illuminated Lir.*

Both men turn their guns to face Lir and he pushes me away from his side. "Go, Jax!"

Go? I can't leave him behind, and it's not going to happen, anyway. I'm frozen in place, my body too tense and on edge to take me anywhere. The leader darts forward and grabs my wrist, pulling me along with him. Once we're halfway down the aisle, the other two men start backing away slowly, their guns still trained on Lir.

Now's his chance—the men are distracted, and he could make his escape. There's no point in us both getting caught up in this. It won't be so bad . . . I will just . . . just breathe in and out . . . block it out. Like before. I don't have to be here. I can—

"Let go of her!" Lir's words can only be described as a snarl. He ignores the guns pointed at him and moves forward, only to freeze when my captor caresses my cheek with a third gun he pulled from his waistband.

The cold metal glides through my tears. "One more step and her pretty little brains will be all over the floor."

Take the step. I'd rather be dead. Eyes close.

"Take me," says Lir. "I have to be worth more. Just leave her be. She's been through enough."

No. No. No. That's not the way to do it. One of us has to get out of here.

"Oh, we'll be taking you anyway. I was just getting the merchandise out of the way 'cause Zach back there isn't a very good shot." Hot breath carries the words past my ear. *Too close!*

A rapid pant is the best my lungs can manage to squeeze past my constricted throat. *In. Out. In. Out. In. In.* No. That's wrong.

A crackle. Lir cries out and my eyes fly open. He falls to his knees, then slumps to the floor, a fourth man standing behind him with a gun.

"No!" My voice shatters the air. I pull away, fly forward, and fall to my knees beside him. He's breathing. No blood.

My eyes latch on the man, the one that shot my friend with the jolt gun in his hands. Only a jolt gun.

Boot. Knife. Hand. I creep forward. Yelling behind me, nothing important. His hands shake. Mine do not. The first shot misses me entirely, but the second sends fire into my thigh. The fire flows up into my hands and down into my feet. I clench my fingers to keep my knife, but it's too much. The jolt sends my fingers outward and me to the ground, where I shake for a while before welcoming the darkness that overtakes me.

Thirteen

I have to blink my eyes a few times before I'm sure they're actually open. The darkness around me is heavy and nearly suffocating. The ache in my leg radiates up through the rest of my body, steady but bearable. What the hell? I sit up, my hands out to either side. My left hand hits a cold, metal wall while my right hand stretches out into nothing.

"You're awake."

I jerk. "Lir?"

"Yes." Another hand connects with my blindly reaching right one and his fingers wrap around mine. "Right here."

Despite the dark, I'm not consumed with terror, no longer frozen in panic. But I have to know. "Where . . ."

"They're not here." He squeezes my hand. "It's been quiet out there for a while."

I swallow and take a deep breath. "They are coming back though, aren't they?"

"I believe so, yes." I feel him move over until his leg is touching mine and I gratefully lean into his side, a small sense of comfort settling into my chest. "We'll figure something out."

If only that were true. Those men didn't seem like the type to make careless mistakes and allow valuable prisoners to escape.

"Why didn't you leave when you had the chance?" I ask. "Now that they know what you are . . . it might be even worse for you."

Lir's hair brushes against my temple as he turns his head toward me. "I was not going to leave you with them. I've been cruel lately, but that is . . . not who I am. I—"

"I don't want to talk about that." I straighten, pulling away from him.

Lir's arm circles my shoulders and he nudges me back down until I'm leaning against him again. "We won't talk about it, then," he says.

Silence stretches out between us, different from before. Our future is bleak and our circumstances are certainly less than ideal, but . . . I'm relaxed, a warm feeling of reassurance washing over me. As if maybe we can figure this out.

"Do you know where we are?" I ask.

"I'm not entirely certain. It looks like we're in a large metal room of some sort. Almost like the place I was held while in your town."

I glance around at the darkness around me. "How can you tell? It's pitch-black in here."

"Superior vision, remember?"

"Oh." A store wouldn't have lab rooms, but it would have . . . "A refrigerator, or a freezer of some type. Lucky for us it's empty, otherwise the smell wouldn't be pleasant."

"They must have set this store up as some sort of supply depot," he says. "Picking through for things to sell as they needed them."

I shake my head. "I can't believe I didn't notice. There's no way this store wouldn't have been looted a long time ago and everything was still so neat . . . I wasn't paying enough attention."

"You were upset. Because of me."

I nod.

"I let you suffer because I didn't know how to reassure you about the rescue of my enemy or even if I could continue helping you in that quest. I let my anger at the situation get the best of me and I didn't even explain . . ." He sighs. "Once the *kitu* has been used to establish a link, it allows us to mentally send messages, words, images, commands . . ."

Mental communication? Did humans ever have something like that? Probably nothing nearly as advanced, at least nothing that could communicate mind to mind. Send images mind to mind . . . Oh no.

My hand comes up over my mouth. "That's how you know. About Jace, I mean. Your friend . . . he sent you an image."

"Yes. Through the link I was able to view Kov's final moments." He pauses and inhales. I can feel his jaw clench above me. "Your brother looks much like you."

Another silence follows, but he doesn't move away and neither do I. I can't even imagine what that must have been like for him, to watch his friend die. Did he experience it as well? Was he looking out through his friend's eyes as it happened? A shudder works its way down my body. How very awful. He must hate us . . . humans, Jace, even me. I'd probably hate him if the situation were reversed, and I don't really have any friends to lose.

And yet he's here. He searched me out when I stormed off instead of leaving. He tried to defend me and got himself caught. It's something Jace would have done. It's what Jace *did* do—let himself be caught so I could escape.

"He's still my brother, you know."

"Yes, I know that."

"I'm going to do whatever I can to get him back."

"I know," he says.

"Will you . . . do you hate me for that?"

"I wanted to. It would make it easier. You are part of the race that would wipe mine out if they could. Your sole mission is to rescue the man I swore to Kov's bondmate I would kill. I probably wouldn't be in this situation right now . . ." He shrugs and a small chuckle breaks past his lips. "No, I don't hate you. I tried to convince myself I did. But I couldn't. You are funny and intelligent. Your strength and loyalty are like nothing I've ever seen. Even when everything is going wrong, you find some way to surprise me. Through all of this you've held yourself together under stresses I cannot even imagine. Even when *I* was the problem, you just kept going. And after the way I acted, you cried on me, leaned on me, trusted me . . ." He trails off, gently shaking his head.

Lir sees all that in me? I'm a lot of things; panicky, hotheaded, impulsive . . . but all that? Maybe his vision isn't as clear as he thinks it is.

"Even without knowing about my brother, with all the other things you could have disliked me for, why did you agree to go with me in the first place?"

"I didn't have much choice at the time," he says. "It was either stay with the humans who I knew would kill me or trust the one girl who might help me. Even then, I knew that there was something special about you. Given the choice again, knowing what I know now and where it would lead, I would still make the same one." His head turns and I can see the shine of his eyes facing me. "You are everything I was taught humans were not."

His fingertips brush across my cheek as he pushes a lock of hair behind my ear. "Jax, I—"

Bang! The sound travels through the small room and we both jump. Two more loud raps on the door send my heart into my throat and my pulse upward. They're back.

I cannot cower in the corner like I want to—not that I can really see where the corner is, anyway. The noise reverberates through the room. I stand and instinctively back away from its origin to my right. My back runs up against the cold metal wall and there's nowhere else to go.

But this isn't like before. I can fight back. I'm bigger, stronger, and I know how to kill.

The fingers of one hand curl into claws, perfect for ripping and tearing. I won't go quietly. Icy fear has no place in my body now. Instead, I'm filled with fire, burning me from the inside out and just waiting to be released. My breaths come quicker, expanding my lungs and filling my body with tension. A buzz starts at my toes and runs up my body. I'm on edge. I'm ready to spring, bouncing lightly on the balls of my feet.

"Stay with me, Jax," says Lir. He is still holding my hand even though he hasn't changed position. His hold anchors me, holding me there and giving me something to focus on. He won't leave me. I'm not alone.

The tension recedes slightly and I squeeze his hand.

"When the door opens, I'm going to push one of these shelves over and out. You just need to run. Get out of here. I will be right behind you." Questions run around in my head, but I can only nod, too busy working on switching from fight to flight.

The door edges open slowly, a narrow line of light appearing on the wall. At first it hurts my eyes, too long in the dark, and I have to squint against it. There's only one shape in the doorway, not four like I'd feared.

It's the young one, Zach, the one who shot us with the jolt gun now wavering in his grip.

Crash! A large metal shelf falls to the ground. Zach jumps backward out of the way and I go. Jump onto the fallen shelf, step level to level until I'm out the door and back on the ground. I take a moment to look from side to side, but the other three men are nowhere in sight. We're still in the store, so I run down an aisle and dart around the corner.

Where the hell is Lir? There's no noise and a quick glance back confirms that he is not behind me, as he said he would be. I should keep going, but I double back down the next aisle over, slowing into a creep as I approach the end near the cooler.

No Lir. No Zach. No one. The satchel, however, is sitting by the door. I'm not leaving it behind.

Five steps take me across the narrow space between the end-cap and the satchel. I grab the strap and pull it over my head as I turn. My forward momentum stops when I crash into someone and bounce backward, crashing back into the wall and losing my grip on the satchel.

The unbuckled flap flies open and I watch the cuff and my knife skitter across the floor to my right. Something else clatters down. The jolt gun. My attention turns back to Zach, the obstacle I ran into.

Zach's gaze travels from my face to my hands to the jolt gun. I'm unarmed, but so is he. This will come down to who is quicker. And smarter.

I fake a step away from the knife, as if I'm going to run, and he's three steps in that direction before he realizes I went for the knife, not the exit.

My knife, the lighter object, traveled farther across the floor, so by the time I've reached it, Zach is almost to the jolt gun. There's no time for me to move in before he'll be able to get the gun up.

Jace is the knife thrower, not me, but he did give me one lesson. I hope it took.

A deep breath. I pull a picture of Jace into my mind, replaying the image of him throwing his knife into a tree trunk. *Flip the grip. Hold the blade. Arm straight down. Don't flick the wrist.*

The knife leaves my fingers and rotates one . . . two . . . three . . . four times before sinking into the side of Zach's neck. He's still moving, but blood wells out around the knife and when he removes it a flood of red gushes out.

After two staggered steps to the side, he falls to one knee and then tilts sideways onto the ground, landing so that the blood pours over his face and pools on the floor under his head. His chest rises for two wet breaths and then stills. His fingers twitch once, as if he's still trying to reach the gun that sits only inches from his out-stretched hand.

So much blood. I close my eyes and swallow three times, then step closer, my face a blurry shadow over the red pool on the floor. The burn starts in my stomach, traveling to the back of my throat, and then I'm on my knees, vomiting up the entire can of cold, congealed beans.

By the time my stomach has stopped heaving, the pool of blood has spread out, wetting my knees and extending under the gun. I grab it anyway and wipe it on my pants. Doesn't really do much, but . . . it's something. I spring to my feet and turn to find Lir standing behind me.

"I told you to run," he says.

"I didn't see you. I couldn't leave without you . . ." My voice is hoarse, and I cough to clear my throat. "I saw the satchel. I didn't see him. He went for the gun. I didn't have a choice . . ." Tremors climb up my arms and the jolt gun vibrates against my thigh with the movement. Tears creep into my eyes. I just want him to understand. "I don't want to be a killer. He was just—and I—" The words get stuck in my throat and my stomach turns again. My breath comes in wheezing gasps and spots form at the edges of my vision.

Lir leans closer until he's right in my face, pinning my eyes with his. "Calm down. I understand. You did the right thing." He turns until he's next to me and puts his arm around my shaking shoulders. "We need to get out of here before the others get back."

As if called by his words, voices sound from the front of the store. Lir pulls me away from the body, gently but persistently. "Let's go."

I could have run. I was faster. I should have left, but . . . "I got the gun." The barrel shakes back and forth when I hold it up.

He picks up my knife from the floor—blood, blood red—wipes it on his pants, and holds it out to me. I shake my head, so he slides it into his pocket. "We need to go."

I let him pull me up the aisle, my feet dragging across the floor. I stop and lean down to grab the fallen *kitu* as we pass.

That kid . . . Zach . . . he wasn't much older than me. And I killed him. But he's not the first man I killed, he's the third. Is this how it started with Jace? Did Jace become a killer because I did first? Maybe that's why I didn't see it in him. I'm a killer, too, a murderer. Blood-splashed scenes flash through my mind until I have to shake my head to get them to stop. It's all I can do to put one foot in front of the other, and I cannot afford to lose myself in the memories I've so desperately pushed aside.

Lir stops at the end of every aisle and listens. The voices are moving away from us, pleasant tones punctuated with laughter. They won't be laughing long. I'm sure it won't be long before they find their comrade and come after us.

And then, "Zach? Zach?" Metal clatters on the ground. A gun dropping? "He's still warm. They aren't far. Find them!" Running footsteps fill the air. "We're coming for you, erk, you and your whore!" The voice breaks on a sob. "You killed my brother. You killed him."

Lir stops and tries to pull the gun away from me, but I don't release it. They'll come after us, but I just can't. "Just run. No more fighting today. No more blood."

The doors aren't far and we break through them and into the cool night air well before the men catch up to us.

§

The signs of abandoned civilization fade behind us as we reach the woods and plunge ahead. I take the lead, jumping and ducking erratically to avoid branches and roots. Lir stumbles, but regains his feet before I even have a chance to look back. I keep my eyes focused on the trees, looking for the right one. I see it ahead and slow. Releasing Lir's hand, I point to the tree and then point up.

My hands scramble against the bark and my feet search for purchase as I shimmy up. I'm able to grab one of the lower branches to help me and climb until the limbs start creaking under my weight. It should be high enough. Lir follows, out of breath and sweaty. He collapses against the trunk of the tree, wedged in a vee where it meets a branch. I'm a few branches above him, so I climb down until I can squeeze in next to him.

It's awkward trying to share the small space with Lir and I end up with half my butt hanging off the branch. Moving to another branch is an option, but I can't bring myself to move away. I need the reassurance that he brings to me. The shot of adrenaline is wearing off and the tremble in my hands has spread to my limbs and escalated into violent shaking.

Lir grabs one of my hands and motions for me to scoot forward. Then he settles me between his legs with my back against his chest. It's calming being so close to him, my body flush against his. My breaths even out and my pulse slows. I relax into him, enjoying the feel of his chest rising and falling against my back. I shouldn't be enjoying it, this strange new closeness between us. I don't deserve it. A warm feeling tingles in my body at his nearness and I try to ignore it.

I'm not an idiot. I know about the birds and the bees and about love and feelings . . . but knowing about something and knowing what it feels like are two completely different things. Obviously, I'm attracted to Lir, but even that is a new experience for me. The only boys I've really spent time around have been my brother and Flint. Of course, I'm not going to be attracted to Jace, but this is different than how I feel around Flint, too. Flint is my friend—really more my brother's than mine—but being close to him has never made me feel like this.

When the men come crashing through the woods nearby, Lir pulls me in closer and wraps his arms around me. My eyes close, almost by themselves. His breath, still coming in faster-than-normal spurts, tickles my neck and he's pulled me so close I can even feel the beat of his heart. I should pull away, reassert my boundaries, some-thing, anything to push him away. I'm dirty and sweaty and covered in another man's blood, but all I can do is think about how nice it is to let someone else take control for a while, how nice it is to be pressed against him with his arm circling me, protecting me. We stay like that for a while, me leaned in close to him, even after the sounds of the men have long disappeared.

"Jax?" Lir whispers into my ear.

"Mmm?" Between the warmth and the feeling of safety, I've almost drifted off to sleep.

"Do you think it's safe to get down now?"

My eyes spring open. What the hell was I thinking? I keep my face turned away so he can't see my embarrassment when I answer. "Yeah. Let's go."

I jerk away from him and climb down a few branches until I can easily jump down to the ground. While Lir works his way out of the tree, I pull myself together. Yeah, we're friends, allies, but any-thing more between me and Lir is just a foolish . . . what, exactly?

Not a dream, not a wish . . . just an idea. A stupid one. He's going back to his city and I'm taking Jace home . . . wherever that may be.

I let Lir lead the way this time and we walk directly opposite the path the men took. Who knows if we're even going in the right direction anymore? I can only hope that come morning I'll be able to find a distinguishable landmark on the map so we can get back on track.

What I wouldn't give for something to rinse my mouth out with. The stale taste of vomit coats my throat and the knees of my pants are beginning to stiffen with dried blood. I don't care much where we wake up in the morning, as long as I can get clean. I cannot walk around with the blood on me. When we finally stop to sleep, my rest will be filled with nightmares for sure.

Even awake, the wet thunk of the knife entering his throat replays in my ears and the creeping chill of anxiety climbs my spine. My hands wipe against my jeans again and again, without me even thinking about it. There's no blood on them, not really, but I just can't get them clean and I need them to be clean. *In. Out. In. Out. Wipe. Wipe.*

It's late. I'm tired. "I've gotta stop. I can't . . . I can't . . ." I slump against a tree. "I . . ."

"You don't have to explain. We can stop here," he says.

Lir backs up until he's beside me and slides to the ground. I follow him down and he adjusts me until we're half sitting, half lying down in a similar position to how we were in the tree, me between his legs with my back resting against his chest. My breaths are still ragged and the sound of the knife . . . my knife . . . hitting its target is starting to drown out everything else.

I sway back and forth, rocking slightly to the beat of my breathing. He doesn't say a word, just holds me until I gain control of myself and lean back against him. *It will be okay. I had to do it. Just like before.* No! I will not think about that. I slam my eyes shut and squeeze them closed so tightly bright lights play behind my eyelids.

Lir rubs my arm and wiggles around a little before leaning his head back against the tree. I rest my head on his shoulder and if I tilt my head, I can just make out his profile. He's still awake. His lashes sweep across his cheek when he blinks and his throat bobs when he swallows. What is he thinking about? I bet he can see now how strong I'm *not*, maybe even regretting sticking around for me. I'm not even strong enough to face the nightmares I know are coming.

I just watch him, studying his face, memorizing his features . . . why? . . . holding my eyes open until I lose the battle and drift off.

When the dreams finally come, they're not at all what I expect. My dreams once again focus on me, me in danger, me crying, me shaking . . . It's not the fear or the blood of those I killed filling my head, but my own. A sense of helplessness as a hand grabs my wrist. Shock at finding me covered in blood, shifting to relief that it's not mine . . .

Many shifting scenes later and I'm back to looking out of my own eyes. Jace stands with his hand out, backed by a bright white light. His mouth moves, but no words come out and then his face twists, a scream flowing out past his lips. Echoing, bouncing, over and over, my brother screams.

My eyes fly open and I break out of Lir's hold, springing to my feet, a silent scream resting on my lips. The rise and fall of my chest is rapid and it takes a moment before my heartbeat slows enough for me to even try to relax. I pace forward and back a few times, trying to work out the shakiness in my limbs. What the hell was that?

Eyes still closed, Lir hasn't moved. I shake my head. Pale, scruffy, and obviously exhausted, he needs the sleep, so I leave him be. If only I could find the same escape back into sleep.

My eyes feel like sandpaper and I'm less than fully alert. Briskly, I rub my hands up and down on my arms. I'm used to the nightmares, but that was something else, something worse. Jace is in terrible danger, he is in pain . . . and there is no possible way for me to know that, but I do. Every piece of me can feel it and a new urgency fills my body. Time is running out.

Red streaks in the sky signal the sunrise and it's nearly light enough for us to set out. If we haven't gotten too far off course, we should now be within two days of the city. Forty-eight more hours for Jace to wait. Hopefully.

I pull the map from the satchel and eye a nearby tree. It's not very tall, but it should get me high enough to make out where we are. The rough bark scrapes my palms as I climb, but I ignore the discomfort.

Once I'm above most of the tree line, I unfold the map and angle it so the eastern side is toward the rising sun. Finding the town we just left is easy; locating where we currently are isn't. I close my eyes and try to retrace our mad dash through the darkness. We left through the front door of the store and traveled roughly north-east . . . maybe.

I scan the area, looking for some landmark that might show up on the outdated map. There's a large body of water about a mile north of us. Another glance at the map confirms my guess. We did travel northeast, and while we aren't completely off course, we over-shot the road that I planned to take over the mountain. Dammit. That might just add another day . . .

Lir calls my name out from below.

"Up here." I look back at the lake. It's in the right general direction and we need water anyway. I need to feel clean again.

I shove the map back in the satchel and make my way out of the tree. "Come on. We're going swimming," I say.

Fourteen

It's not a lake, more of a reservoir that we find on the other side of the trees. It's large enough for swimming, at least, large enough to wash the feeling of blood off me and for me to dip my head under and feel clean again.

I take off, half running and pulling my shirt off in the process. I have to sit to remove my boots, but it isn't long before they're left behind me as well. My fingers stall on my bra strap and an uncomfortable feeling gathers in my stomach. Lir is staring at my shirt, still fully clothed and looking less than enthusiastic. Meh. I shrug and shed my bra and pants. His hang-ups aren't mine. Most of my clothes are covered in blood and I just can't be in them any longer.

The water cools my skin instantly, just on the edge of being too cold, but it's wonderfully refreshing. I swim out to the middle and tread water, stirring up some sediment and clouding the water, and I'm almost grateful for the coverage. Lir is still standing there and my face is heating at his obvious stare.

Of course I've swum with Jace before and even Flint a time or two, though Jace asked me to keep my shirt on then. But this . . . Lir's eyes skitter across my skin and it's like nothing I've ever felt before. Maybe this wasn't the best idea. Lir is not my brother and his darkened gaze proves it. I've gotten comfortable with him, but the way he's looking at me now . . . part of me likes it, likes the power I have to draw his gaze, but then there's also a scared cornered animal that wants to hiss and back away. I settle for turning away from him and swimming all the way across to the other side.

It's quiet out here, peaceful, even, and I let out one extended breath, releasing as much tension as I can from my body. On my next inhale, I suck in as much air as my lungs can hold and plunge my head under the water. The dark silence of the underwater refuge clears my mind enough that I feel almost sane again. I'm better, but not perfect. I don't feel the blood against my skin and my hands are pale and just starting to wrinkle. More tension leaves me as I slowly release my breath into tiny bubbles that climb to the surface. Though the push to go get my brother sits in the back of my mind, the wrenching guilt over taking a life starts to recede and my worries slow and stop spinning around in my head.

I rise back into the air-filled world and lean back until I'm floating. The dream still plays behind my eyes, but it's fading now, getting hazier with each lap of the water against the shore. "Just a dream. Just a dream." The chant continues in my head.

The dark form of a bird drifts high in the cloudless sky. I lift my arm from the water and trace its flight with one finger. What would it be like to swoop and dive in the air? To be so far above everything and just go where the wind takes me? *Peaceful.*

As the bird disappears in the distance, I realize I've been out here for a while. I swim closer to shore, lower my feet, and stand on the muddy bottom. Pulling my hair back from my face, I comb my fingers through it and braid it down my back in one long tail, just about touching the curve of my backside. Now that I'm clean and my head is a little clearer, the chill of the water starts seeping into my limbs. Indecision stalls me. How do I get my clothes back?

There aren't many choices—only two, actually. I can either stroll over and pick them up like it's nothing, or cower here until . . . until what? Crap. Looks like there's only one possible decision.

I take a deep breath and stroke over to the other side of the pond, staying as submerged as possible until the last possible second. My eyes count the rocks at my feet as I retrieve my clothes. No chance of sitting out in the sun and drying here. I use my shirt to towel off and pull my jeans and boots back on, ignoring the dried blood that flakes off the pants.

The air is too heavy and my face is starting to heat. "If I'd known it would make you be quiet, I would have taken my clothes off sooner," I say, nervously laughing at my own joke. Lir hasn't moved, so I nudge him with my shoulder. "Can't swim, huh?"

He shakes his head. "No, uh, it's not . . ." His eyes are everywhere but on me. "We don't have any lakes in the city, so . . ."

"You never had cause to learn." I snicker at the flush creeping up his cheeks. I missed teasing him. "It's a good thing I'm around, then. Sheesh, forget bears and hostile humans, you would have died the first time you fell into water over your head."

His eyebrow goes up and a smile spreads across his face. "I am quite capable of swimming. You just distracted me." I must be full-on blushing now, but I smile anyway and then pull my shirt over my head.

"So what was it that you were saying out there about a dream? Did you have an interesting one about me or something?" He's teasing, but my stomach still lurches and my hard-won calm starts to recede.

"It was nothing. Just . . . a nightmare. About Jace." Lir's flinch at my brother's name is slight, but still there. This isn't something he wants to hear about, but now that he's brought it up I can't stop the words falling from my mouth. "He was there, reaching for me, trying to tell me something . . . but there was no sound until he started screaming, just screaming and screaming and screaming . . ." I trail off and brush my hands on my thighs and rusty specks stick to my palms. It's not even something *I* want to hear about, to face, to realize. "It was awful. And I just know he's in pain. He's in danger . . ." Clenching my hands, I fight back the tears struggling to fall. I raise my eyes and find his, pleading for understanding with my gaze. "I don't know how I know, but they're hurting him."

He thinks for a moment before responding. "You don't know that."

His denial only increases my conviction and anger. My hands move into tight fists. Yes, I've tried to discount the dream, too . . . but he doesn't get to patronize me. "I do know it. Maybe it's only a twin thing and not as sophisticated as your alien link thingy, but I do know." I narrow my eyes, preparing the verbal barb that is itching to leave my tongue. "Isn't that what you would have done? A little bit of torture before killing him?" His shoulders straighten and the muscles in his jaw pop. It's my turn to be cruel. "Seems your friends like to cause a little pain. Maybe you're just like them. And you called us savages."

"If I'd known who he was then, I would've just killed him in the clearing." His words are loud and rushed. They jumble together and it takes a moment for the truth of them to hit me. I step back, the air leaving my chest like he punched me. Lir rubs the back of his neck and looks away. "Before . . . that's what I would have done before I knew you. The ones that took him, they're not my friends. If anything they're just as much my enemies as yours." His head comes up. "Things have changed for me. I don't plan on taking vengeance on your brother. To inspire such dedication and loyalty in you . . . he must be redeemable. There must be more to the story than I know."

The confession shatters my anger and leaves me speechless. I settle for nodding in acknowledgment and then heading back into the woods, my wet braid swinging against my back. "Come on," I call back over my shoulder. "We've got to get going."

Lir's feet pound up behind me and he falls into step beside me. Neither of us speaks.

A few minutes later, we're scrambling across some rocks and I hear it—the unmistakable sound of a rattler. It must feel threatened, so it's not hiding in one of the crevices, it's somewhere where it was frightened by us. My eyes scan the rock bed, looking for a variation in the pattern, something that sticks out. I find the snake about a foot to Lir's left.

He keeps walking despite my stilled frame. I throw out an arm to stop him and he turns with both his body and his feet, bringing his foot even closer to the snake. Almost in slow motion, the snake rears back to strike and I yank Lir by his shirt toward me. His body bowls me over and I fall to my back, legs extended right into the path of the snake's strike.

$$\S$$

My breath hisses in through my teeth when Lir places the ragged piece of his shirt against my leg. Pain radiates up from the wound, the pressure building until I want to scream. A drop of sweat traces down the side of my face and falls onto my shoulder.

"What do I do?" Lir's voice pounds in my ears, his tone frantic.

"Let it bleed," I say. "And get my knife."

Lir pulls my knife from his boot and wipes it on his shirt before handing it to me. The steel is cold against my leg as I run it up the seam of my jeans, parting the leg up to midthigh. I hack off the now loose pant leg and cut a strip from it. I tie the strip around my calf, just above the bite, loose enough I can still get my finger underneath. The blood is slowing, so I wipe the wound with the wet cloth.

We're out in the open and that just won't do. Even though rattlers don't always inject venom when they bite, the burning sensation traveling up my leg and the slight swelling already forming around the wound leave no doubt. There was venom in that bite and it's bad.

"Help me up. We have to find shelter. Now."

He pulls me to my feet and I sling an arm over his shoulder. With a slow hopping movement, avoiding putting much weight on the bitten leg, we struggle through the forest. My eyes scan constantly for someplace, anyplace that might be safe for the next day, maybe two.

Dad was bitten by a rattler once, when I was ten. He was alone hunting in the forest and stumbled back to the cabin and fell into bed. The brief instructions he was able to get out before he went completely delirious weren't very comforting. I did the best I could, but his leg still swelled and he tossed and turned for two days before coming back to himself. He was strong enough to fight off the venom; now I have to be, too.

Each step sends a shot of agony throughout my body. I cannot keep going. The exertion is just going to make the venom spread faster and it needs to be contained as much as possible.

"Put me down. Find a cave. Someplace safe, and then come back." I grit my teeth as another blaze of pain shoots up my leg.

Lir's receding back wavers in my vision, joining the tree trunks in a dizzying dance. Closing my eyes doesn't help. Colors blaze behind them, pulsing with the pain in my leg. The waistband of my jeans grows tighter, pressing into my flesh. My leg is swelling worse and I need to get the pants off while I can. My hands shake as I use the knife to cut the pant leg the rest of the way. Chills rack my body and my limbs jerk against the ground. There's no way I can hold the knife steady enough to cut them the rest of the way. I clench my teeth to keep my yells in. No point in alerting anyone who may be around that I'm here. That I'm injured. That I'm helpless.

Fear follows the chills, seeping into my bones slowly. Is it real fear or the start of delirium? Helpless. *Helpless.* The word chokes me and leaves me gasping for breath. My racing heart beats a steady cadence of terror and pain.

Minutes . . . or hours? . . . later, a tall form separates from the trees and approaches me. The sunset behind it shines on reddish hair and my heart jumps. "Jace?"

No. The colors change again and it's just green with golden sunlight pouring around it. Lir. When he gets closer, the gold in his hair shines and for a moment I just watch the sunbeams coming from him. Then my heart beats again and another searing pain travels up my leg.

The pain coils in my stomach and I lean over and vomit into the bushes until my stomach can't push anything else out. My back continues to heave and Lir leans toward me. At first I flinch away, not sure I want the golden light to touch me, but it's okay. His hand rubs my back until I'm shaking with the exertion of dry heaving and collapsing back to the ground.

"Jax," he says. "There's a cabin ahead. Can you make it?"

I nod, not trusting my mouth to form the right words. He helps me to my feet. If my body wasn't a constant throbbing pain right now, all the wavy colors would be pretty.

"Where'd Jace go?"

"Huh?"

He is playing dumb, but I know I saw Jace. "Where'd you hide him?"

"You aren't making any sense," says Lir.

I stop walking, swaying on my feet a little. "He was here."

"No," he says. "He wasn't. Remember . . . uh, they took him." He pulls my arm over his shoulder. "Come on."

Just like that, the cold heat of fear is back, turning my stomach to mush and speeding up my heart. "They . . . aliens . . . You, you're an alien . . . you took him!"

"No, I didn't."

I pound on his chest with my fist. "Give him back!" The tears come now, the wet soldiers of fear and pain. Heat radiates up my leg and I stumble forward. Lir catches me and presses me against his chest. I continue to beat ineffectually at him with my fists.

"It's not much further, come on." My arm follows him, but the rest of me stills. My wobbly feet won't hold me. The ground is shifting and I can't find a place to walk.

Lir is too far away. He's leaving me behind. Alone. "No! Don't leave me here alone," I yell. "I don't want to be alone."

He's in front of me again. Pulling my chin up to look at him. Green seas float on his face and I lose myself in them, drifting away from my throbbing body. Can I lie down now? Good idea. But I can't. Lir scoops up my legs and cradles my body in front of him and then he's moving through the forest and the trees are blurring around me.

Seconds later I'm in a bed, the musty sheets cool against my skin. No, that's not right. They're hot. I kick them off. My skin is too tight and it's going to pop. I'm alone and I have no pants. No, not alone . . . Screaming. Is that me? Shaking. That is me. Crying. That's me, too.

Strong hands grab my wrists and pull me back against a rock-hard chest with my arms crossed. I'm bucking and kicking, but nothing breaks his hold. A quiet breeze carries into the room, against my neck, against my ear.

"Jax . . . please . . ." Not wind. Words. Lir. Safety. I still and a peaceful blackness takes over my vision.

Fifteen

S ound returns. Brightly bouncing in my head. Jumping on my achy joints.

Snippets of sentences wander my brain. Not from my mouth. That doesn't work.

Shaking again. So. Damn. Hot. Not flames in my veins now. Just a glowing ember that flares with each movement, each brush of something against my stretched tight skin. Somebody should put me out already.

"Does she know?" No. I don't. Who said that?

" . . . about her?" Same strange voice.

" . . . be okay?" A familiar timbre made of green-gold light.

Cool, cold wet against my face, my forehead. Gentle strokes down my cheek.

"So sorry." Green words again.

A lick of flame, smaller but growing, shoots up my leg and out my mouth in a scream.

§

Next is sight, but it's not right. Oh, goodness, now I'm rhyming.

Things are too fuzzy, too vague. Solid shapes move and moving shapes stay still. Blinking doesn't help, so I just close my eyes again.

Ah, that's better. Closed eyes work better than open ones.

The familiar barrage of metal and buildings resolves into one simple room. White walls. White floor. White. White. White . . . and red.

Red hair, tousled, too long and limp. Jace. Thin and pale, but there. Or here? Then he's gone again.

Open eyes and all I see is soft and safety green. Warm lips press against my forehead, followed by the cold wet over my face, down my arms. Relief until the fire flares up again.

§

Floating. Shooting. Sobbing. Cool cloth on my forehead, my arms, my legs. Concerned green eyes hovering over me. Water trickles down my throat, driven there by the force of his words.

"You have to drink." So I do.

Shivers rack my body, but I'm quickly wrapped in warmth and held tightly there. When my eyes open, the emerald eyes are inches from me and I smile. *It will be okay.* Is that me or him?

Someone else breaks into my head and I'm treated to a wonderful slide show of bright colors and shiny ships. My warmth pulls away, but not far.

"You have to fight this." So I do.

"You have to come back to me." So I do.

§

Sand scrapes the roof of my mouth. No, that's my tongue. My eyes open into slits and I immediately shut them against the searing brightness. A breath and then another. Heartbeats without pain.

My mind's turning back on. I'm still floating for a while, drifting right on the edge of full consciousness.

I wake up in a strange bed and almost wish I hadn't. Every part of my body aches, even my fingernails and eyeballs. I shift with a groan and sit up. The effort nearly makes me pass out. Once the stars have cleared from my sight, I look around the room. Where the hell am I?

The memories come back in waves, starting with the rattle and ending with Lir's plaintive begging in my ear. How long have I been out? Light shines in the room even through the closed curtains, so it's not nighttime. It's a low light. Afternoon? Early evening? I've been out of it at least overnight, but somehow I think it's been longer.

I'm alone in the room and a small prick of concern pokes at me. Where is he? There's no way I can get up, but I'm dying for a drink.

"Lir?" My voice is hoarse, scraping past my dry throat and coming out as barely a whisper. I clear my throat and call for him again.

The door flies open and I jolt. "Jax?" A variety of emotions cross Lir's face, settling on relief. "You're all right?"

"Is that what this is called?" My voice cracks and Lir hands me a cup. "Thanks." I guzzle the water and then push my back against the headboard. "Where are we?"

"Some cabin in the woods."

"How long?" My fingers clench around the glass. Every minute I've been out is another minute that they've had with Jace.

"Two days," he says. He runs one hand over his face, exhaustion showing clearly on his pale skin, and slumps down on the bed beside me. "I thought you were going to die."

"For a while I did, too," I say. He cracks a weak smile. "Have you gotten any rest?" Every bone in my body screams that I should set out immediately back on my path to rescue my brother, but I'm still weak and Lir is clearly exhausted.

"Not really," he says.

"Lie down," I say. "We'll set out tomorrow."

If Lir knows how much that costs me, he doesn't mention it. He simply lies down on the bed and closes his eyes.

Another night of sleep helps. When I wake again, I feel much more like myself, though there's still a lingering ache in my joints and the side of my left leg throbs. Lir has pulled me back against him in his sleep, cradling me against his chest.

"Morning," Lir mumbles into my neck. "Feel better now?"

"Much," I say. I turn until I'm facing him, our faces only inches away from each other. "You?"

"Yes." His gaze moves from my eyes to my lips and my face heats. Mental alarms ring in my head. This is not a position I should be in. I pull back and he slowly lets me go.

Sitting on the edge of the bed, I look around the room while my face cools. Lir's hand finds my lower back and I want to lean back into him, but we've wasted enough time and we have to get going.

"Thank you for letting me rest," he says softly.

I don't turn around. "Why wouldn't I have let you rest?"

"Because you want to get to your brother," he says. "And I'm holding you up right now."

"Holding me up? You saved my life . . . or at least made the whole thing a little less unpleasant. I may be a lot of things and I might not always make the best choices, but I try very hard to not be selfish."

"You're the opposite of selfish. I don't think I've ever met someone more loyal and selfless. You're amazing." His voice grows serious. "I know you don't want to talk about what happened to you and I'm not going to pry, but I know it must have taken a lot for you to set out on this quest to rescue your brother. I admire that."

What do I even say to that? *I'm glad you like me?* I settle for a shrug and say, "Thanks."

I move to my feet for the first time since I was bitten and nearly fall when my muscles don't want to support me. I hold steady through the weakness and walk across the room. Goose bumps rise on my bare legs when they're brushed by a breeze. I'm wearing only an oversized T-shirt, not mine, and underwear, mine. "Where are my pants?" I ask.

Pants are a must. I haven't had time to be embarrassed by my nearly undressed state, but the feeling is certainly settling in, heating my cheeks—again—and making me uncomfortable.

"I don't know," says Lir from behind me.

I turn toward him. "You don't know? How can you not know? Wasn't I wearing them when we got here?"

"You cut one leg all the way up. They were pretty much useless." He shrugs. "Your whole body was swelling. We had to take them off you."

"We?"

"Peter and I. This is his cabin. He—"

A small gray-haired man enters the room, cutting Lir off. "Oh, she's awake. How wonderful!" Blue jeans, black shirt, white collar. A priest? "Are you hungry, dear? Lunch is just about ready. Do you feel up to coming out here to eat? I could bring it in to you."

"Uhh . . ." My mind is still catching up with the world and his—Peter's?—exuberance is just a little too much for me to process.

"Goodness, where are my manners? It's nice to finally meet you, Jax—well, more officially, at least. I'm Father Peter." He thrusts his hand out and I shake it weakly. "You can call me Peter. Really, the whole *Father* bit is . . . not quite the way of it anymore, yes? But I wore this collar for over a decade before the Collapse and I just can't bring myself to part with it. So Lir here has told me that you're from Bridgelake. Well, not both of you, obviously"—he waves his hands at Lir—"he's not from around here. What is it like in Bridgelake? I've thought for a long time about joining a settlement and just haven't gotten around to it. So much to do around here . . . Oh, my, there I go again, chattering your ear off. What can I get you to eat, dear?"

Behind him, Lir's shoulders shake with silent laughter.

"Can I get some pants first?"

Peter turns a bright shade of red. "Oh, yes, of course, of course. We can't have you wandering around half-dressed." He points at my legs. "They'll have to be short though, off the wound on your ankle. Nasty thing, that. Thought we were going to lose you there for a bit. Sorry about cutting into you. It won't heal pretty, but you're still alive and that's what matters, yes? We were quite worried. Your young man there wouldn't leave your side for hardly anything. Getting him to eat was as difficult as getting you to do it. Of course, he was conscious, so that's not really true . . . Anyway, pants! I'll go find you some."

After Peter leaves, I slowly make my way back to the bed and sit down next to Lir. "Wow." I shake my head. "Peter is very . . . enthusiastic. Must have been an interesting few days for you, huh?"

His grin lights his eyes and he raises a single eyebrow. "You have no idea."

Sixteen

Peter convinces me to come to the table for lunch and with Lir's help I'm able to hobble out there and sit with my leg propped up on a chair. With the constant stream of chatter flowing around me, I stuff myself until there's no more room. It feels good to be full, almost good enough that I can forget everything else.

The chatter is mostly from the strange priest, but Lir also contributes to the conversation. Amazingly, my alien friend is nearly as talkative. Maybe Peter's rambling nature is contagious, or maybe they had plenty of time to get to know one another. Either way, I relax into my chair and enjoy just watching him talk and smile and laugh—Lir, not Peter.

Whether it's my still-fuzzy brain or just me, Peter is a little much. He starts off babbling on about one topic and then switches, often midsentence. In one verbal explosion, he can cover three different topics and ask at least five different questions, none of which he actually gives me time to answer. Lir seems to have developed an ability to keep him somewhat on track, but I'm just working on perfecting my smile and nod—that, and not falling asleep on my plate.

"Huh?" I force my drooping eyelids up. "What was that?"

"Oh, my, you're quite exhausted again aren't you, dear? I was telling you young people that I've got an old truck in the shed. I've kept it up and it still works, converted fuel and all. Might help you get to your destination sooner if you'd like to borrow it. That is, you do know how to drive, yes? Silly me, probably not. When would you have gotten a chance to learn, after all?"

My tired mind at least picks up on the important bits. "You have a truck?" This is the best news I've gotten since this whole ordeal began.

Though I know Dane keeps a fleet of at least five trucks, working vehicles are few and far between in this post-Collapse world. At least vehicles in the human sense of the word. There are plenty of ships that fly overhead carting around alien passengers.

"That's what I just said, wasn't it?"

Yeah, among a whole lot of other noise. It's hard, but I resist rolling my eyes. "Driving can't be that hard. I can learn."

Peter's brow furrows and he looks at my leg. "It's a manual, though—you know, stick shift." At my blank look, he continues. "You have to use both legs, for driving. One for the pedals and one for the clutch. Probably wouldn't matter much if it was your other leg, but the clutch on the old biddy is difficult, sticky—you've really gotta work it. With your injury . . . nope." He turns in his seat. "What about you, my boy? Fancy learning how to drive a stick shift? Shouldn't be too hard. I mean, the driving bit, at least. I'm sure you all could get out on the road with no problem. I've even got a map that can take you right to the city. Gotta watch out for that band of ruffians. Very unpleasant. Just the other day—"

"What ruffians, Peter?" Lir smirks at me.

Hardly missing a beat, Peter continues. "There's about ten, maybe twenty. They don't tend to bother me—I'm too old for their interests—but they aren't anyone you want to run into. Mostly they stick to the old Walmart a few miles over, but lately they've been going further afield. A few of them crashed through the woods nearby a few hours before you showed up. Didn't say much, just asked if I'd seen a girl traveling with"—his eyes go wider—"an alien. Oh, dear, they were looking for you. Those were the men you told me about, yes? The ones you had an altercation with? Well, thank goodness you escaped. Nasty characters, those are."

Lir leans across the table. "You say there are maybe as many as twenty of them? What else do you know about them?"

Peter fidgets in his chair and twists his fingers together. "The leader, his name is Lenny, I believe. Big man, likes guns. His oldest son, Stuart, recruited some of the other guys and . . . I'm not entirely sure what their purpose is. He's got a younger son, too. Just a kid, really. Zach is his name. When he was younger he used to spend a lot of time here with me. I tried to teach him right from wrong. The Lord knows his brother hasn't. Haven't seen him in a while, though. I think he's joined up fully with whatever Stuart's involved in now. I try to stay out of it mostly, but they've come through here . . ."

"And you've fed them. Or whatever else," says Lir.

The rest of their conversation fades out around me. I don't care that we missed them by mere hours. I focus on three simple words: *Just a kid.* Zach was just a kid and I killed him. Thunk. A gush of blood.

My stomach turns, the food now a lead weight. I stumble to my feet and limp quickly back to the bathroom. The cold tile makes my knees scream, but I have to get down there to puke up my lunch. Dammit. Just a kid.

Once I've relieved myself of my stomach contents, I sling my arm over the toilet seat and rest my forehead on it. Am I trembling from nerves or weakness? Sweat beads on my brow and my leg is screaming. Bed would be nice right about now.

Someone crouches down beside me, but I'm too tired to turn my head. Lir's warm hand makes circles on my back and comfort flows from his touch.

"You did what you had to. It's normal to feel guilty for that, but don't let it tear you up like this."

"I'm trying . . . it's not just Zach . . ." I almost choke on the name. "He's not the only one. It just brings so much back to me and I don't want it. I don't want those memories."

"I know." I tilt my head to the side and he smiles softly. "They're part of you, though. You can't shut them out forever."

I'm sure he doesn't mean it that way, but his words sound like an accusation. I close my eyes. That look of his, searching, pitying . . . I can't see it right now. "I think I need to go back to bed. Rest up. I want to get out of here tomorrow."

"Isn't that a little soon? Your leg—"

"Jace has waited long enough." My words are fast and harsh. "Besides, the *ruffians* are bound to come back by here. We need to be gone well before they do."

Lir nods. "Fine, then." He helps me to my feet. I want to protest, but there's no way I'm getting there on my own.

Once I'm settled under the covers, he turns to leave the room. I know it's wrong. I know that, despite Peter's words, he's not mine, but I can't help the words that fall out of my mouth. "Don't go."

Lir faces me, eyebrow up, with a curious look on his face.

He's been my life raft, my rock, and I'm just selfish, too broken to have anything to offer him, but I need him. Some part of me calls out to him, craves the comfort he offers, and I'm not strong enough to deny it. "I don't want to be alone right now," I say.

Without another word, Lir crawls into the bed beside me and wraps his arms around me. I rest my head on his chest and the rhythm of his breath sings me to sleep.

My sleep is restful and my dreams, though odd, aren't frightening at all. I'm back at the cabin I shared with Dad and Jace, feet propped up on the table and a book in my hands. Dad is cooking dinner and Jace is making silly faces over the edge of my book, trying to make me laugh. Normal enough scene—well, at least years ago it was—but Dad and Jace aren't quite solid, almost like shadows. I, however, am solid, and I'm not the only one. My back rests against Lir.

Lir studies the cabin with wide eyes and then his emerald gaze focuses on me. That eyebrow of his rises and he smiles, a mixture of amusement and amazement on his face. He leans over me and strokes my cheek once before the dream shatters into green and gold and disappears.

§

The morning light slanting through the window wakes me. There's still a dull pain in my leg, but I feel ten times better, stronger, even. I hop out of bed and pause for a moment, waiting for the dizziness, the tiredness, something, but there's nothing. It's as if that one night of really good sleep and pleasant dreams restored me. Weird, but good, especially since I want to hit the road today.

Lir, still sleeping, looks so very peaceful, the most relaxed I've ever seen him. Tousled green curls frame his face and his lips are turned up in a lazy half smile. That look—it's almost like the one he gave me in the dream, tender and sweet. If only he'd look at me like that when awake. What am I thinking?

I dash out of the room and into the kitchen. Thankfully, Peter must still be sleeping, too.

Living room. Kitchen. Hallway. Repeat. My pacing doesn't help my racing mind, but it gives me something to do. Why am I dreaming about Lir? Why do I care? Do I care if I care? The doubts and worries just keep piling on, getting even more nonsensical. What if I like him? Do I? Why don't I even know? Shouldn't I know?

On my next circuit, I run into Lir, who's exited the bedroom and stands in the hallway. He blinks a couple times and runs his hand through his sleep-mussed hair.

"Morning." The little half smile. The eyebrow. *Stop staring, Jax. It was just a dream.* "I think there's something we need to talk about," he says.

Oh, no. Was I talking in my sleep? What if I grabbed him or something? I can't deal with this right now. "Yup, there sure is . . . uh . . . your hair."

"My hair?" His brow furrows.

"Yes, your hair." More confident now, I smile and nod. Those guys are looking for an alien. Lir looks normal enough in Jace's clothes and long sleeves could cover his *kitu*. He can almost pass for human. But then there's his hair. I've seen some interesting hair colors—I mean, mine is deep red, after all—but I've never seen anyone with green hair. I reach up and feel a few strands, studying the color and the shape. "How would you feel about a haircut?"

"A haircut." He goes from confused to almost . . . disappointed?

"Yeah, come on. I bet I can find some scissors." I'm in luck. I find a large pair of poultry shears in the back of one of the kitchen drawers. I pull out a chair. "Sit."

The eyebrow arches upward. He's transitioning back to amusement. Too bad it's at the expense of my discomfort. "Should I be worried? I mean, I'd like to keep my ears, please."

I laugh and nudge his shoulder. "Just sit. I've got this." Okay, so I really have no idea how to cut hair, but how hard can it possibly be?

It's harder than I expected. Once I get the green tips cut off one side, I cut them off the other—it's completely uneven, so I remove some more from the opposite side . . . and so on. I can't cut it too short at his neck, otherwise his scales will be visible, but when I step back I have to burst out laughing at his new look.

Shorter on the sides and top and then curling down his neck. He looks ridiculous. Lir looks at me out of the corner of his eye. "Do I even want to look in a mirror right now?"

"It might be best if I evened it up at your neck and we found you a bandanna or something to tie around it. I believe right now you have what's called a mullet."

"A mullet, huh?" Lir smiles. His eyes meet mine and I suck in a breath.

Without the oddly colored hair to distract from them, his eyes shine out like emeralds set in gold. They are amazing and clearly nonhuman. Too bright. Too perfect. And I lose myself in them. "Your eyes . . ." I whisper.

Lir fidgets on the chair. "I can't really do anything about those."

I reach out and put a hand on his cheek. He freezes, studying my face, his eyes the only thing about him that's moving. "No, you can't," I say. "I hadn't . . . They're amazing." Lir chuckles nervously, but doesn't move away. There's a lock of hair resting on his eyelash. "Close your eyes."

Without a word, he does and I purse my lips to blow the hair away. Our faces are only inches apart and I can see every detail of his features. Without him watching me, I take the time to take it all in. Strong cheekbones and an angular jaw. A dusting of stubble, which, this close I can tell has a hint of green in it. Long eyelashes lining his still closed eyes. Golden. He's truly gorgeous. I brush another lock of hair from his face and before I know what I'm doing, I lean forward and press my lips to his. The heat of desire flares through me, but almost as quickly is extinguished by the sudden chill of fear. What am I doing?

Lir jerks back and opens his eyes. "Jax?"

My hand slaps over my mouth and I jump up and run out of the room. Out of the house. Just out. I can't believe I did that. I've done some pretty stupid things, some pretty impulsive things, but this was topping the list. What that hell was I thinking? I wasn't, that's the problem.

Lir runs out of the house calling my name. He sees me at the end of the gravel drive and starts toward me, but I turn and run into the trees. "Jax, come back."

I run full-out, not caring, not wanting to think. Just run. I want to go home. I want to find Jace. I want . . . to kiss Lir again. My feet almost squeal against the dirt with my abrupt stop. Where did that thought come from? Random bursts of thought start to coalesce in my head, making more sense than before. I can't run from this. I need Lir to get to Jace. Somewhere in the back of my mind, a whisper: *I need Lir. Period.*

Turning back the way I came, my steps are much slower now. I'm not looking forward to discussing this with Lir. I round the corner and have to retreat. Lir is standing in the middle of the yard and four men have guns pointed at him. His hands are up, but it doesn't look like the men are backing off. I haven't been gone that long. How did they find us?

The bushes shield me from their view, but there's not really anything I can do to help Lir. I can't outrun a bullet and I'd be no good in a fight against all those guys. One man motions downward with his gun barrel and gives a command I can't hear. Lir kneels. It's beginning to look an awful lot like an execution.

Seventeen

I'm really too far away to make out their faces, but none of the men look like Stu. That's a start. Lir's *kitu* is covered and his hair is mostly disguised. They might not know what he is.

Or maybe they do. A blond man kicks Lir in the stomach. His shout is loud enough to reach my ears. "Erk bastard."

Lir doubles over, clutching his stomach, and the man who kicked him raises his gun. The kicker's voice is lower now and I can't make out the words. Lir shakes his head rapidly, interjecting with more words too low for me to hear.

Peter runs out of the house, throwing himself between the gun and Lir and frantically waving his arms. One of the other men, this one brown haired, steps forward and grabs Peter's arm. He pulls Peter out of the way and points his gun at the priest.

There's no way I can sit here and watch them be shot. I have to do something to stop this. The moment I start toward the yard, Lir's head springs up and he searches the tree line until he's looking right at my location.

Stay back! I stumble backward at the force of the words echoing in my head. What the hell? No time to worry about it now.

Lir's prone on the ground, the blond's gun resting on his temple, and Peter is frantically waving his arms and chattering away while being held back by the other.

"Where is she? What did you do with her? Where is she!" Each question from the blond rises in volume until I can almost see the angry spittle flying from his mouth.

They want me? They can have me. At least I can buy some time.

I pop out from behind a bush and yell from my position in the trees, "Hey! Stop that!" Not the most brilliant plan, but at least their attention is drawn away from Lir. Two men stay with their guns pointed at Lir's crouched form and two move toward me, including the blond. I raise my hands and move slowly out of the trees. The gun barrels stay on me, but I'm more angry than scared. "The guns are uncalled for. I'm not going anywhere."

One gun barrel shifts away and the other drops completely as the men move closer.

"Jax? Oh, thank God." The blond runs forward and gathers me into a hug. His—Flint's—arms squeeze me until I can hardly breathe. "Dammit. I was so worried. Did it hurt you?"

The vise around me loosens a little and I'm able to speak. "How did you even get here?"

"We've been tracking you." He runs one hand through his hair. "It's bad enough that they've got Jace. I wasn't going to let some erk take you hostage and not come after you."

I wince and wiggle out of his arms. Maybe we should have come up with a different story. "Let them go, Flint. I'm here willingly. It's not what you think." He glances over his shoulder and then back at me, a questioning look on his face. "Just do it," I say.

His brow furrows and he places one finger in the center of my chest, tapping it to punctuate his words. "You better have a really good explanation."

"I do. Just release my friends." My gaze doesn't waver from his until he turns around and tells the brown-haired man—Daniel, shudder—to release Peter and the rest of the men to lower their guns.

And my very first instinct is to run to Lir and crouch down on the ground beside him. No blood, a little pale and winded, but he's okay.

As I look him over, he's got eyes only for me. "Do you ever listen to anyone?" he asks. His hand comes up to my cheek. "They could have killed you."

"Flint wouldn't have shot me."

"You didn't know it was your friend before you made your move. What if it had been Stu or one of his men?" He moves into a standing position. "I was getting through to him. If you'd let me talk to him awhile longer, I could have gotten the message across with no danger to you at all."

"Yeah, your way looked like it was going so well." I roll my eyes. "Was it the gasping on the ground or Peter's ramblings that were supposed to convince them of anything?"

He laughs and plants a kiss on the top of my head. *What?* Lir looks even more amused when heat gathers in my face. The laughter settles and the amusement slowly leaves his face as he looks around us. I should probably be paying more attention.

A variety of facial expressions surrounds us: wary shock from Flint, disgust from Daniel, glee from Peter, and confusion from the rest of Flint's men. I imagine I look the most like the latter.

Lir's hand tightens where it has fallen on my shoulder and he pulls me in to his side and slightly behind him.

Daniel's gun inches back up and Flint steps forward, narrowing his eyes. At his next step, I end up even farther behind an increasingly tense Lir.

"I told you she was fine." Lir smiles with clenched teeth.

"So she is, physically at least." Flint's eyes sweep over Lir's hand on my shoulder. "Mentally? I think I'll need to talk with her myself for a while before I can decide that."

"What exactly are you implying?"

"I'm not implying anything, erk. I'll come out and say it—I don't know what scheme you're running, but I know you've injured two of our soldiers, killed another, tied up a helpless girl and taken *my* Promised as a hostage and somehow"—he studies my face and his brow furrows—"somehow you've gotten her to trust you."

Of all the things for Flint to bring up, like I'm his possession or something. Stupid male posturing. I'm about to lay into him when Lir's head tilts to the side and his arm drops.

"Your . . . Promised?"

Flint takes another step forward. "Yeah, as of the day you murdering scum stole my best friend. Someone has to look out for her."

Lir's face falls. He sends a glance my way, hurt flashing across his features for a moment before a mask of indifference slips into place and he steps to the side—away from me. "I apologize for the injured soldiers. Emily volunteered to be tied up to aid in my escape and I did not kill anyone. Jax came with me of her own free will, the hostage thing was just a story, a lie . . . it seems not the only one. I was not aware of the circumstances of your bond and, therefore, I also apologize for any familiarity with your mate."

Flint steps to my side, but keeps his eyes on Lir. "Let's talk, Jax. I think you have a lot of explaining to do."

"But what about—"

"Keep an eye on these two, Daniel." Flint grabs my arm and pulls me toward the house.

"Now, young man, this is just uncalled for. Just put those guns away. I've minded my own business out here, but I have to protest at the treatment of my guests." The shortest statement I've ever heard from Peter.

"Shut up, old man," says Daniel.

I wait for Lir to look up, to protest, to do something, anything, but he just keeps his eyes averted. Any fight has gone out of him and he won't meet my eyes, won't even look my way.

My only choice is to lead Flint into the house and hope I can convince him to let us complete the rescue mission.

§

Flint and I sit at the kitchen table and I tell him everything—well, almost everything. I don't tell him about the kiss, or the cuddling . . . or the aching need I have to go to Lir, who came inside about fifteen minutes into our conversation, walked to a bedroom, slammed the door closed, and hasn't made a sound since. I definitely don't tell him about that, but I tell him about the whole rescue mission idea, the hiking, the bear, Stu and his boys—I leave out Zach's fate—and the snakebite, leaving out the whole naked swimming part. So maybe I leave out a little more than I tell, but he gets the pertinent parts, right?

Flint's happy enough with my explanation. At least, he seems so; he doesn't question it, anyway. When I unwrap the gauze and show him the large bundle of scar tissue—*What the hell? How did that heal so quickly?*—on my lower leg, he curses.

"You've had a rough couple weeks." He runs his hand through his hair and rests his elbows on the table.

"No kidding."

"I just don't get it . . ." Blue eyes bore into my hazel ones. "Why didn't you trust me? Why didn't you wait? I had it under control."

A small snort escapes me. "Under control? That's what you call getting Promised? I'd hate to see what would have happened if you hadn't had it *under control.*"

His face hardens. "Actually, you would have. You saw what happened to the girl before you. Remember? The old guy? You don't even want to know what my father had planned for you." He runs his hand down his face. "There's no time for this. My father's probably already—"

"Your father? What does he have to do with this?"

"Did you really think he'd let you escape, let you embarrass him like that?" Flint scoffs. "I had a plan, and now—"

I lean across the table. "And your plan nearly screwed up my plan, the one that was working!"

"Oh, yes, your plan that worked out so well for you!" His voice starts to rise. "Piss-poor planning, Jax. You wandered into the woods with an unknown alien, nearly died how many times, exactly! Almost got yourself sold to breeders . . . and dammit!" His fist hits the table with a bang. "You were my responsibility."

"I am not your responsibility!" My voice edges up into a yell and the heat of anger starts flowing into my body.

"You are when I promised Jace I'd take care of you! He knew . . ." Flint trails off, shaking his head, his voice going softer. "The stupid bastard knew something like this was going to happen. He made me promise . . . dammit!" He turns away, rubs the back of his hand across his face and then faces me again. "It's the only thing I can do for him now."

I clench my hands into fists. "No, it's not! I can go get him!"

Standing, leaning inches from my face, he screams with nothing but naked anguish. "Jace is dead!" His voice catches on the last word and he slams back down into the chair.

"He. Is. Not!"

Our eyes meet and we just stare at each other, chests slowly rising and falling with our anger.

"She is correct. Jace is not dead." Oh, now Lir decides to join in on this lovely conversation.

"Don't you even say his name!" Flint's on his feet, across the room and pushing Lir against the wall with his arm over his windpipe almost before I can blink. "How would you know? This is all your fault!"

To his credit, Lir maintains the stoic calm he adopted outside. "Release me and I can explain."

Two loud inhales and exhales and Flint drops his arm and steps backward. "Explain."

"Perhaps we can do this civilly?" Lir's eyebrow goes up—it's the mocking one, not the amused one. "Sitting around the table like . . . civilized members of our species?"

Flint jerks his head in a nod and comes back to the table, taking the seat next to me and gesturing for Lir to take the seat across the table. "Okay, we're sitting. Now explain."

When he turns them on me, Lir's eyes are even more like emeralds, hard, with pointed facets. "Jax, tell him about your dreams."

"My dreams?" Now he wants to have this discussion? He didn't believe me when I told him . . . does he believe me now? And if he does, why?

"Yes, your dreams. The ones about . . . your brother." Lir's composure cracks for just a second. He tenses his jaw and studies the wood grain on the table.

"The ones you told me weren't real? Are those the dreams you mean?"

"I believe I was mistaken."

"You believe . . ." Argh! I hadn't really paid attention to Lir's prim and proper formality when we met, but after spending time with him relaxed and laughing, the return of his prissiness is grating on my last nerve. It reminds me of our last argument. "What is wrong with you?"

He still won't even look at me. "There is nothing wrong with me."

If I could do the eyebrow thing, I'd be doing it. "I'm sorry that Flint assaulted you . . . *twice*." I glare at Flint. "But that's done with now. And he *will* apologize. I can't deal with the two of you fighting right now. Can you please drop the prose and just speak?"

His eyes finally come up to mine, his gaze icy and intense. "I have no argument with your mate—that is, as long as he has none with me. I do, however, have an argument with you, and I will talk any way I damn well please."

"With me?" My voice is a squeak. "What did I do?"

His eyes flick to Flint and then back to me. "This is not the proper venue for this discussion."

"Not the . . . what?" Confusion wars with anger and I'm left with a strange mixture of the two.

Lir sighs and shakes his head. "Maybe it is different for you, but where I come from, we do not *conveniently* forget to mention that we are mated." The last few words leave his mouth through his teeth. His nostrils flare as he waits for my response.

"Mated?" His eyes go to Flint, who is watching our conversation with interest. "You mean Promised?"

Lir's eyes narrow. "If that is what you humans call it."

And then I get it. Laughter bubbles up from my chest and out of my mouth. "You think . . . no. It was just a stupid ceremony. I had no choice . . . his idiotic father and his asinine Promising. It's not what you think . . . Why do you even care?" That's actually a wonderful question. Is it about the kiss? He can't possibly be jealous, can he?

Any semblance of control on Lir's features vanishes. His face cycles from disbelief to anger to confusion and even a tiny flash of something that looks like hope. He blinks slowly. "You really don't know. I'm sorry. I didn't realize." A hint of a smile. "That *is* a discussion we should have in private. But first you should explain to your friend about your dreams."

§

After I explain the dreams I've been having about Jace, Flint leans back in his chair and lets out a long sigh. He doesn't question. He doesn't look confused. He just looks relieved. Flint is taking this whole dream-connection thing better than I did. Strange.

Since I'm the one who did the explaining, why am I the one who's left confused? "So, you believe me? That I'm really dreaming about Jace?" I ask.

"Yes." He nods and clasps his hands together behind his head, tilting the chair backward onto two legs.

"Just like that? No surprise? No argument? No telling me I'm crazy?" Flint's taking it better than Lir and the alien actually has experience with something like it. Unless . . . "Has this happened to Jace before?"

Flint sits up again and swallows loudly. "There's something you should probably know."

The words send ice into my body. Whatever he has to tell me is bound to be something I don't want to know. "And what is that?"

He exhales and looks at his hands. "You should know about your mother." His eyes slide over to Lir and he swallows again. "About what she was."

All I can do is stare at him blankly. Things are clicking into place in my head as I put it together for myself, but . . . no. That can't be right. I shake my head softly.

When I don't say anything, he continues. "She was one of them, an erk. Here on some sort of early arrival program." He purses his lips and stares into my eyes. "My father thinks you're some sort of weapon. Quicker, able to blend in, and not dependent on the cuffs."

A rock settles on my chest and I close my eyes. *Breathe.* If my mother was E'rikon, then . . . I open my eyes and search out Lir.

"Did you know? Is that why . . ." I clench my jaw and breathe slowly, fighting the burn in the back of my eyes. "Is that why they took him? They knew what he was. They were looking . . . they were looking for us?" I try to ask the question as calmly as possible, but my voice almost breaks at the end. The pain of betrayal is ten times worse than the snake's venom. "You lied to me."

Lir steps forward. "No. There are rumors. I had suspicions . . ." He places his hands on my cheeks, peering into my eyes. Searching. Waiting. I look away.

"So you knew?" Hope dies in my chest, leaving a hollow feeling.

Lir pulls my chin up until I'm looking at him again. "About the rumors, yes. About you? No, not for sure." He runs the back of his hand down my cheek and I fight the urge to lean into it. "If I'd known I would have told you. This changes everything. We have to get to the city right away."

I pull away from him. Confusion rolls through me. He wants to get me to the city. He wants me to be their weapon. "I'm not doing it. I won't. I'm not a weapon."

Understanding washes over his face. "No, that's not what I meant," he says. "You weren't meant to be a weapon. You were meant to unite us."

Flint breaks in. "How do you know all this, alien?"

Sliding his eyes to Flint, Lir tenses. "Considering it has more to do with my race than yours, you seem to know quite a bit about it as well, human. How do *you* know all this?" I'm interested in Flint's answer to his question as well.

Flint shuffles his feet against the floor and his eyes dart between me and Lir. "Jace told me." I don't know if I'm more surprised that Jace told Flint or that Jace knew at all. "After . . . what happened . . . Jace didn't know what to do. He was taking care of you by himself and you needed him almost constantly. You couldn't even sleep without him, wouldn't let anyone else near you. He had no time to hunt, no time to do anything really but care for you. I helped as much as I could . . ."

"I don't remember any of this," I say. Lir gives my shoulder a gentle squeeze from his position behind me.

"You were completely out of it. Eventually you'd let me sit with you for short periods so Jace could gather supplies, but never long enough for him to really get ahead. Winter came. There was no food left and he had nothing to trade. He turned that cabin upside down for something he could use to barter for food. Your father had a little hiding place under the floorboards. Not much was useful to him at the time, mostly a few old notebooks, but there was something he thought he could trade—a bracelet. At least, that's what he thought it was." He takes a deep breath. "My father knew what it was and put the pieces together almost immediately. I don't know how, but he knew . . . things . . . He'd been searching for the alien hybrid child for years, only to find out there were two. He offered Jace the chance to move into Bridgelake. Jace accepted."

"But I was only out of it for a few days . . ."

Flint's eyes hold a mixture of remorse and sadness. "No, you were near comatose for months."

"Why didn't he tell me?" Had I known, I would never have chased after that ship, never led Jace right into their trap. We would be at home right now and Jace would be safe.

Flint shrugs. "Even when you woke up, you were so distant and just broken. Once he figured out what was going on, he also figured out that you weren't . . . functional? Jace was already paying the price. We decided it was better to leave it be."

"Functional? *We* decided . . . What the hell, Flint?"

His face goes red and his words start hissing through his clenched teeth. "You have no idea how hard it was for him, what you went through . . . He wanted to tell you about this, but he also wanted to protect you. We didn't think any more complications would be good for you."

"Who were you to decide what was best for me?" The realization that Jace could hide so much from me stings like salt in a wound.

"You checked out. You left him. He didn't know what to do. He did the only thing he could—for you. No matter how much it hurt him, he protected you. Took care of you. Watched over you. My father is not a good man and the price he asked of your brother was high. The things he did to assure *your* safety have about destroyed him." The bitter anger in his eyes cuts like a knife. "It was always about you."

Suddenly I see our last conversation at the lake in a new light: Jace looking forward to a shopping trip, Jace telling me it couldn't be just us forever . . . Jace stepping in to distract the aliens. Bile rises in my throat. I stand and half step, half stumble backward with my hand over my mouth. Always for me. Always about me. All my fault. Everything. I don't even bother trying to hold back or hide my tears; I just let them trail down my cheeks and I bite down on the side of my hand, shaking my head back and forth.

Flint moves up from his chair and moves toward me.

"Get away from her." Lir steps up to stand in front of me. "She doesn't need to be yelled at for things beyond her control."

"And I bet you know just what she needs, erk. To be carted off to live as a prisoner in your city? To fix all your problems? I'm sure Jace is having a swell time with your friends." He steps forward, inches from Lir's face. "What do you even care? What she doesn't need is you."

"I care about *her*," Lir yells. The air leaves my chest in a whoosh. "Yes, I care about my people, too, and she's obviously a part of that, but I won't make Jax's choices for her. You and her brother seem to have done enough of that."

Lir and Flint glare at each other, their muscles visibly vibrating with tension. The pressure in the room rises another level, so I step between them, putting my hands out. "You two fighting is not going to help anything. I don't like that you and Jace kept me in the dark, but I can't do anything about it now." I drop my hands and grasp Flint's shoulder. "But there is something I *can* do. I can bring him back. It's my turn to protect Jace and I'll do it or die trying."

"He wouldn't want you to do this." Hope and anguish fight for control of his features. "Jace wouldn't want you to die for him."

"But he would die for me." I lower my hands and step away from the two boys. "Time is running out and there's a lot we have to do."

Eighteen

Between Peter and Flint, my choice for a driving instructor is obvious. Being in an enclosed space with the chatty priest with my already frayed nerves would not work out well for Peter. The truck has to be running first, though. Peter's upkeep apparently wasn't very recent.

We're all standing outside now, Flint enforcing the uneasy truce with Lir.

Daniel is the only one here with any mechanical knowledge and he refuses to help with the truck. He keeps narrowing his eyes at Lir and then sending Flint loaded looks. Both are better than his expression when his gaze rests on me. Flint ends up pulling him aside and talking to him in low tones with a lot of head shaking going on. The other two soldiers follow.

Peter fusses over me, claiming my leg won't be able to handle the stress of the clutch. I pull up my pant leg and show him the now healed wound. His eyes widen and he opens his mouth, but Lir pulls him to the side over by the truck and the two of them put their heads together, deep in conversation. Their conversation over, the four Bridgelake soldiers eye the duo and Flint breaks away and comes to stand with me.

"You sure about this?" he asks.

"I'm getting Jace. There's no other choice for me."

He sighs and runs a hand over his face. "Yeah. I know that. I meant, are you sure about . . . the alien? Can you trust him?"

I watch Lir and Peter. Can I trust him? If Flint had asked me yesterday, I would have said yes without hesitation, but he's been distant and strange since the soldiers got here. Since he found out what I am. Of course, having guns pointed at me wouldn't do anything good for my mood, either.

Green eyes meet mine over the top of Peter's head and he gives me a weak smile before shifting his gaze to Flint.

"He's not too fond of me," says Flint. I snort and the side of his mouth goes up. "Rather fond of you, though. Wanna explain that?" He leans forward and turns his head to look at me.

Why is Lir fond of me? I mean, we've made huge strides lately and there was that super-embarrassing kiss, but what is his interest in me? It's not like anything else is possible between us. He's got his world and I have mine—at least, I will as soon as I get Jace back. I shrug. "We've had to depend on each other. I've saved his life. He's saved mine. We're friends."

"Friends?" Flint does his own version of the eyebrow thing.

"Yeah." I try to avoid the heat that fills my cheeks and look away. "What else could we be?"

Flint doesn't answer, just presses his back against the wall, folds his arms over his chest, and watches Lir. "I'm worried about you," he says after a few moments. "Something isn't right in this situation. What was he doing out there? Why was he left behind? If you go into that city, they have both you and Jace. What if they won't let you back out? Especially since that one knows what you are?"

"Lir's different. He's not like the rest of them."

"How would you even know?"

He's got a point. Lir and I have spent over two weeks together and he knows an awful lot about my life, but I know virtually nothing about his. I know how old he is and that he has a younger sister. I've slept curled in his arms, cried on his chest, even kissed him, and I don't even know his last name. Do the aliens even have last names? He's known all along what my mission is, but never given me any idea of how or where I might find Jace, never even hinted at the layout of the city and how he's planning on getting me in there.

We'd been shoved into an intense situation—well, I dragged us into one, anyway. It's only natural that we'd develop a strong connection, right? Only natural that guilt eats at me for not defending him to Flint more. Only natural that I'd like nothing more than to be curled in his arms right now. Have I been a total fool?

Flint breaks me out of my roaming thoughts. "There's something we need to discuss before you head in there. Away from the alien."

"Your buddies going to refrain from shooting him while we're gone? I don't trust Daniel."

He presses his lips together and his eyes go back to Lir. "I'll talk to them."

I narrow my eyes and nod slowly. "Okay."

Flint walks back to the rest of the soldiers. After a few minutes of intense discussion, Daniel and the other two walk away down the driveway.

Lir breaks away from Peter and opens the hood of the truck. Maybe that's his job in the city, an alien mechanic. I can hope, right? He props it open with a block of wood the priest hands him and rests his hands on the raised hood, staring intently into the engine compartment. He turns his head to talk to Peter and I study his profile.

His hair looks ridiculous, but it doesn't detract from his other features. He stands tall and confident even under the glares of the other humans. I've seen him scared and he doesn't look like he's worried, but I feel just the slightest edge of unease rolling off him and curling in my stomach. The familiar heat of anger is buzzing in my body, too, but it's not mine. It's more of a slow burn than the sudden, intense flare that signals my own emotions. What is happening to me?

My breath stutters in my chest. This has happened before. Someone else's emotions, someone else's thoughts burrowing into my head. Unwelcome. Hurting. Knife. Blood. *Hands.* Hands on hair. Hands on neck. Hands on . . . Nonononono.

A screech. Palms pressed to temples, I fall to my knees. *Get them out. Out. Out. Out.* Banging hands on head. I forget to breathe again. *Breathe. In. Out. In. Out.*

Slowly my breaths even out, oxygen bringing reality back into focus, bringing Flint's gun back into focus, the gun that's pointed at Lir.

"Get out of her head." Flint's words are a hiss beside my ear.

"I'm not—I didn't—blazes, do you really think I would do *that* to her?"

With one shaky hand, I push the barrel of Flint's gun away. "Stop. Not his fault." My tongue loosens with each word I manage to push out. "A flashback. A panic attack. Old news now, right?"

"Jesus, Jax." Flint puts his arms around me and pulls me back into his chest. "Since when do you have them when you're awake and no one else is anywhere near you?"

"Since today?" Breathing is still work right now. "At least one that bad. It's been a rough couple weeks." I clutch his arms folded in front of me and close my eyes as my heartbeat stops racing.

The gray sludge of sadness laps at me from across the driveway. Lir. I wasn't imagining it, then. I open my eyes and meet his. There are so many emotions there I almost drown. Sorrow. Anger. Regret. And even something else that I don't want to face. I see a realization cross his face and the flow of emotions from him slams shut, leaving me strangely empty.

§

I spend about twenty minutes getting my bearings back before following Flint to the other side of the house and walking into the woods. He glances back behind us as he walks until the house cannot be seen through the trees.

"Are you sure you're okay?" He places a hand on my shoulder and comes to a stop.

Still a little shaky, I almost dodge his touch but I pull myself together before he notices. "Yeah. I'll be fine." Squinting at him, I tilt my head to the side. "Why did you assume Lir was doing something back there? What did you mean by *get out of her head*?"

Flint blows a loud breath out through his lips and paces a few steps with his hands clasped together behind his back. He pauses and looks up at me from under his brow before taking a few more steps. "They have some sort of mind connection thing. Jace can . . . he does it, too. That's how he's always able to calm you. He can push emotions at you or something." He shrugs and shakes his head. "I don't really know how it all works, but I figured you were looking at . . . him . . . when it happened. He all but admitted to being in your head. You realize that, right?"

"Yes," I say. Up to this point, I'd been handling the whole half-alien thing rather well. I don't *feel* any different, but the idea that Jace has been in my head—outside of whatever twin connection we share—sends my mind reeling. *How different are we? Am I? What other strange abilities will manifest? How much did Jace keep from me? How long has he been manipulating my emotions? And has Lir been doing the same?*

"Though, as much as I don't want to admit it, I don't think he was trying to hurt you," Flint says, breaking me out of the escalating cycle of worry spinning in my brain. He rubs the back of his neck with one hand. "He seemed genuinely upset to see you in that much stress." I raise my eyebrows and he frowns. "Doesn't mean I trust him. There's a lot more to the situation with Jace and the aliens, a lot of things you don't know . . ."

"You'd be surprised about how much I do know. I know about Jace. What he's done."

He flinches and purses his lips together. "He didn't want to do any of that. That's not him."

"I know that." I fold my arms over my chest. "As much as he's obviously hidden from me, Jace is not a bad person."

His mouth turns up into a small, sad smile. "When did you find out?"

"A few days ago."

A wrinkle forms on his brow. "But . . . you've been gone for weeks. How'd you find out about it?"

"Lir told me."

Flint stops pacing altogether and gapes at me. "He *knows*. He knows who he's helping and he's still doing it?"

I shrug. "Yeah."

His eyes roam back toward the house and he shakes his head softly. "That's interesting." Another noisy exhalation. "How much do you trust him?"

Good question. I trust Lir with my life, but with Jace's? I'm still not so sure about that. "Why?" I ask.

"Jace was assisting my father with an attack plan."

"A plan to attack what?"

"The city. The aliens."

I scoff. "Impossible. There's no way he could get through the barrier."

"The alien ships get in and out," says Flint. "How do you think they do that?" When I don't respond, he continues. "He hasn't told you much, then. There's a small device installed on each ship that lets them pass. That's what Jace stole off the last downed ship. That's what got them all worried and trigger-happy. They know we can get in now."

"Why hasn't Dane already attacked? What's he waiting for?"

Flint laughs nervously and rubs his hand over his head. "That's a funny thing. Seems the device disappeared the same night you did."

The little metal object I took from the locked desk drawer. Has to be. "So his plan was, what? Send you out to drag me back?"

"Uh, not exactly. He doesn't know I'm here."

"Then why are you here?"

"Well, I was planning on rescuing you from the erk," he says dryly. I open my mouth to respond, but he holds up a hand to stop me. "Obviously, that's unnecessary. But . . . I'd like you to give me the device."

"So you can take it back to Bridgelake and hand it over to your father?"

He shakes his head. "No. I'm a lot of things, but I'm not stupid. The second he's got that thing back, he'll attack and he won't be selective about targets." He pauses and swallows. When he looks at me again, his eyes are shiny with the start of tears. "Jace is in there and . . . for now . . . he's at least alive. If there's any chance . . . I can't lose him." He bites his lip. "I promised him I'd protect you, but instead I'm begging you to go in and get him. I'll hold on to the device only as a backup plan, just in case . . . I need to come in after you. In case you can't get out on your own."

"Lir won't let anything bad happen to me."

"You don't know that. I know you think he's being up front with you, but what if he's not? You have no idea what you're getting into in that city. They might look like us, but they're still aliens. They came here and never offered to help us, never suggested integration, nothing. Just holed up in the city and ignored us. But it turns out they've been here awhile—you and Jace are proof of that. What if they've been here even longer than that? What if they caused the Collapse and now they're just biding their time while the rest of us die off?"

The implications of that make my head spin. *What if . . . ?*

He must take my silence as understanding. "As crude as it is, there's a reason for the breeder camps. Fewer children are being born and those that are, they're sickly. Every child born in the last ten years." I fill in the rest of that thought on my own. Every child born since the aliens moved into the city . . .

I'd known there were tensions between humans and the aliens, but it had never been something I paid attention to. Dad hadn't raised us that way, though I guess I now know the reason why. Even levelheaded Emily didn't trust Lir, yelled at him, called him *it* like the others. Once again, there's so much more going on that I've been completely oblivious to. What else have I been blind to?

Flint sighs and studies his feet. "Unless you can talk the erk into bringing me in, too, I *need* you to do this. Jace would never forgive me if I let you walk into that city without some kind of backup plan." He raises his face, anguish etched into his features. "You know what they've been doing to him, you've seen it. What if they get their hands on you, too? I don't think you'd come back from something like that, Jax, not again, and we have no idea how much damage they've already done to him."

As I study his features, pain and longing obvious on his face, another thing I'd been too selfish to see becomes clear. "You and Jace, huh?"

Shock crosses his face and he shakes his head frantically and takes a step back. He watches my face for a beat and then his shoulders slump. He sighs and nods. "Nobody else knows. My father would . . . not be happy."

"How long have you guys been . . . together?"

"There's always been something between us, but we didn't . . . act on it until about a year and a half ago." He meets my eyes. "I love him. I would do anything for him."

"That makes two of us, then." I smile. "With the two of us on his side, no one can stand in our way."

He laughs and wipes at his eyes with his sleeve. "So you'll do it? Give me the device to hold on to?"

"Yes, I trust you. Though I might have to smack my brother around a bit for keeping this from me," I say, throwing one arm over his shoulders. "You guys could have told me, you know."

Flint brings his other arm around and pulls me into a hug, resting his chin on my head. "Yeah. We were just so used to hiding it and we thought—"

"—you were doing what was best for me." His chin bobs. "Do me a favor. Next time you and Jace decide to do 'what's best for me' without consulting me, smack yourselves upside the head."

"Will do," Flint says, chuckling.

Nineteen

Two hours later, I watch Flint's form recede into the distance as Lir drives us down Peter's driveway. Flint and I spent a while in the woods discussing our plan and by the time we got back to Peter and Lir, they had the truck running. Peter was chattering away to Lir in the passenger seat as the alien drove around in a circle. So, by default, Lir will be doing the driving.

Flint raises one hand in a wave, a somber expression on his face. When he lowers his hand, he pats the front pocket of his jacket lightly—the pocket that contains the small metal object from Dane's desk. The reassurance I get from knowing he'll do what's needed is barely enough to edge out the gut-twisting guilt from not telling Lir about any of it. One week and then Flint will come in after me. I only hope I don't need that time. I return his wave and send a second, happier, wave to Peter.

The silence between Lir and me borders on uneasy. He hasn't said more than a few words to me since my breakdown in the driveway. Actually, the whole bordering thing isn't true; it *is* uneasy. My mind still reels from my stupidity for kissing him and, even more important, the new knowledge of my heritage and potential abilities.

Obviously, the alien part of me can connect with Jace and has connected to him in my dreams. That part sounds similar to the mental communication Lir described to me, but it is the emotion thing that really worries me. Jace used it to control me. Even if he was trying to help, the fact that he did it without my knowledge has nausea brewing in my stomach. How do I tell what thoughts and feelings are mine?

Back at Peter's, I recognized the foreign emotions coming from Lir, but they were strong and almost overwhelming. I can't pinpoint any other time when. I . . . connected with Lir, but would I have even noticed something more subtle? Jace managed to use the connection without any training and Lir would be used to it, he would understand it, know how to use it . . . Pieces fall into place. The calm I get from his touch. The shorter nightmares. The draw I feel toward him. That stupid, impulsive kiss . . .

I burrow back into my seat, pull my legs up, and tuck them under me. Flint's words dance in my head, poking at my own doubts and fears. I've spent barely over two weeks with Lir. Is that really long enough to know someone, to trust someone? Especially considering we weren't speaking for a few days and I was out of my mind for another few.

When not sleeping or ill, I've been the one doing most of the talking. He's been a steady, quiet presence, giving very little away. Or has he?

He said he'd heard rumors, but rumors of what, exactly? The aliens, as far as anyone knows, stay in their city. How would the possibility of my heritage, my existence reach their ears? If they knew . . . that would mean that, as Flint said, they have been here far longer than anyone realized. But why hide that? What isn't he telling me?

Driving is much quicker than hiking and it's a little over an hour before we reach the outskirts of the city. The closer we get to the towering buildings in the distance, the more his muscles tense.

His shoulders push back and he sits straighter. I can see his hands clenching around the steering wheel and I want to comfort him, reassure him that this is going to be okay, offer him the same comfort he has offered me before. But I don't know how to bridge this distance forming between us, how to cross over the gaping chasm of my uncertainty and newfound distrust.

The wind has pulled my hair from its braid, so I run my fingers through it and redo the plait, twisting it into a bun on the back of my neck. Waves of tension cross the car and roll into me. I wipe my sweaty palms on my jeans and try to focus on keeping my breath steady. He's doing it again. Has he been doing it all along? I want to ask, but icy trails of my own fear are starting to climb my spine as we draw even nearer to the city.

As my pulse ratchets up, the flow of . . . whatever it is coming from Lir cuts off abruptly, and even more abruptly, the tires move into the gravel on the side of the road as he pulls the truck to a stop.

"What are you doing?"

Lir turns to meet my eyes, a nervous expression on his face. What now? "Before we go in there, there are some things you should know." My face must do something strange, because he is quick to reassure me. "Nothing bad. Well, not . . ." Lir blows a breath out through pursed lips. "There are a lot of things that I haven't told you."

"No kidding," I say dryly. "If we're getting things out in the open, how about we start with the whole emotion-sharing thing or whatever it is, because that kinda creeps me out."

A shocked look crosses his face for a moment and then he nods. "Fair enough." His teeth press against his lower lip. "The emotional connection is called the *dhama*. It has various purposes, and although we can use the *kitu* to link to any within our race to some degree, the *dhama* develops between those with family ties . . . or, uh, emotional ties."

Emotional ties? No time to dwell on that now. There are more pressing questions rushing past my lips. "Does this mean that anyone in the city can get into my head? Can they read my thoughts?"

"No."

That was a very quick answer. I narrow my eyes. "You seem awfully sure about that."

He becomes rather fascinated with the dashboard in front of him and rubs the back of his neck with one hand. "I told you before about the functionality of the *kitu* as a communication device, so we can communicate mind to mind, but unless you send the thoughts out there, broadcast them, no one else can pick up on them. Well, not without a *kiun*, anyway."

"What—"

"Not something you need to worry about."

"That's not what I was going to ask." Actually, it was, but then a pretty clear image of some sort of fancy headband popped into my head. Wasn't anything I've ever seen, so it had to be from him. Can't read minds, my ass. Or maybe . . . I can? I squint my eyes and stare at him, but nothing happens.

Lir gives me a confused look and raises an eyebrow. "There's something else. I—"

"How did you hear rumors about me, about what I am, if you guys are supposed to stay in your city?"

He presses his lips together and shakes his head. "I will get to that, but what I have to say is more important right now. The—"

"No. Answer my question." I fold my arms over my chest.

"The rumors aren't from the humans. We have rumors of our own about what your friend called our 'early arrival program.' Your half-alien heritage isn't exactly an accident." At my silence, he continues. "When our planet started to fail, we sent scouts here, to research, blend in, find out if this planet was compatible. They arrived about ten years before what you call the Collapse. The team found that although their *kitus* allowed them to live comfortably, the atmosphere wasn't quite right and would not be compatible for any children born here. There were efforts to create a hybrid"—he squeezes his eyes shut and drives his teeth into his lower lip—"an organism our scientists could study to help us make any necessary adjustments to our own biology. The last transmission we ever received from Earth declared the attempts to combine human DNA with ours a failure. That was only days before the events that led up to the almost total decimation of this planet and the human race. But we had no other options. We came to Earth anyway. Put the dome in place to protect the *kitu*-less children until a solution could be found. But you . . . you're going to change everything. They'll let you stay—"

Any other words crossing his lips don't even register to me. Three phrases echo in my head. *An experiment. An organism. For study* . . . Flint was wrong about the weapon part but spot-on about the carting me off to be a prisoner in this city. Almost before I can blink, I'm across the seat, my back against the door and my fingers scrabbling for the handle, far, far away from the traitorous boy who pretended to care. I dig my nails into my palms until the backs of my eyes burn, desperate to stop my hands from shaking.

"Jax . . ." His voice is soft and his eyes plead with me to understand. What the hell am I supposed to understand? "Let me explain."

Lir scoots forward. Once he's in reach, my hand flies out, landing across his cheek with a loud crack. For the lies? For the manipulation? Or for the humiliation of thinking he actually cared about me?

"I don't want your explanation." I'm lost, alone and cornered, my words bitter barbs meant to cut and hurt and stick. "Have you been lying the whole time, or just since you figured out what I am? Thought you'd just toy with the stupid, stupid girl you could manipulate with a wink and a kiss. And all along I'm some sort of experiment for you to toy with."

"No! That's not what you are to me!" The blazing green fire of his eyes stands out against his cheek, bright red with the imprint of my hand. He reaches forward, but I bat away the hand he raises to touch my arm, my cheek, my *something*.

"Get back!" He doesn't listen.

"Jax . . ."

"When they take me, will you hear my screams in your head like I hear Jace's? How far could I broadcast? Can I make you all hear it, feel it?"

A lukewarm cocktail of worry spiked with guilt pours into me. Not mine. I flush it out with my own flaring rage, but without the heat of my anger, frosty fear takes over. Ice in my veins, freezing my limbs but leaving my head to spin. They're going to put me in that white, white room.

Jace! My brother's name becomes a chant in my head and my hands start to shake. I'm too frozen to move away when Lir grabs my upper arms and pulls me toward him.

His arms wrap around my back in a tight hug, pressing me against him. "Just listen to me. Please!"

The urge to relax into his embrace wars with my raging desire to flee. Flee the vehicle, flee the road, flee . . . to where? There's nowhere for me to go, not without Jace. I force my limbs to relax and pull back.

A heated intensity brews in his eyes. "That's *not* what you are to me." And then his mouth is on mine.

My body freezes at first, but then gradually relaxes against him and his lips move softly against mine. The movement is gentle and unsure, fiery, but not demanding. I tentatively move my hands to his hair, trailing my nails over his scalp, and Lir makes a sound in the back of his throat and pulls me closer. When my hand reaches his neck, I trace the scales there with one fingertip, making small circles against them. Every part of him that touches me causes tingles to rise up and race over my body.

There's more to this kiss—a tiny shift, a spark, a rush of something that I don't understand—but I lose myself in it anyway, giving myself the luxury of pushing aside all the worries and questions in my head. The connection—the *dhama*—flares to life and it's almost disorienting, feeling his desire, his elation, and his worry all mixed together with my own emotions in a swirling whirlpool that pulls me down and makes my head spin. But I see the difference now. I can tell his emotions from mine.

Lir pulls away, presses another soft kiss on my lips, runs his hand down my cheek and then turns back to the steering wheel. "This isn't going to be easy. I will do everything in my power to protect you and get your brother back, but you have to trust me. Please." I nod slowly and he pulls back on to the road without another word.

Stunned into silence, I sit with the fingers of one hand brushing against my lower lip. In the heat of the kiss, my panic receded, so it's not fear that has left me reeling but the niggling sense that something major just happened. And not just to me. What was that?

Twenty

The large buildings that towered when they were in the distance seem even more impossibly large as we get closer. I've never seen anything like it and my eyes widen with awe. Bridgelake, always so large to me before, is dwarfed by this place. I'm not entirely sure what the city looked like before, but I can't imagine it was anything like it is now. Shiny, clean, and perfect, the city stretches out for at least a few miles. Small buildings line the road, increasing in size toward the center, where three large towers are arranged in a circle. The design is almost too uniform. The E'rikon must have done much more than just rebuild. To achieve this, they would have had to raze the city to the ground and recreate it how they wanted it. This is no longer a city built by human hands.

My eyes are pulled from the beauty of the city ahead to a shimmer in the air. I gasp at the wall of—energy?—blocking the road and any further progress forward. So that's the barrier that has kept humans out all these years. It's situated around a mile out from the first building and rises upward into the air quite a ways before curving over toward the city. I guess calling it a *thingy* was understating it a bit.

Lir stops the truck a good distance from the barrier and clenches his jaw before speaking. "I have not had the time to prepare you as I would have liked to, especially considering . . ." He shakes his head softly and then continues. "You have to trust that I will get you through this. In a way what you are will make this easier, but there are those that are not going to like that I brought a human into our city, and until I can get my father to call a Council meeting, that is what you need to be, a simple human. No matter what happens, know that I am on your side and I am doing what I can to get you to your brother."

I nod slowly. His green eyes search my face, as if memorizing it. Leaning forward, Lir presses his forehead against mine. "It won't be easy. There are procedures, rules, *expectations* . . . I will need to abide by those as much as possible. Keep your head down and your mouth shut as much as possible, especially around any others."

Irritation fills me. "I know how to handle myself. You don't have to protect me."

"Yes. I do." He brushes his hand down my cheek and then straightens his shoulders and steps out of the truck.

I nod silently and exit behind him.

As we draw closer, two E'rikon move up to meet us, their *kitus* glinting in the sunlight. Both are dressed in uniforms similar to what the other aliens in the clearing wore, form-fitting gray pants and high-collared jackets with tall boots. "State your business," says the shorter one.

Shoulders back and with an arrogant tilt to his head, Lir manages to look every inch the soldier he was when I first met him. "Steliro Vestra reporting in." *Steliro?*

A quiver of shock rolls through them. "Vestra?"

"Yes." Lir's short, simple words manage to convey an authority I didn't think possible.

They snap to attention and salute with their cuffed arms. "Sir." They relax with a nod from Lir. What is he, some sort of alien big shot? Does this make my rescue mission more or less difficult? Does he have enough power to just order Jace to be released?

"I need entry and transport immediately. My *kitu* is not currently functional."

"Yes, sir." One of the guards steps forward and through the wall of energy shimmering in the air. He lightly grasps Lir's upper arm and steps back through.

The three of them turn to walk away. My mouth opens in protest and I'm about to ask Lir what the hell is going on when he speaks. "And the girl. Bring her."

The other alien steps through the wall, grabs me, and yanks me through. Electricity zips along my nerve endings and tingles in my fingers. The sensation isn't exactly unpleasant—more uncomfortable—but I don't think my experience is normal. On the other side, the alien pauses, tilts his head, and narrows his eyes at me for a second before shaking his head and continuing, never letting go of my arm. When his fingers dig in a little too hard, I inhale sharply.

"Do not get overzealous. She is not to be harmed," Lir says, without even looking back at me. A brief sense of betrayal fills my belly, but I calm myself. What could I expect? Certainly not that he'd fawn all over me in front of these two after what he just told me. His disregard still stings, though.

The walk isn't long, maybe a hundred yards, before we reach a shining transport vehicle. It's more of a pod than a car, bright silver with expansive windows. The interior seats face each other and I assume it operates on some kind of autopilot, as there's no steering wheel or anything else that I can recognize. Lir enters the vehicle first and I'm pushed in after him. I don't slide into the seat next to Lir; instead, I sit on the bench seat across from him, huddling as far into the corner as I can get. The two guards pile in, one next to me, still holding my arm, and the other across from me. When my knees brush his, he sneers a little and adjusts his legs to avoid touching mine.

The air in the vehicle is thick with tension. I keep my eyes downcast and stay silent, but my mind is racing. This is nothing like I expected. Despite the warning—if you could call it that—Lir's sudden stoicism unnerves me. My heartbeat picks up and I can almost feel the walls of the transport closing in on me. Was this all a horrible mistake? There's no escape now. My lungs constrict and it's getting harder to get a proper breath. I have to stay calm. It's one thing to freak out in private, or even in front of humans, but I can imagine the aliens would not take it well if I started screeching and banging my hands on the walls.

Most important thing right now: breathing. If I get that in line the rest should follow. I focus on my breaths. *In and out. In and out.* Gradually my racing pulses recedes and I feel normal, or at least as normal as I can feel locked in this tiny space with three aliens, all of whom refuse to even acknowledge my presence.

Riding in the pod thing is much different than riding in the truck. It's smoother, for one, and there's no engine noise. What makes it run? I distract myself with trying to figure out how it might be powered and directed, staring out the window at the ever approaching city. No conclusions come to me. I might be smart, but this is technology I'm sure no human has seen up close and it's probably much more advanced than anything we had even before the Collapse.

We . . . I'm still thinking of myself as a human, but I'm really not, at least not entirely. Of course, if I have to identify with one race, I've spent much more time with humans and I'm not even sure which of my characteristics stem from my alien heritage. Besides the weird mental stuff, what sets me apart from humans? I don't have scales. My blood isn't green. Would anyone even know unless I told them?

The pressure gets to be too much and I drum my fingers on my thigh, tapping out a rhythm to distract my frazzled brain. Still no one talks. I look up from under my brow, darting my gaze around the vehicle. The aliens, Lir included, look almost bored. Even in human clothes, Lir stands apart from the other two. Taller. Leaner. More . . . something.

The dirt caked under my nails makes me blush. I didn't even take the time for a bath at Peter's. Lir has been traveling just as much as I have—hell, he was even a prisoner for a while—but he manages to be clean and put together. How did I not even notice this before? I am not either of those things and it makes me feel even more out of place. The creeping sense of unease returns and I have to go back to looking out the window. I wish I had clothes to change into, or even a bath.

The vehicle stops with a gentle deceleration, barely even a bump in the passenger area. We're in front of one of the larger buildings, a silver monstrosity that's at least forty stories high. A ship flies past and docks on the roof. I'm busy staring up at it when one of the aliens grabs my arm and pulls me out. "Come on," he says gruffly.

Lir stops our two escorts at the door. "I will take her from here," he says. "Notify my parents that I have returned."

"Yes, sir."

Both aliens salute and Lir pulls me up to the door. He presses his *kitu* against a metal square to the right of the door and frowns when nothing happens. A quick glance confirms that our escorts have already disappeared into the pod, leaving us stranded out on the sidewalk, apparently unable to enter the building. The stiffness in his posture relaxes and he lets out a loud huff.

"Didn't really think this bit through, did you?" I ask. My head tilts down and I keep my voice low.

He chuckles under his breath and glances up and down the empty street. "Not exactly. Would you like to give it a shot?"

"What do you mean?"

"In theory, you should be able to open the door by linking into the system."

"In theory, I should be able to do a lot of things." I snort.

He shrugs. "It shouldn't be that difficult."

"Says the guy who can't even open the door." A smile works its way across my face.

"Just put your hand on it or something and link in."

I roll my eyes. "Just like that, huh? Flick a switch and access my mental superpowers? I'm sure—"

Lir's fingers wrap around my arm and squeeze as his whole body tenses. I look up from my toes to see that one of our escorts has returned and he's looking between us quizzically.

"Is there a problem, sir?"

Soldier Lir is back again, shoulders back, looking down his nose at the other alien. "I am unable to link in without my *kitu*. Escort us to my quarters."

"Yes, sir." The alien nods briskly and places his *kitu* against the pad. A moment later, the door slides open and he leads us into the building.

§

We take an elevator to the top floor. After opening another door, the alien salutes and scurries back down the hall. Lir walks through the door and into an open living room filled with a couple chairs and a couch. All in white. I'm barely through the door behind him when a small form comes bounding across the room and throws itself at him. It's a little girl with sparkling green-and-gold hair. He catches her with an oomph.

"I'm so glad you're home! I missed you!" Her voice rises into a squeal.

Lir lifts her from the floor, swinging her in a circle, and pats her back. "I missed you, too, Stella." The little sister he told me about. He walks farther into the room, leaving me staring after him, not quite sure what to do or say. "Have a seat, Jax."

I sit, my mind reeling with yet another rapid shift in his persona. He kissed me and stroked my cheek before we got here, then ignored me in the pod, joked with me downstairs, and now his demeanor just went from emotionless soldier to adored big brother. Which one is he? The rapid shifts in his mood bring an edge of unease trickling into my body.

I try to sit on the very edge of the starkly white couch, hoping to save it from my dirty clothes. My joints ache with the desire to run, to hide, to escape, and I have to clasp my hands together to keep them still.

The child's chatter echoes from down the hallway and I hear a door open and close. Seconds later, the girl is running back out to the living room, Lirless.

"Hello," she says, cocking her head to the side. "I like your hair."

"Um . . ." How articulate of me. I reach up and pat at my head self-consciously. "Thanks?"

"What family are you from? You're red like the Revas, but they have black too and sometimes yellow. And your eyes don't match," she states matter-of-factly.

I'm at a loss and have no idea what she's asking me, so I just smile, silently screaming at Lir to come rescue me. Almost as if he hears my silent plea, he appears in the hallway. "Stel, please leave our guest alone," he says. He disappears back down the hallway and I hear the sound of running water.

Stella stares at me, a mischievous glint in her eye. "I don't care if your eyes don't match. I think you're pretty."

A flush heats my cheeks and I twist my hands in my lap. "Thank you."

Lir instructed me to keep quiet, but sitting here with the bubbly little girl, I'm not sure what to do. If she keeps staring at me, I'm going to crack. Interrogation by child. I lift my eyes and smile at her. She perks up and leans closer to me, as if she's imparting a secret.

"Do you want to play with me? My brother always hogs the best dolls," she says. She backs up a little. "You're not a doll hogger, are you?"

I can't help but laugh. The ride in the transport, the open hostility of the escorts, and my doubts about Lir fade into the background. Right now, this little girl has given me just enough normality to make me comfortable. My jittery limbs finally relax fully and I smile at Stella. "No, I've never even had a doll to hog."

Stella gapes at me. "Really? What do you do for fun?"

The sound of a throat clearing brings my eyes up. Lir stands in the hallway watching us, a subtle smile on his face. With that expression, he looks like the guy who kissed me in the truck, the guy who held me while I slept . . . the beautiful boy I saw in the clearing. It's nice to see him again. I'm not fond of the icy-cold soldier Lir. He has ditched the jeans and T-shirt and another charcoal-colored uniform, like the one he wore when I met him, hugs his frame. Stella's clothes are the same color. Huh. Must be an alien thing.

Part of Lir's hair, leftover from my pathetic attempt at a haircut, hangs over his forehead in wet curls. I would like nothing more than to go tousle them. His eyebrow goes up and I blush. Am I that obvious? But Stella is looking at me strangely, too.

"Why do you like my brother's hair so much?" she asks. "Mine is much prettier."

My breath catches. How did she know?

Lir's eyes go wide and the color leaves his face. "Stel," he says calmly. "Can you go play in your room for a bit? I need to speak with Jax."

Stella bounds off down the hallway without further question and Lir settles in next to me on the couch. "What was that?"

"You're asking me? I have no idea. Was she reading my mind? I thought you said you guys couldn't do that. Though I'm pretty sure there are some worse thoughts in my head she could have gotten, so . . ." A blush overtakes my face when I realize what that sounds like. "I mean . . . about the whole half-alien thing and Jace . . . and stuff."

He smiles softly. "Did you know you were doing it? Were you broadcasting to the others in the transport pod?"

"To the others? You mean the guards? I don't know." Another realization dawns on me. "Was I broadcasting to you?"

"A little."

I run through the trip in the transport pod, desperately trying to remember what I thought about, if I gave anything away. Am I supposed to be policing my thoughts now? I wouldn't even know where to start with that. Am I doing it now? I don't have time to figure out the answers to my questions, because a tone sounds near the door and Lir jolts to his feet as two more people enter the apartment.

Decked out in clothes the same shade as Lir's, the teenage boy and girl stand there for a moment with their mouths gaping before the boy's mouth climbs up into a grin and the girl rushes across the room and throws her arms around Lir. His arms settle around her waist and she presses her face into his chest. He whispers against her ear and one hand comes up and strokes her long, yellow-gold hair. It suddenly feels like someone punched me in the stomach.

It doesn't get any better when he releases her and she turns around, enabling me to get an even better look. Pure golden perfection, from the shining waves of her hair to the perfect matching shade of her luminous eyes. Her lithe body fills out the form-fitting uniform . . . perfectly. There is just too much about her that is perfect.

Acid churns in my stomach and I study my hands in my lap—my filthy hands with ragged, uneven nails. When did I start caring? Better yet, why? Did I really expect . . . *No. No. No.* That kiss in the truck is still a bit of a mystery to me and I'm even more mortified that *I* kissed *him*, but it's not like there's any chance for . . .

Lir clears his throat and I look up to meet his eyes. Did it get hot all of a sudden? Heat rises in my face as that single eyebrow goes up. How much of that little freak-out did he hear? One side of his mouth curls up. That too? *Turn it off. Turn it off.* Thankfully the other two don't seem to notice my embarrassing mental commentary, but the boy glances back and forth between us and what I can only call a mischievous smile takes over his face.

"What the blazes happened to your hair?" His golden eyes stay focused on me even though he directs the question to Lir, as if he's waiting to see a reaction from me.

Lir clears his throat. "Just a poor attempt at a human disguise." He ruffles his hair forward and turns his head from side to side, posing. "I've been told it's what the humans call a mullet."

The boy laughs, but the girl scoffs. "Why would you want to look human? It's not like—" She breaks off and takes a close look at me, her hand rising to cover her mouth as her eyes widen. "Lir . . . what have you done?"

The boy's eyes narrow at my face before widening as well and shifting to Lir.

He clears his throat again and runs his hand back through his hair. "Rym"—he gestures to the boy—"Trel"—waves a hand to the girl—"this is Jax." Two incredulous pairs of eyes bore into me. "She assisted me in my return. I could not have done it without her."

Four long strides bring Rym to the couch with his hand out. "Well, Jax, let me be the first to formally thank you for returning our cousin to us. Full of himself as he is, we missed him." He winks. Humor shines from his eyes and it relaxes me enough to accept his hand. He promptly lifts the back of my hand to his lips, waggling his eyebrows at me over my knuckles. "This is how it's done in the human world, yes?"

I pause at the touch of his mouth on my hand just long enough for my breath to catch in my throat and my limbs to tense, before I snatch my hand away and offer him a small smile. "Yeah. I guess so."

If he thinks my actions are strange, he doesn't comment on it. "You the one that massacred his hair?" At my nod, his smile gets even bigger. "Well, good for you. That wanker was always a bit too pretty with all those curls."

"Wanker?"

Lir shifts over until he's standing next to me and rests one hand on my shoulder. "Please just ignore him. My cousin has spent too much time watching the vids from the London team." *London team?*

"They have all the best slang," says Rym with a chuckle. He springs up and musses Lir's hair. "At least now I've got a chance with the ladies. Do you know how tough it is to be in competition with this guy?" He jerks his thumb at Lir.

Lir just rolls his eyes. Trel is still standing there with a bit of a dumbfounded look on her face, watching their interaction.

Really, Rym has nothing to worry about. Although his looks are different than Lir's, he's no less attractive. Close-cut hair and the same brilliant eyes as his sibling. He's perfect and golden just like her.

Lir swivels his head to me and the eyebrow goes up again. Then again, there's an intensity to my alien boy, something special in his emerald gaze that pulls me in more than his cousin's friendly nature and good looks. I'm obviously not immune to physical attraction, but Lir is the only one I've ever felt it for.

"So tell us about yourself, Jax. Why are you here?" Trel's voice is almost overly sweet, but her eyes bore into me.

What am I supposed to tell her? My gaze slides to Lir.

Staring straight at Rym, Lir speaks, his words careful and precise. "We have had a long trip and my parents should arrive soon. I think it's best if I speak with you later. Jax will be here for a little while." *I will?*

Rym nods slowly and grabs Trel's sleeve and pulls her toward the door. "Come on, sister. We should let Lir get settled." He sends me a wink as the door slides shut. "Very nice to meet you, Jax."

Twenty-One

Lir sits next to me on the couch. "Are you okay? Rym can be a little . . . exuberant . . ." His voice trails off and he looks away. "You could have turned down his hand. I know touching makes you uncomfortable. He wouldn't have been insulted. Casual touching is different for us anyway because of—" At the sound of the door sliding open, Lir breaks off, jolts to his feet, and distances himself from me. A pang of disappointment hits my stomach as the stoic mask covers his face again and he nods to the male and female who have just entered.

"Mother. Father."

"I am so happy you are home, Steliro," says his mother. There's kindness and a genuine happiness in her gold eyes as she looks at her son. "Have you spoken with the techs yet?"

"No, Mother," Lir answers. "I have barely had time to bathe, must less wander down there."

"But . . ."

"Don't worry, Mother. I'll be fine," Lir says. He gives his father another subtle nod. "Sir."

"Good to have you home, son," says his father. His nose tilts into the air arrogantly, but there's a softness to his face that suggests he really is happy to see his son. "You will have to tell us all about your adventures with the humans." He says the last word with disgust and Lir's eyes darken slightly.

"Yes, about that . . ." Lir straightens and brushes his palms over his pants. "This is Jax." His hands gesture to me. "Jax, my mother, Vira, and my father, Stellan."

If his parents could have been any more shocked, they would have fainted. Both of their mouths drop a little, but they recover quickly, Lir's mother with a small smile and his father with a bit of a sneer. This isn't going very well.

I stand up and copy Lir's previous movement, brushing my palms over my pants. Holding my hand out to his mother, clearly the lesser evil in the room, I work up my best friendly smile and say, "Pleased to meet you."

Vira makes every effort to return my smile, but the effect is not quite there. She ignores my hand, shooting glances at Lir and Stellan and avoiding my face. I awkwardly lower my hand and turn to greet Stellan, but the glowering look he's sending at Lir stops any words from exiting my mouth.

"What were you thinking?" Stellan says. "Bringing a human here? To our home? Where your sister is? She's already fragile, Steliro. Are you trying to kill her?" His voice rises with each word until at the end he's yelling, punctuating each syllable with a shake of his finger.

I shrink away from the irate alien, my heartbeat sounding in my ears and a tremble returning to my hands. Lir catches my eye and a warm sense of comfort flows over me. Indecision flickers on his face for a moment before he speaks. "There is something—"

"Who else knows she is here?" snaps Stellan.

"The two that escorted us here, Stella, of course, and Rym and Trel just left."

Stellan closes his eyes and rubs the bridge of his nose between two fingers. "The twins know? There is no way to hide it now." He opens his eyes and narrows his gaze at me and then turns to his son. "My office. Now." He spins on his heel and strides down the hallway, Lir following close behind.

I'm left standing in the middle of the living room with Vira. She watches Lir's retreating back and then flicks her eyes to my face. It takes a lot of effort to keep some semblance of a neutral expression on my face when I feel like I want to puke.

Eventually she takes pity on me and leads me down another hallway to a bedroom.

"There is an attached bath if you would like to get cleaned up. I will see what I can do about finding you some clothing." She meets my eyes and looks away quickly. "Thank you for returning my son to me." A soft smile and then she walks away.

The bathroom is just as clean as the rest of the quarters, sparkling white, and I'm like the mud somebody tracked in on their shoes. Can't complain too much, though—the shower is amazing. Showerheads extend from both walls so they rinse both sides of my body at the same time. Steam fills the bathroom and I inhale the warm, relaxing scent of the soap that Vira found for me. When I tilt my head back to wash my hair, some soap leaks into my eye and I yelp, twisting away from the spray and feeling around for a towel.

My hand hits open air instead of the wall I was expecting and I stumble, falling to my butt in the water and knocking over the line of bottles on the edge.

"Jax?" Lir's voice from right outside the bathroom. "Are you all right?"

"Fine," I yell, scrubbing at my eyes with my hands. "Just fine."

I hurry through the rest of the shower, rinsing my hair this time without getting any more soap in my eyes. When I step out, fog covers the large mirror over the sink. A single bottle of lightly scented lotion sits on the counter next to a folded towel. The thick fluffy towel is a luxury in itself and I almost moan when I rub the lovely lotion over my skin. I don't think I've ever felt so clean and pampered.

I fold the towel back up and set it on the counter, but I still have no clothes. Thankfully there's a robe—a white one, of course—hanging on the back of the door. It's short and reaches only halfway to my knees when I wrap it around me, but I don't have any other options unless I want to wander around naked. I half stumble out of the bathroom—stupid door sticks—and stop in my tracks when I see Lir sitting on the bed. The robe was a good choice.

"I had to tell my father about . . . what you are," Lir says, gaze fixed firmly on his hands. "I just . . ." His eyes come up, trailing from my bare feet up my damp legs and landing on my face. "Where are your clothes?"

My face heats and I grip the robe closer to my body. "They seem to have run off."

Lir grins and chuckles, shaking his head. "I'm not really complaining." The tension in my body releases at his relaxed attitude. "Can we talk?"

"Uh, sure," I say. I plop down on the bed next to him and his face flushes.

"I meant later, you know, with clothes on?"

My head tilts and I shrug. "You're here now. Let's get this over with." I'm not sure what I expect him to say, but it can't be good. Lir fidgets and looks away. Maybe clothes would be a good idea. There's no barrier between us, nothing protecting me from the words he's about to say.

"Jax . . ." he starts, "I haven't been fully honest with you."

"No kidding. I think we've already had that conversation," I say in monotone.

He sighs and pinches the top of his nose. "First of all, let me apologize for my father. He's . . . under a lot of pressure right now and bringing you here is just going to complicate it even more."

"Then why'd you bring me here? Why am I lounging around your house instead of finding Jace? How is this helping?"

"It's not . . ." A loud exhale pushes past his lips. "I thought this was going to be the easy way. That my family's position here might . . . be of assistance. But the tensions between us and the humans have gotten too far out of hand. My return hasn't exactly escaped notice and the fact that I brought you into the city . . ."

"And which camp am I in? The 'us' or the humans? Because I didn't ask for any of this. I just came for my brother."

His eyes flash. "You seem to forget the things your brother has done to end up here. In our eyes he's a criminal." I guess I'm solidly in the "them" category, then.

"That still doesn't explain why I'm here lounging around instead of out getting Jace back."

Lir's hand moves up, ruffling his hair in a gesture I've come to recognize as frustration. "About that . . ." The hand on my back freezes when my muscles tense. He can't possibly back out now. I'm depending on him and I'm completely out of my element here. "I don't know where he is."

"What is that supposed to mean? You promised."

The hand goes to his hair again and he sighs. "I didn't promise anything, Jax. I said I'd get you here," he says. My head tilts to the side and I blink once slowly. "No, that's not coming out right . . . I want to help you, but after I found out what you were, I knew we had to come here first. It's a good thing we did, because there's been absolutely no news of your brother's arrival here. My father has a good idea about why that may be, and so do I, but there are steps that have to be taken. You can't go running around trying to find him by yourself. It's going to take time."

"Time? I don't have time. *Jace* doesn't have time. I need to find him now! Who knows what they're doing to him!"

His brow furrows. "I am doing all I can . . ."

I turn and poke my finger into his chest. "You don't get it. They're torturing him. Your people . . . I can't just sit here . . ."

He wraps his hand around mine and gives it a gentle squeeze. Warmth trickles into me, lowering my heart rate, slowing my breaths and . . . calming me. "It will—"

I snatch my hand away like it's been burned. "Don't do that! What gives you the right to shove your emotions on me?" Springing up off the bed, I stalk to the other side of the room.

"I didn't mean anything by it. I just thought—"

"You thought that you'd control me? Manipulate me?"

Redness creeps up his neck and he stands. He stalks across the room until he's standing right in front of me. "No. I thought I would *help* you. You don't understand—"

"I don't want your help!" The words explode from my mouth before I can stop myself. "I just want to get my brother and get out of here!"

There's a flash of pain in his eyes, then he flexes his jaw and a visible wave of tension flows through him. The chilly soldier persona has returned. "I have arranged a Council meeting to discuss my return and allow you to present a formal request for Jace's release. Get some rest. We will discuss this in the morning." He strides out of the room without looking back.

What did he expect me to say? *Yes, please, crawl around in my brain.* The prickling heat of irritation slowly gives way to a wash of guilt. It's not his fault I'm not . . . like him. He's had his entire lifetime to get used to this emotional thing and it's probably instinctive for him. We're both exhausted and stressed . . . I'll apologize in the morning.

After searching through a few drawers I throw my hands up in frustration. My clothes disappeared and there's no— A small gray stack of folded fabric on the edge of the dresser catches my eye. I fluff out the clothes. No surprises here—simple gray shirt and pants. Socks and underwear, too. I sure hope Vira was the one who dropped this stuff off.

The fabric slides easily against my skin, softer and smoother than anything I've ever experienced before. If not for the fact I'm virtually alone in this alien city, having seemingly pissed off my only ally here, I'd be reveling in all these little luxuries. I collapse onto the bed, sinking into the mattress as it molds around me. Maybe I'll revel a little anyway.

Despite the comfort of the mattress against my body, when I close my eyes and try to sleep, it won't come. I pull the pillow over my face and close my eyes, searching for that elusive peace and failing. My mind is too busy bouncing from thought to thought and every one leads me back to a different worry. Where is Jace? What if I can't get him out? Have I completely screwed things up with Lir? What *things*?

I'm lost in thought when the sound of giggling comes from the end of the bed and Stella pops up into view. "Hi!"

I sit up and smile at her. "Hi, Stella. What are you doing in here?"

"I just wanted to talk to you. No one would let me talk to you . . ." She makes a pouty face and shakes her head. "So, are you really a human? I've never met a human before."

"Yes." What else am I supposed to say? I don't want to scare her, and if her parents' attitudes have anything to do with it, she'll probably never see a human again. "I'm human." It's only a little stretch of the truth.

She nods as if satisfied with my answer. "I like you, Jax. Don't worry, Lir will forgive you." Leaning closer, she whispers the next part. "I have tantrums too and he always forgives me." Such a simple statement, but it is enough to reassure my racing mind, and my chest moves with laughter.

I impulsively reach forward and hug her. As her little arms go around my waist, I realize there's no *kitu* on her wrist. Does that mean she has to stay within the city or she'll die? But . . . then how did I broadcast to her? Didn't Lir say the mental communication came from the *kitu*? Have the E'rikon altered the atmosphere within the barrier and that's why they stay in the city? But then . . . how did Lir survive outside it when his *kitu* wasn't working? The questions just keep coming, swirling in my head until Stella releases me and hops off the bed.

"I better get back to my room. Night, Jax!" She scampers out of the room with a wave and I settle back against the pillow.

Somehow, I manage to fall asleep despite the steady stream of questions marching around in my brain.

Twenty-Two

I'm at the cabin again, but without the shades of Dad and Jace. Instead, Lir stands in the center of the living room, his hands clasped behind his back and his head bowed. He uses one hand to gesture around the room. "This is the second time you've brought me here. You feel safe here." His chest rises with a deep breath and he lifts his head to meet my eyes. "Does this mean you're finally ready to listen?"

What's going on? Am I dreaming?

"In a way, yes," says Lir. Alarm crosses his face as I take two scrambled steps backward. "No . . . please don't shut me out. You *are* safe here." He bites his lip and extends a hand to me. "We need to talk. I know I haven't exactly gone about things the right way, but this is new to me, too."

The hand stays out, a silent plea, but it's his eyes that draw me in. Open, entreating, caring. Besides, no real harm can come to me in a dream world, right?

I walk forward and place my hand in his. "Okay. But this better be good."

Lir laughs and pulls me forward. "You never fail to surprise me." He leads me to the couch and we sit.

"So . . . is this another E'rikon thing? The dreaming?"

"You could say that. Honestly, I didn't realize until recently that humans don't share connections like we do. This shared dreamscape"—he circles his arm around the cabin—"is the product of a bond. It's a place for us to regroup, heal, communicate. Really, whatever we decide to use it for."

"We as in you and me?"

"Yes." There's more to that statement, so I just raise my eyebrows at him, waiting for him to continue. "This is our place. Only ours."

I narrow my eyes.

He lets out a nervous chuckle. "I didn't think it was possible, not without the *kitu*, much less when I thought you were fully human. I'm still not sure how it happened." Green eyes find mine and hold my gaze. "I do know it couldn't have happened if you hadn't let me in. I didn't force this. I couldn't and wouldn't have done so."

"What exactly happened?"

"The emotional link, this place . . . it means we're bondmates."

"And that means . . ."

Another uncomfortable laugh. "It means we have a special connection. Most bondmates are coupled . . ."

I inhale sharply.

"But if that's not what you want, we don't—you don't . . ." He trails off and shakes his head. "I am really messing this up, aren't I?" He gives me a crooked smile. "I tried to talk to you this morning. I thought it would be good news. You were so agitated and then you kissed me . . . I felt your confusion, your panic. Not what I was expecting. You had no idea what was happening and then, of course, other things got in the way."

He runs his hand over his head. "When you had a panic attack in Peter's driveway, I knew things were not going to go well. I've been trying desperately to keep it in check so you aren't subjected to things you are unprepared for. I lost control in the truck because *I* needed the reassurance. *I* needed that connection to get *me* through. I was selfish and I'm sorry for that and pretty much everything that followed. I didn't take the time to reassure you in a way you understood. I didn't really stop to think and I sure as hell didn't consider how what I told you earlier about . . . the hybridization . . . would sound before I opened my mouth. Especially after everything else that you'd been through today."

What to process first? The bond? The apology? My brain can't seem to focus on either one of those. Instead, it grabs hold of the first question to form and ejects it out of my mouth. "Is this bond thing permanent?"

Lir's smile falters and he winces as if I hit him. "No. It's rare, but it can be broken." He swallows and then closes his eyes. "Is that what you want?"

"I don't know. I don't understand it." I pull my hands away from him and throw my arms up. "Is this what you want? Why would you want this bond with me? There have got to be more . . . suitable girls for you, ones your parents approve of or . . . not broken ones."

"I can't say this is an ideal situation, but if I hadn't wanted it on some level, the bond would not have been formed. It doesn't work that way."

"How will this even work? You know I can't stay here, right? My plan is still to get Jace and leave. Are you going to come with me?"

He shrugs. "I was hoping I could convince you to stay, but I haven't really thought that far ahead."

My legs are itching to get up and start pacing and my fingers begin to drum on my knees.

He moves his hands over mine and gives them a gentle squeeze. "Don't think, just feel." With two fingers he lifts my chin until I'm looking into his eyes.

A subtle warmth starts in my hands and flows up my arms. I tense up for a moment, but then I close my eyes and float on the sensation, letting it move through my body. Comfort. Peace. Connection.

One of Lir's hands comes up to cup my cheek and his thumb brushes across my lips. *So beautiful.* He leans in, his breath brushing across my mouth before he presses his lips down over mine. This kiss is not born from my confusion or from his fear. It's a careful exploration, a hesitant reverence. His hand moves back to twine in my hair and he darts his tongue along the seam of my mouth. He pulls back and gives me one more light peck before settling back onto the couch, his face red.

"Sorry," he mumbles. "I wasn't trying to take advantage."

"You're sorry for kissing me?"

The half smile turns almost into a grin and he raises one eyebrow. "Do you want me to be?"

"No. I want you to do it again."

This time I lean into him, wrap my hand around the back of his neck, and pull him to my mouth. His hand goes back to my cheek and then trails down my arm, igniting the subtle warmth into a steady burn everywhere he touches. Wrapping his other arm around my lower back, he pulls me forward until I swing my legs up onto the couch and over his lap. His heart pounds against my other hand, now resting on his chest. A sound somewhere between a plea and a groan rumbles in his throat when I nip at his lower lip.

Images begin to flash through my head as his lips work against mine: me in the forest. Me in Emily's dress. Me swimming across a pond. My leaning close while hair clippings float down in front of my face. The sound of my laugh. The humor of my scowl.

I pull back and wait for Lir to open his eyes. When he does, they're like molten jewels, swirling with green-gold fire. He leans forward to reclaim my mouth, but I put the tops of the fingers on my right hand over his lips and shake my head. "It was you. The entire time. How?"

"The entire time? How long have you been getting images from me?" The words are muffled by my fingers, but he doesn't back away. He presses little kisses to my knuckles and the palm of my hand.

"Since the first night in the woods," I say.

"I've never heard of anything like that happening." He stares at me in wonder. "That means . . . you're probably linking to Stella, not just broadcasting. That connection might be enough to save her."

"Save her?"

"You didn't really let me finish explaining things earlier. The children born here, like Stella, cannot survive outside the dome. None of us could without the *kitus*." His eyes widen. Cool excitement starts to splash out from him. "But you can and you linked to me, *bonded* with me even without a functional *kitu*."

"Because I'm half-human." But that also means . . . "You would have died out there if you hadn't been with me. They disabled your *kitu* before they left. Did they know that you'd be as good as dead? Were they trying to kill you?"

"I'm not entirely sure, but that would be a logical conclusion."

"But then you had to have known . . . something . . . when you weren't dying. You said you had no idea what I was."

"I didn't." He grabs my hands again. "At first I just thought it was taking me a very long time to die. I didn't understand why and I really didn't care. I let myself get close to you even though I knew it was a bad idea. And then you were bitten by that snake . . . I never sat around asking myself, 'hey, why aren't you dead yet,' but when the delirium hit you, I felt something. I knew somehow that you were different, that it was you keeping me alive and me helping you fight the infection. I didn't really understand all the implications of that until your friend explained what he knew about your heritage."

"So I am just an experiment, then?" I yank my hands away and stand. "I wasn't wrong. They're—*you're*—never going to let me and Jace leave, not when we can do this thing that none of you can do. Not when you can use us. They've obviously already been experimenting or something on my brother." Agitation rises in my stomach and crawls up my throat. "What Flint said . . . I'm not even functional. I don't know how to use this link thing and I'm unstable with my own emotions, much less anyone else's."

"Work with me, with us. We're meeting with the Council tomorrow. We just have to show them we have nothing to hide."

"But I do have stuff to hide, Lir. Where is Jace? If your return has caught everyone's attention, then wouldn't they already know about Jace's arrival?" My feet carry me back and forth in front of the couch.

Lir rubs the back of his neck and looks up at me. "Maybe it was kept secret. I don't know, but we'll need the Council's help to find Jace and get your link working correctly."

"What if it never works correctly? Then I'm useless, expendable. What then, Lir?"

"I'm not going to let anything happen to you, I promise."

"What if you can't stop it? None of this makes any sense. This link, this bond . . . How do you even know that this thing between us is real and not just some consequence of what I am? I'm just a broken girl who inadvertently managed to keep you alive."

He jumps to his feet and grasps my biceps. "You're more than that!" Eyes like green fire bore into me and hot conviction shoots through the link.

I may not have figured out how the link works, but I do know how to get my own emotions to the forefront. I use my fear to cool the link. "How would you even know that for sure? How would I know?"

"Because I fell for you well before I knew what you were. Even when you were just the stupidly brave girl waving a knife at me, I knew that you were special. Are you going to deny that you felt it, too?" The next words whisper across my cheek as he leans in even closer. "Don't lie. I can feel you even if you won't admit it to yourself."

His emotions merge with mine, wrapping us in a vortex of heat, and my already volatile state only needs that slight increase in temperature to combust. I slam my lips onto his. His arms wrap around my back and press me tight against his body. Somehow I end up with my back against the wall, his mouth still firmly attached to mine.

This kiss is hunger. He devours me with the press of his lips and the touch of his hands. One hand brushes down my side and curls around my waist, pulling me closer, erasing any space between us, every hard plane of his body glued to mine. The other hand tangles in my hair to control the angle of my head while he sucks my lower lip into his mouth, releases it, and then slides his tongue into my mouth.

I moan and run my hands over every part of him I can reach, his shoulders, his arms, his hands, his cheeks . . . One of my hands manages to find the bottom of his shirt and slip up between the fabric and the smoothness of his stomach. He pauses, his abs tightening, his arms tensing as if to pull away. I whimper and slide my hand farther up until I can feel the rapid beat of his heart against my palm and he groans into my mouth, continuing to kiss me with white-hot desire flowing around us.

He's right—I do feel it, *have* felt it. And it terrifies me.

A thought. A shuffle. A hesitation. Those three things are enough to let a sliver of frost form. The wispy tendrils of ice spread and suddenly I'm much too hot. Lir's arms are too tight, his mouth too demanding, his hand tugging too hard at my hair. A soft, scared noise travels up my throat and he pulls back, the lust in his eyes transitioning quickly to worry when he sees my face.

"It's okay. You're safe." *I would never hurt you.* He thinks he's helping when he pushes the words at me, letting them float into my head through the link on a gentle current of comfort.

But. That. Means. He's. In. My. Head. And they are, too. Those men I killed with their platitudes, their *pretty thing*s, their *little girl*s . . . and hands and hurtandbloodandpain. They were in my head. How did they get in my head? This thing that I am let them in and I want them *out*!

The cabin dissolves around me, fading into nothing until I am alone in the blackness of my mind.

Twenty-Three

S tella!" The shout brings me to instant awareness. Not so for the little bundle curled against me and fast asleep. When did Stella come back in here? I nudge her, but she doesn't even budge.

My face is sticky and when I wipe at it, my hand comes back wet with blood. A nosebleed? The stark white pillow has a sopping patch of red. There's another shout from the hallway and I hurriedly scrub my face with the pillowcase. Without a mirror I can't really tell if all the blood is gone, but I'd better get my visitor out to her worried parents. This is already not going to go over well with them.

I pull Stella into my arms and carry her into the hallway. "Um . . . Mr. Vestra? She's here."

Vira flies up the hallway and gathers Stella into her arms while Stellan glares at me over his wife—no, his *bondmate's* shoulder. "What was she doing with you?" Ice laces his words and I can tell nothing I say is going to satisfy him so I just shrug and avert my eyes. He advances up the hallway, a predatory look in his eyes. "So help me, if you've harmed her—"

"Father!" Lir steps out from a door to my right, tousled from sleep and wearing a worried frown. "Stop it. She wouldn't hurt Stella."

If only the carpet would swallow me. The door to my room is behind me, so I slide slowly backward, hoping to get away from the father-son confrontation about to take off in the hallway.

"You don't know that, Steliro. She may have some of our DNA, but she was raised with humans. They're no better than animals," says Stellan, redness creeping up his neck and into his cheeks. "I don't know what possessed you to bring her here, but you need to get rid of her today, now! She's completely unstable. Who knows what she's capable of? I want her out of my house and out of this city!"

"*I* know what she's capable of. I—"

"How could you possibly—"

"She's my bondmate!" Lir's face is just as red as his father's and his words come out in a shout. At the shocked look on his father's face, Lir backs down and repeats it, this time softer. "She's my bondmate, Father."

Stellan shoots a glare my way, but I'm sliding back into my room before he says anything else.

My first stop is the bathroom, where I wet down my sleeve and scrub at my cheek. The dried blood comes off easily, but my skin is left red and irritated, the dark circles under my eyes standing out against the bright color. I look like I haven't slept in months.

I turn away from the mirror too quickly. Black stars flash across my vision and my legs falter. One elbow smacks into the countertop, but I catch myself on the doorway before I fall all the way to the ground. I rest my dizzy head against the door frame and take a few deep breaths, waiting for the room to stop spinning before I trust my legs enough to hold me. Stellan is right. I am unstable, and not just mentally. Whether it's the bond, the city, the chaos, or some other variable, the panic attacks have been hitting harder and more frequently since yesterday. Though my mind feels clearer this morning, my body appears to be failing me.

The slam of a door sounds through the house like a shot and then the door to my room opens slowly. Lir pokes his head around, his eyes finding me in the dim room. "Jax?"

I find a weak smile for him and he comes farther into the room, slowly. His eyes take in the tears on my cheeks and he moves to my side. He places a hand on my back, softly, carefully, and rubs it in a small circle. "Are you okay? What's wrong? I didn't mean . . . the dream thing . . . I'm sorry . . . I—"

"Stop." I release the door frame and rest one hand on his chest. "Not your fault."

"You're bleeding and you look like you're about to fall over. The bond is not supposed to be like that. It's supposed to heal, to give strength, to be a good thing."

I give him a wry smile. "And we all know how good I am about doing what I'm *supposed* to."

He smiles, but it's nothing more than a simple upward twist of his mouth, a nervous reflex to my awful attempt at a joke. His hands drop to his sides and he sighs. "My father would like to speak to you . . . If you're not up to it, you don't have to."

"But there's still a Council meeting to get through later, right? Might as well get some practice."

"He's just worried about Stella. He's mad at me, not you. Though it might be prudent to discuss the bond issue with him before presenting it to the entire Council."

The puff of breath that escapes from my nose is like a near silent laugh. "I'm pretty sure your father's feelings about me are clear, but he can't possibly dislike me any *more*."

The four of us gather in the living room, Stellan sitting in a chair, Vira perched on the arm, and Lir sitting next to me on the couch. I stare at the floor, twisting my hands in front of me.

"Now, explain to me why you think this girl is your bondmate," says Stellan.

"It is something I *know,* sir. I've linked to her. Met her in her dreams. A severe wound on her leg healed from one dream session that lasted barely five minutes." That's what he meant by healing? The bond fixed my leg?

Everyone looks to me.

"Yeah, my leg—" My voice cracks and I clear my throat before trying again. "I was bitten by a rattlesnake—"

"A bite she protected me from," interrupts Lir.

I shoot him an irritated look. I'm already about to climb up the walls; if he wants me to talk, then he needs to be quiet. Vira closely watches the silent exchange between us.

Stellan interlaces his fingers and gives me a bored look. "And?"

"The bite got infected and Peter, the guy we were staying with, had to cut into my leg to remove the infected tissue. When I first woke up I could hardly walk, but then . . . well, look." I pull up the leg of my pants to show the golf ball–size scar on my calf. "This happened only a few days ago."

"How were you able to do this when you have no *kitu* and my son's was not functional?"

Simple is probably best. "I don't know," I say. "I just found out about it myself. Somehow . . . I don't need one. But there's something else you need to know. I—"

"Is that how Steliro has survived with you? Can you help the children?" Hope shines in Vira's eyes and uncertainty turns in my stomach. I don't know how it works. I don't know how to use it and I don't know what, exactly, it does. How to explain it to them?

"Yes," says Lir. I look at him in confusion, not sure what he's agreeing with, and then it dawns on me that he's answering his mother's questions. "She linked to Stel last night, Mother."

Stellan looks intrigued, Vira ecstatic, and Lir . . . I don't know, maybe apprehensive.

"Link to me," says Stellan, his voice hard. It's not a request.

"I—I can't. I don't know how."

"Then how did you do it with Steliro?"

A thrum of panic spreads into my limbs. "I didn't even know what I was at the time. I just . . ."

Stellan turns to Lir and up goes the eyebrow. "Steliro?"

"I don't know, Father . . . sir," says Lir. His gaze stays trained on the floor.

Stellan's eyes harden and his voice goes quieter. "Then explain to me your theories. You must have at least one."

"I . . ." Lir's eyes come up and I can see the conflict in them. Pain flashes across his face for a moment and I can feel him try to reach out to me through the link, but he shies away from it when his gaze catches on my face. He sets his face and Lir the soldier, the obedient son, returns. "It might be brought about by strong emotions."

Strong emotions? I suppose that could be true, but why won't Lir even look at me? I get my answer when Stellan stands, watching me like a hawk. He steps toward me and I shrink back at the cold calculation in his eyes, my heart climbing into my throat, choking me. Something cold, hard, and sharp pounds at my defenses, battering against my mind. It's not the subtle, liquid connection I get from Lir—more of a very large, very solid rock bashing against the link, trying to force its way in no matter the consequences to the rest of me.

Attempting a deep breath only leaves me with short gasping pants in and out of my nose, and a warm stream of what can only be blood drips from my nostril. The booming of my pulse starts to drown out the world around me and a whimper escapes my mouth.

It's enough to break Lir out of whatever trace or sense of duty that was stalling him. He opens his mouth, but Vira speaks up first.

"Stop it, Stellan," she scolds. "You are scaring her." Vira reaches my side and pulls my face to look at her, compassion flashing in her eyes as her gaze falls lower. "It is hurting her." She turns her view back to Stellan. "We will figure this out without tormenting the poor child."

Stellan gives a curt nod and his body relaxes into a less threatening pose. Vira grabs my arm and, brushing past Lir and her husband, leads me out of the room and into the bedroom I slept in.

Vira sits down on the bed and pats a spot beside her. "Sit," she says. "Relax."

I sit. "Thank you." I twist my hands in my lap and bite at my lip. "I really don't know how it works. . . . . ."

"Hush now," she says. "We will figure this out. I realize Stellan may seem hard, but he is really just worried about Stella . . . about Lir, about us, about the city. My bondmate just takes the world's problems on his shoulders and he does not always think things through." She watches as my limbs relax. "My son does not, either. He was not trying to betray you in there. Please do not think that of him."

"I wasn't."

"Really? You were quick to believe the worst of him yesterday." Her words are not unkind, just assessing.

"That was . . . a misunderstanding. He was supposed to help me find my brother. Not bring me here."

"Your brother? Is he . . . like you?"

"Yes. We're twins."

Vira's head tilts and she smiles. "That is wonderful. We do not often have twins, though I know you met Rym and Trel. Do you know which of your parents was one of us? You might have family here."

Family? The thought had never even crossed my mind. Even now that I knew who and what my mother was . . . it never occurred to me that I might have family here.

"My mother," I say. "She died. When we were born." Vira reaches toward my hair, pulling one of the long, deep red strands to her and running her fingers over it. "Stella said I looked like I was from the Reva family."

"Yes, that is a possibility." She studies me, measuring me with her gaze. "I do not know how much Lir has told you about us, our society, his father's position here, or even his own, but I do see the connection between you two. However, I do not see how you might form a future together. The people will not accept you, not as a bondmate for our son."

"But—"

She holds a hand up and gently shakes her head. "Even your heritage would not be enough for them. The balance here is fragile and Lir has many responsibilities. Just bringing you here and arranging for a meeting with the Council was a huge risk, and the repercussions of that are yet to be determined. My son's actions were impulsive and I do not wish for either of you to suffer for that." She pauses and picks up one of my hands. "Please do not mistake my words for harshness, Jax. I wish things were different. There is just too much distrust between our species and Lir cannot put his own interests over those of his people. It is the price of leadership."

"I understand." I do—well, kind of. I've gathered that Stellan is important, and as his son, Lir is, too. I'm not quite sure how the whole thing works, but it's not as if I expected this brief happiness of mine to last anyway. Last night, the dream was wonderful, but I know I could never be what Lir would need me to be, no matter how much I wish I could. Despite everything, Jace has been my goal and the only thing I've given myself permission to hope for. I blink quickly to dispel the tears I won't admit are forming.

"Stellan has always preached isolation, segregation from the humans, and up until recently the relations between our species have been not so much peaceful as mutual indifference." She pauses and presses her lips together. "My son has openly defied his father by bringing you here. This comes after a series of acts that went against Stellan's wishes and his orders, the first of those acts being joining the patrols to search for Kov's killer. To do this, Lir had to align himself with certain others, most notably Vitrad, my brother—the most outspoken of Stellan's opponents and the head of our military."

"Why are you telling me this?"

"Lir has too much faith in his uncle and not enough in his father. Had he come to us before parading you through the city and announcing his return to the Council, we might have been able to help. Even with Stellan's position as chancellor, our hands are tied now and there is no time to prepare you for everything that might happen today. I do not know how your request will be taken and Stellan cannot cancel this meeting. I am frightened that Vitrad is going to use it as an opportunity to tip the fragile balance in his favor. I do not know what that may mean for you, but it puts my family in an even more precarious situation than it is now."

"And you want me to . . . ?"

"The Council does not react well to unknown variables or things they do not or cannot understand. Currently that is exactly what you are. If you cannot make your link work, it is best for you to appear as human as possible, to make yourself seem like less of a threat."

"I'm not a threat."

Vira smiles softly. "I do not believe you would do any intentional harm, but just by being what you are and because of the connection you have formed with Lir, you are a threat to our society, our way of living, and simply our basic beliefs. The bond you have managed to form with my son is nothing short of amazing, but most will not feel the same. It will set Lir apart from us, his family, and his species, and will garner too much attention from the Council. That is, if bringing you here has not already."

"Long story short, the Council is bad, cower like a lowly vermin, and whatever I do, don't say anything about you being my potential mother-in-law. That about right?"

Vira laughs, covering her mouth and looking surprised when the loud sound exits her mouth. "My goodness, you certainly are direct. I think I may understand what my son sees in you."

I shrug. That makes one of us. "If you're trying to avoid attention, you might want to tell him to do something about his hair before this meeting. I'm not exactly a barber and I can't imagine that look is standard around here."

"He does look a bit ridiculous, doesn't he?" Her smile is warm and she looks at me with something like affection, as if, were things different, she would have welcomed me into her family with open arms. It would have been nice to have a mother like her. As it is, we can only share a common desire to protect the boy we both care about.

Twenty-Four

After a quick, bland breakfast, getting ready doesn't take long and before I know it, I'm whisked out of the apartment and through the city, following behind Stellan and Vira. Lir walks slightly behind his parents but still well separate from me.

His father admonished him about "appearances" when he tried to hold my hand. Lir opened his mouth to argue, but I shook my head and indicated for him to walk in front of me. It was quick, but Stellan shot me a grateful look, his blank face softening into worry for just a moment before he turned his head. My stomach churns with every step, and even though I can tell he's trying to stop, waves of anxiety are flowing from Lir to me.

We aren't taking one of the silver pods. Though I'm curious, I don't question why. Maybe me walking through the city, unrestrained and following meekly behind, is meant to show how nondangerous I am. Or something.

The other aliens stare at me as we pass, their gazes skittering over me like tiny bugs, itchy and uncomfortable. It's not . . . vicious, not like they want to hurt me or anything, but there's a lot of curiosity in their eyes and maybe some of them look a little disgusted or confused. That changes when Stellan brings us to a stop in front of one of the three towers.

The two aliens flanking the door look at me with open hostility. They're dressed in the same bland uniform as everyone else, but like the other aliens in the clearing, their jackets are decorated with symbols. Perhaps this is how they designate members of their military? They allow us passage after sending a few narrow-eyed glares at me. Stellan leads the way through a large lobby area to a bank of elevators. The four of us board one of the elevators and I slink into the corner, while Lir and Stellan stand stiffly near the door.

Seconds later, there's a ding and the doors slide open. Stellan steps out first, then Lir, who links arms with Vira. I follow behind, my head down, studying my surroundings with subtle glances from the corners of my eyes.

Two aliens in light-gray uniforms stand outside the door we are approaching, snapping to attention as our group gets nearer. The respect isn't for me, though. A simple nod from Stellan and the two soldiers relax slightly and pull open the door. Stellan motions for me to enter, in front of everyone else for the first time. As soon as I enter the large, high-ceilinged room, I wish I were still in the back.

I don't know what I expected, but it's certainly not what I find. It's a large atrium with seats lining the walls in staggered sections. There's a raised dais in the center of the room with a large semicircular table facing outward into the room. On the outer edge of the circle and just slightly elevated above the table, four chairs sit. Lir's family members file toward the four chairs. When I move to follow, Lir shakes his head at me and motions toward a single chair sitting within and facing the semicircle.

I walk to the chair, but I don't sit. No one else is in the room yet, but already my heart rate is climbing and my palms are sweaty. Once Stellan has sat, Lir and Vira follow suit, one on either side. As if on cue, the room begins to fill, aliens filing in from the sides of each row and filling the seats as they go along. Last to enter are five men, who walk up to the table in the center, one sitting in the larger center chair and the others sitting two on either side of him.

Soon, everyone is sitting but me. I try to catch Lir's eye, but he stoically ignores me, as do Stellan and Vira. The alien in the center seat at the table gestures for me to sit, a glint of something in his eyes that I can't read.

I sit and place my hands in my lap, fighting the urge to wipe my sweaty palms on my pants.

"You have called this meeting, Stellan," says the center alien without turning around. "Please state your reason."

"This girl assisted my son, Vitrad," says Stellan. "She would like to make a request of us." So formal, almost as if scripted.

So this is Vitrad Linaud, alien military leader, Lir's uncle, and the person Vira so desperately warned me against. He doesn't look so frightening. Tall and slim with golden hair and silver-ringed pupils.

His eyes have not moved from me. "Is that so? And bringing a human into our city was your idea?"

Lir speaks up. "No, that was my doing."

I fidget under Vitrad's heavy gaze, meeting his eyes and quickly looking away. There's a subtle gold ring around the flashing silver of his eyes that I hadn't noticed before. As those hard eyes drill me to my chair, Vira's fears seem much more understandable. Whatever else is going on, Vitrad is not on my side.

"But why?" His voice is mocking. "I still do not see any logical reason for her presence here."

"When I was . . . left behind, the unit I was with took her brother prisoner. She is requesting that he be returned," says Lir, his voice faltering slightly.

"Are you referring to the human we have in custody? The one who killed Teskov, your friend and my daughter's bondmate? The one who has admitted to knowledge of a forthcoming human attack?" *What is he talking about? Flint said Dane had plans, but not that anything was going to happen soon . . .*

Lir's eyes dart to me for just a second before he answers. "Yes." The simple syllable sends murmurs throughout the room.

A slimy smile crawls across Vitrad's face and triumph flashes in his eyes. "And yet you bring one of them here . . . Did it ever cross your mind that she might be a spy?"

Lir gapes for a moment and his brow furrows in confusion, just enough to shatter the illusion of his confidence. It appears Vitrad has gone off script. Not only was Lir not expecting that ambush, he'd never actually taken that idea into consideration and he has no possible response. Not without revealing the bond between us, at least.

My eyes shoot back and forth between Lir, who is still just sitting there, and Stellan, who is slowly going pale while watching the exchange. When my gaze lands on Vira, I give her a subtle nod, permission to tell my secret to protect her son.

Vira rises and sends me a reassuring smile. "Vitrad, there is more to this situation than my husband and son have already stated. It is our belief that the girl is not fully human."

Vitrad tilts his head and narrows his eyes at her. "Then what is she?"

"She is a hybrid. E'rikon and human." Vira slowly steps to the side until she is standing behind Lir as another, louder murmur travels through the room. Vitrad is the only one who looks unaffected.

One alien stands up in the back of the room. "That is impossible. That program is a known failure." Voices of agreement sound throughout the room, many others standing up to voice their concerns.

Vitrad waves them all off and waits for the noise in the room to die down before speaking again. "Explain yourself, sister," he says. "That is not a statement we can afford to take lightly."

Vira looks to me, but I don't know what she's asking now. "Her hair is one thing, but the main reason is what's inside her, what she can do."

"What she can do?" Vitrad tilts his head again and studies me.

"She can link to my daughter."

More voices sound out in surprise, the whole room growing noisy. A new light grows behind Vitrad's eyes and a sinister smile crawls across his face. The look is quick, gone almost before I notice it, but a cold feeling of dread curls in my stomach. What's worse is that Vitrad never, not for one second, looks even remotely surprised. He knew. He *knows*. His eyes meet mine and he looks at me as if he's a hunter and I'm his prey.

"Not possible," Vitrad says, waving Vira off. His expression closes off, a mask of disinterest falling into place.

Lir speaks up next, ignoring the not-so-subtle grip his mother has on his shoulder. "It's quite possible, Uncle." Lir pulls up his sleeve and holds out his arm, putting his *kitu* on display. "I was hit with a pulse, my *kitu* nonfunctional. Without her I could not possibly have survived."

These aliens sure like to mutter in surprise. Or maybe this has just been a very interesting day for them. Vitrad waves his hand again. What is with this hand-waving thing? The room quiets and Vitrad stands for the first time.

"Let us test this theory of yours, then." He walks around the table and approaches my chair, his face closed and nonchalant. When he draws closer he leans down until he's staring directly into my face. "Well?"

Wide-eyed and unsure, I just sit there. "I don't know what you want me to do," I stammer.

Vitrad straightens and walks back to the table. "You are wrong. She is nothing but an ordinary human."

"But—" Lir shoots to his feet. The two guards come up on either side of him and pull him back down.

Vitrad spins around to face Lir and his family, the first time he's really looked at them since he entered the room. "You, Steliro, are a traitor. Bringing this human here." He stalks closer. "And you, Stellan and Vira—I expected more from you. Harboring her?"

Redness creeps up Lir's necks and into his cheeks. "I am no traitor. There's a reason—"

"Silence!" Vitrad bears down on Lir, stopping when he towers over Lir's seated form. "This is my room. You are here as a courtesy. I suggest you hold your tongue."

Stellan rises until he is eye to eye with Vitrad. "This may be your room, Vitrad, but you do not rule here."

"And neither do you," says Vitrad. Stellan glowers, but doesn't respond, and Vitrad turns his attention back to me. "Take the girl into custody."

My stomach twists and ice water trickles into my veins. The two aliens flanking Lir move around the table and take position on either side of me.

Lir stands up quickly. "There's no need for that."

"Now, Steliro," says Vitrad, a cold grin forming on his face, "this is for the best. We know the humans are preparing to attack. It is only logical that we take her into custody so she cannot warn them we know they are coming."

Lir tries to step to me, but is blocked by a guard. He steps up to Vitrad instead. "No. This is not what we agreed upon. I forbid it."

What they *agreed* upon?

Vitrad's eyes flick down to Lir's wrist and he sneers. "I think your issue has made you confused. Perhaps you should head down to the medical section and get your head back on straight." The sick glee in his eyes makes me shudder when he turns them to me. "Take her."

"There is no need for this," says Lir, his voice beginning to rise. "She is contained here. She is no danger to us."

"That's what you don't understand. Contained or not, she is a danger to us all." Vitrad motions to the guards. "Besides, was not the human initiative your proposal? Were you not the one that advocated the obliteration of the human race? I seem to recall it was your vehemence to bring Teskov's killer to justice that has led us here today."

The obliteration of the human race? What? My head jerks toward Lir. Betrayal, ice-cold and complete, coils in my stomach when he won't meet my eyes.

The two guards grab my arms and pull me back. I send out frantic signals, trying to make it work, prove what I am. But nothing works. I don't know how to access the link and I've never hated that fact more. My feet kick out and I get one arm free. I pull against the other hand on my wrist and I can feel my breath coming faster. Blackness crawls on the edges of my vision and I'm helpless to stop it. My heart pounds against my ribs, but not even the adrenaline is enough to free me. As my body shuts down, I see Lir struggling against two other guards with one hand out, calling my name.

Twenty-Five

When the world returns, I'm nearly blinded by the stark white of the room I'm in. White walls. White ceiling. White sheets on a white bed. My head pounds behind my eyes and I raise my arm to rub my temples. It only gets about halfway up before it's stopped by what can only be a restraint. I wiggle my feet, but they're locked down, too. As my breath speeds up again, I close my eyes and focus on calming myself. I do not have time for another breakdown.

Besides me, the room is empty. And cold. Goose bumps rise on my arms and trickle down my body. Except for the light sheet, I'm naked. Although the thought concerns me, I don't focus on it, instead studying the room around me.

The walls are circular and a large mirror takes up nearly half the wall space. Must be a one-way mirror. Now my nakedness bothers me. The thought of a bunch of aliens studying me on the other side of the mirror . . . I shudder.

Time passes slowly and I have nothing to occupy my racing mind. Thoughts and ideas bounce around and I sing softly to myself in an effort to stay calm. My effort is failing. The longer I lie here alone and restrained, the more my heart beat increases and the faster my breaths come. I squeeze my eyes shut. Maybe if I can shut out that glaring white, it will get better. Gritting my teeth, I chant to myself to calm down in my head.

I don't know how long I lie there, but a portion of the wall slides away and a gowned, gloved, and masked alien enters. His pale blue eyes hold no kindness for me and I cower away from him as he approaches the bed. I don't notice the ring-shaped object in his hands until he starts sliding it over my head and fitting it in place over my temples. He shakes it—I assume to make sure it's secure—and then nods toward the mirror. There are definitely people watching me.

When he tightens the restraints and steps away from the bed and just watches, I panic. I don't have time to fear for long.

Bright light screams into my head and I close my eyes, trying to shut it out. But it's not really there and closing my eyes does not bring any welcome darkness. The light sharpens, burning across my brain and shooting pain through my entire body. When it darkens, I start to breathe out in relief, but almost as quickly it pulses brighter, even more painful than before. I hold out against the pain, biting my tongue and willing it away. On the third pulse, the brightest yet, I can't hold back my screams anymore.

I lose count after the fourth pulse and am almost thankful for the restraints, as they keep me from clawing my eyes out. The room fades back into place and I have tears running down my face. The alien still stands, observing me, and I turn to him. My voice, hoarse from screaming for who knows how long, doesn't even sound like me.

"Please." It's the only word I can say.

He steps forward and hope rises in my chest. His hands pull my eyelids back and he shines a small flashlight into them. When he reaches for my wrist, my hope dies a slow death. There's no pity—no humanity—in his face; he's just taking my vital signs. My stomach drops when he steps back from the bed and nods to the mirror again. I don't bother trying to hold anything back and start scream-ing immediately this time.

Each pulse of light smashes against the narrow pathway of the link like a hammer. Each clang of the blunt tool they're using to smash their way into my mind reverberates through my entire body, brewing and churning with heat. The light is too hot for my fear, but my anger thrives on it, growing and expanding until my veins are filled with molten lava. There's no outlet for it, so I burn from the inside out.

Ages later the pounding in my head stops and my eyes struggle to readjust to the room, the normal illumination seeming closer to darkness to my overstimulated brain. My face is wet—not just with tears, though those do drip down my temples and into my hair and ears. There's a warmer liquid trailing out of my nose—and my ears—thicker and coppery, as swiping my tongue over my upper lip determines. Blood, then.

I'm alone again, silence surrounding me like a blanket. Exhaus-tion settles into my limbs and I can't even bring myself to turn my head when the door slides open again. What does it matter? I'm never getting out of here.

"I see you fight the *kiun* just like your brother," says a voice that skitters down my spine and settles into my stomach. Vitrad. His face appears in my vision, leaning over me with a cold smile. It takes all my effort to make sense of his words. "Resisting it has not done him any good."

Words scrape past my dry throat. "Hasn't done you much good, either, I imagine." There's some fight left in me after all, if only in reaction to his cold, satisfied smirk.

He snorts. "I suppose you are correct, but this process will go so much smoother if you would only cooperate."

"And what would my cooperation get me?"

"Your life."

"A life as a lab rat? No, thanks, I'll pass."

"I am certain I can think of something to entice you. Until then, please enjoy your accommodations, Miss Mitchell. I shall see you again soon." The brisk click of his boots echoes around the room. As the door begins to slide shut behind him, he leaves me with an even worse thought than the return of the *kiun*. "I certainly hope you are not depending on your *bondmate* to save you."

Vitrad knows about the bond. How? Was it Lir or Stellan? An attempt to save me or to condemn me? Lir made an *agreement* with Vitrad. What could he have possibly agreed to? Does it even matter now that it resulted in me being strapped down in this room of nightmares?

A sound works its way up my throat. It starts as a puff of air and evolves into a chuckle. Not really a funny situation, but something has to come out, slide past that pressure valve in my brain, and I'm about screamed out. The burning anger has steeped and brewed into something else and every pulse of light just drove it deeper, slicing into my very core until a dark hatred has started congealing deep inside me.

Sometime later, I find a restless sleep.

§

The nightmares are back. Held at bay for too long, they're even worse than before. What was scattered images has become a reenactment in which I am both observer and participant. My body flows through the same motions as it did that day . . .

Water sloshes against the edges of the laundry tub and wets my bare legs. With a huff, I turn off the pump and toss the pile of clothes into the water. I add soap and scrub a shirt against the washboard.

"Hello there, pretty thing." The raspy voice of a man in his forties.

I grimace at the stench of his body odor as he leans closer and his bloodshot eyes travel up and down my bent legs with twisted desire.

The other man is younger, maybe early twenties, and his clothes are cleaner and he's not really looking at me. I focus my attention on him.

"Hello," I say. "Are you looking for someone? Just passing through? Do you need some food?"

The now wiser part of my brain, knowing what's coming, screams at my body. But it doesn't listen. It's an odd feeling to be stuck inside a dream, mind frozen in fear, while your body acts out your greatest horror.

"There's something we need, al'rght," slurs the older guy, taking another step toward me until he's only inches away.

I take a step back, away from his reaching hand and toward the younger man. "I can give you a meal. That's all I have to offer."

That was my biggest mistake, thinking that youth and hygiene meant that man was somehow safer.

A callused hand grips my bicep. "Oh, no, little girl. There is so much more you have to offer." His fingers dig in, hard enough to bruise.

I can't. I can't. I can't.

Jace!

That day I didn't scream for my brother's help for the first time until much later. But thankfully this is just a dream and my call is answered.

"Jax!" Warm, strong arms wrap around my huddled form, the voice familiar and welcome. "What are you doing here?"

I slowly open my eyes. The men are gone, their images scattered and sent back where they belong. Far, far away from me.

When I meet Jace's eyes, a sob rips out of my chest. I wrap my arms around him and bury my face in the side of his neck.

Small soothing noises rumble in his chest as he rubs one hand in circles on my back. "It will be okay." A subtle warmth washes over me, comfort lapping at the edges of my frayed emotions, and I relax into it.

Then my breath catches in my throat and I pull away. "You're doing it. The emotion thing."

His eyes widen and he averts his gaze. "You know, then."

I smack his shoulder. "Why didn't you tell me? Why hide it from me?"

"I wasn't even sure that I was doing anything for a while. It just seemed to help you when I was nearby. Then there was one time with Flint and—"

"With Flint? I thought it was an E'rikon thing. It works with humans, too?"

"Of course it works with humans." His brow furrows and then I can almost see the realization hit him. "Wait a second. Too? Who the hell have *you* been spending time with that . . . isn't human?"

"How do you think I got here? Just waltzed up to the dome and said *please*?"

Jace's body goes rigid. "You're here, actually here. In the city."

"Yes."

He stands and runs one hand down his face. "For God's sake, Jax, why?" His hands shake as he takes two steps back and his expression morphs into utter despair. "Why?" he repeats in a whisper so soft I can hardly hear it and then my brother, my rock, the *strong* one, collapses to his knees with his head in his hands. And all I can do is sit there with my mouth open and watch him fall apart. Finally, a deep breath shudders through him and he raises his head to look at me. "You shouldn't have come."

"Did you think I was just going to leave you here?" Each word rises in volume until I'm nearly shouting the last one. Everything I've gone through to get here and he tells me I should have stayed away?

"I hoped you would." He flinches. "I knew . . . after everything, I deserve to be here, but this is not what I wanted for you. I wanted you safe, and being here is anything but safe."

"What about what I want? Don't you think you've made enough decisions for me?"

"I was trying to protect you. I—"

"No. If you were so worried about trying to protect me, you should have spent a little more time thinking about how I would handle life without you," I say.

"I did. I made Flint promise to do whatever was necessary to keep you safe."

"Flint? Your boyfriend was your master plan?" I slide closer to Jace and throw my hands up. "You knew about the emotional link, so obviously you've been calming me for a while, keeping me whole, chasing the nightmares away. Was Flint going to do that for me, too? If it wasn't for Lir . . ." My hand comes up over my mouth as the thought completes. *If it wasn't for Lir, I would have fallen apart.*

Jace wasn't the only one to feed me emotions. Whether Lir used it to manipulate me or not, the link with him kept me together in a way I could not have done for myself. It's also the only way I ever could have made it here.

"Who's Lir?" My attention snaps back to Jace, who seems to have regained some of his bearings.

Good question, actually. Who exactly is Lir? I struggle to find the right answer before landing on simply saying, "He's my friend, the one who brought me here."

"And he's E'rikon."

"Yes."

"You can't trust them, any of them." He paces, running an agitated hand through his hair. "You need to get out of the city. If they find out you're here . . ." He shakes his head rapidly. "They can't find out, Jax. There's this whole 'initiative' they have. I don't know much, but I know it involves wiping us—and I do mean humans when I say *us*—completely out."

"The human initiative." My stomach drops.

"Yeah. I'm pretty good at playing a vegetable at this point, so they talk sometimes when they think I'm not listening. There's a general guy or something—"

"Vitrad."

He shoots me a quizzical look. "Yeah. He heads up their military division, but there's this other group—"

"The Council."

A pause. "The Council, and it's run by this one guy—"

"Stellan."

Jace stops his pacing and crosses his arms. "Do you want to tell this story? How do you know all that, anyway?"

I shake my head mutely and he continues. "This is important information you'll need to get to Flint once you leave. So the Stellan guy, it's his family—the Vastras, the Vantras . . . something like that—they are kinda like royalty or something and they're related to Vitrad somehow. There's some sort of power struggle going on with the Council against Vitrad, but the kicker is that Stellan's son has sided with Vitrad in the whole thing because he has a vendetta . . . well, against me." His shoulders droop. "I've done horrible things, Jax. Dane used me, my abilities, that nonhuman half of me, just as much as these aliens would like to do." He curls his hands into fists and closes his eyes. "But that's not the big picture here. The Council has been staying Vitrad's hand, but it's only a matter of time before the balance shifts. It's already happening. And when the E'rikon make their move, it will be the end of us. They have things we couldn't even dream up . . ."

The fire in his eyes bores into me, vehemence lacing his words. "As much as they've . . . studied . . . me, they still have no idea what I'm capable of, what *you're* capable of if you put your mind to it. You and I, Jax, we're the only weapons, the only hope the humans have against the E'rikon. I'm not sure exactly what it is we're supposed to be able to do, but the aliens cannot be allowed to figure it out. No matter what they've done to me, I've given them nothing. They figured out what I was when they landed in that clearing. If they find out about you, especially that you're my twin . . . Get out of the city. Find Flint. Tell him about what's going on and have him take you far away from here."

He jolts and cocks his head to the side. "They're coming. I have to get out of here. Whatever happens, remember I love you." He pulls me in for a hug and kisses the top of my head.

"But they already know . . ." My protest is too late; his shape has already dissipated and I'm left alone in my dreamscape. Getting out of here just became even more important. I'd always thought the E'rikon hadn't attacked before because we were at least evenly armed, or they just didn't care. That illusion has shattered with my brother's revelations.

What would Jace think of me if he knew that I gave Flint the key to his own destruction and set him on a path directly here? And if he knew that all his pain and screams were for nothing, that they had me anyway, that I'd *delivered* myself here based on the promises of the very boy who was the catalyst for what could be the end of the human race? He'd hate me. My only hope to redeem myself is to get us both out of here before the sky falls down around us.

Twenty-six

When my eyes open, the thing I most want to do is close them again. I'm still in the white room and I want more than anything for it to just go away. I raise a stiff arm to push my hair out of my face and realize that I'm no longer restrained and I'm dressed in a simple gray gown. A nervous feeling—a smaller, lesser cousin to hope—crawls into my stomach. They aren't going to bring the light back, at least not right now. My sigh of relief puffs my lips out and I close my eyes again.

The hiss of the door brings me to full alertness and my limbs tense in preparation. Preparation for what, I have no idea—my legs are much too shaky to even hold me up, much less allow me any sort of defensive position.

The smell of bread wafts into the room and my stomach clenches and growls. Aching hunger brings me up to a sitting position and I curl over my still rumbling stomach. How long has it been since I've eaten? Is this a new form of torture, letting me smell the food? But no, a loaf of bread lands on my cot and I snatch it up with greedy hands. I don't even bother looking up until the bread is gone and I am searching out the crumbs on my blanket with a wet finger. A disgusted snort brings my head up and my eyes narrow on Vitrad's face.

"You." The word comes out in a snarl.

"Save the theatrics for someone who cares, Miss Mitchell," he says. "You may have caught the attention of the Vestra family, but their allegiance is fickle, as is their power here. Stellan may be swayed by his bondmate for now, but without results, we will just have to go back to the way things were."

Vira did something for me. At least she bought me time.

"I don't know what you expect me to do. I don't know what you want from me," I say.

"Yes. You do. You just refuse to help us." He stops my retort by raising his hand. "At least, that is the report I will present to the rest of the Council. How quickly do you think the people will turn on the Vestras when they find out that Steliro has bonded with a half-breed spy who tricked her way into our city in order to get information on our defenses? Perhaps she even assisted her brother in the murder of my dear, dear daughter's bondmate." He makes an exaggerated swipe below his eye with one finger and raises his eyebrows.

My next words catch in my throat. Vira was right. Vitrad is using this as an opportunity for a takeover. The level of deception and lies leaves my mind spinning. Who can I trust?

He continues. "Both you and your brother have managed to keep us out of your heads, but you can only imagine how fascinated I was to learn that there really is some truth to the rumors that you are capable of something special—at least according to your brother's pleas to keep that information from us. There is a weapon inside you, Miss Mitchell, and I want it." The cold smile that slithers across Vitrad's face sends ice through my veins. He laughs, a hard sound that screeches in my ears. "I can see the realization forming on your face. Yes, Steliro gave me this information. Did no one tell you that you cannot block out your bondmate?"

Freezing tendrils of dread and betrayal twist through me, twining around my stomach. Lir let him into my head? There's no other way Vitrad could have known . . .

"Such a passionate boy. So easily led into hatred for the humans. Did you perhaps think Steliro was out there by accident? Mechanical problems? And such luck to come across your brother . . ." He lets out a mocking chuckle.

Further conversation stops as a rumble works its way to my ears and the room shakes. The light flickers and in the stuttering darkness, Vitrad's brow furrows and he almost looks worried. The expression is gone quickly, replaced with a hard resolve.

"This was not supposed to happen yet. Seems the humans have arrived sooner than expected." He says the words under his breath, more to himself than to me. Then his full attention turns back to me and a cold smile crawls across his face to match the icy look in his eyes. "I look forward to continuing our conversation."

He spins on his heel and strides to the door. The sound of his voice shouting orders drifts in through the closing door, but it's cut off as soon as the door slides shut.

He didn't put my restraints back in place. I'm alone and somehow I doubt that there's anyone behind that mirror watching me when there are much more important things going on out there. This is my chance.

§

It's ten steps from one side of the room to the other. I've counted the one hundred and thirty-three tiles on the floor at least five times . . . really slowly.

After I sat up and swung my legs over the side of the bed, it took me a while to gather enough strength to rise to my feet. I promptly crashed back down on the bed. Stretching helped and so did flexing my muscles and rolling my ankles, at least enough that I was finally able to stand without my legs shaking out from under me. I don't even know how long it took until I could take a few faltering steps. Gradually, I worked my way across the room once, and then again, until my steps evened out and my legs stopped protesting at holding me up. It's not like I had anything better to do.

Now it's been hours, and no one has even come to check on me. There hasn't been any more rumbling or shaking and it's almost too quiet. Thoughts of Lir slip in and I push them away. I can't deal with that right now. I finally have a hope of escaping and I'm stuck in this room pacing back and forth. It's boring and monotonous, but at least if the door opens I'll be able to run. Of course, there will probably be someone on the other side of the door trying to keep me in. What I really need is a weapon.

The tiles are all glued down, not even a broken corner to allow me to wiggle one loose. Smooth walls, unbreakable mirror . . . the bed frame is plastic. I make another circuit of the room. The light is too high. Unless . . . I shove the bed into the center of the room and stand on top of it, reaching for the fixture. Dammit. Still out of reach.

Lying down on the bed, I let out a sigh of frustration and throw my arms out to the side. A sharp pain in one wrist brings my eyes to the restraint on my left. I focus on the large metal buckle and smile. It's not much and it certainly wouldn't be fatal, but if I pull the restraints off the bed and bundle them together somehow with the buckles on the outside, I might be able to cause enough pain to distract someone.

I'm putting the final touches on my buckle bludgeon—three restraints balled up at the top with the fourth providing me a method of swinging it—when I hear a thud outside the door. I slink closer and press myself against the wall next to the door. There's no way for me to hide in here, but I should be able to escape notice long enough to surprise whoever comes in.

The hiss of the door opening is nearly drowned out by the pounding of my heart. This is it.

He enters slowly—black boots, gray uniform, clearly E'rikon— and my arm swings forward. Just before my makeshift weapon makes contact with his head, he shifts sideways and the buckles fly by only inches from his temple.

"Blazes, Jax," says Rym. "I'm here to help." I narrow my eyes and wind up for another swing. Rym puts his hands up and takes a step back. "Vira sent me. Well, really, she told me you were down here and implied very strongly that I should come get you." He eyes the protruding buckle prongs and then glances at me. "Resourceful, aren't you? That looks like it might be painful."

I nod and step closer, letting the warm coils of fury expand in my body.

"I won't hurt you. I'm not even armed." He holds out his empty hands, palms up. "There isn't much time . . . I know where they're keeping your brother. I can take you to him."

I clear my throat. "Why should I believe you? Maybe this is all part of the plan?" Buried anger bubbles up and heats my words. "He twisted the bond, used it against me. He let that thing into my head!" I swing; he dodges and circles around. "He lied to me. He manipulated me. All to get me here." Another swing, another dodge. "To use me." Swing. "To break me because my brother is too strong." Swing. "Joke's on you guys—I was already broken!" My voice has risen to a screech and my arm swipes erratically through the air. The burn behind my eyes gives way to tears that blur my vision. Just one hit. I just want to land one.

As if he understands, Rym stops moving and lets the buckle hit his chest. He flinches, but doesn't back up even when I raise my arm again. "Lir didn't understand what he was doing." He peeks at me through one eye. I drop my arm and he continues. "He was sucked into my father's delusions after Kov's death and never even thought to question the reasoning behind my father's plans. Yes, it started as a vendetta, but things changed. Lir changed. He's done nothing but fight for your release . . . well, he did until he was locked up down here, too."

"Then what was the agreement he made with Vitrad? What was he talking about at the meeting?"

"He agreed to bring you before the Council so the request for your brother's release could be made formally. Nothing more. Lir thought he was helping." His shoulders relax and he steps forward, his eyes glued to mine. "What they've done to you . . . it wouldn't be condoned if people knew. This is not what we are. This"—he gestures to the room around us and the restraints in my hand—"is what my father has twisted us into. I'm not asking you to forgive any of it, just let me help you."

He's been quick enough to dodge my strikes and could have hurt me easily if he wanted to do so. Besides, I don't really have any other choice. "Okay," I say. "Take me to my brother."

Rym grins. "Ace!" A wink. "I'll let you go in first, though."

Twenty-Seven

Rym leads me confidently through the empty halls until we reach a recessed silver door. He opens it with his *kitu* and steps to the side to let me enter. Once inside, I recoil, nearly knocking Rym over in my backward motion. Seeing my brother in my dream did nothing to prepare me for the actuality of his condition.

The skinny, pale form on the bed barely resembles the Jace I know. His wrist bones jut out visibly even under the dark purple bruises covering them. No cushy leather for him. Instead, metal chains wrap around his limbs and hold him in place. He doesn't even move when a noise somewhere between a gasp and a sob works its way out of my mouth.

I rush forward and fall to my knees next to the bed, brushing strands of greasy red hair away from his face. Patchy facial hair covers his cheeks, but despite its vivid red color, it does nothing to pull my attention away from the gauntness of his face. I run my fingers over his forehead, his nose, his lips, silent tears streaming down my cheeks. What have they done to him?

Reaching down, I grab one of his hands and squeeze, flinching at the feel of the bones under his skin. "Jace. Wake up." Not even a twitch. "Please. We have to go now." Still nothing except for the slow rise and fall of his chest. "Please . . ." I rest my head next to his and whisper my pleas directly into his ear while stroking his cheek with the back of one hand.

A guttural moan finally passes his lips. I raise my head and lean over his face as his eyelids flutter and he moves his head slowly from side to side. "I'm here, Jace. I'm here. They won't hurt you anymore. I won't let it happen."

"Jax?" The raspy noise is nearly unintelligible. "I thought I dreamed you."

"You did, but I'm here for real now. We're going to get out of here. Go home."

The chains rattle when he tries to move a hand and he instantly tenses and starts struggling against his bindings. "No! You're not really here. It's just a trick. I won't do it." He squeezes his eyes shut and batters his wrists against the metal.

"Jace, stop!" *Stop!*

His eyes fly open and focus on my face. *It really is you.*

The sound of his words in my head shocks me, but some instinct in me recognizes the connection between us and I find it easy to form my response. *Yes. Now* please, *we need to get out of here.*

I thought I told you to get out of the city. He scowls and I recognize the expression that he's given me since we were kids, the one he gives me when I don't do what I'm told. I can't help but smile.

And if you'd stuck around long enough to listen to me, I would have told you it was too late for all that. I give him an exaggerated eye roll. *Besides, you know I never listen to you.*

You're such a pain, sis. He grins. The smile is weak and there's still darkness in his eyes, but it's a relief to see the teasing twinkle there, too. *Now stop bawling all over me and let's get out of here.*

Rym speaks up from the doorway. "Jax? You might want to move things along here." He steps forward into the room, into Jace's line of sight.

My brother's whole body tenses and he snarls, clenching his fists and thrashing at the restraints, his eyes glued to Rym. *He's one of them. Get away. What's it doing here?*

The barely coherent words pound at my head. I place one hand on Jace's shoulder. "It's okay." A quick glance at Rym. "He's here to help."

"They aren't to be *trusted*," Jace hisses, his black hatred visible in the strain of every muscle in his body. "They lie. All. The. Time."

Rym gives me an uneasy smile. "Good thing I decided to get you out first, huh?"

I let out a nervous laugh that sounds more like a grunt. "Yeah, good thing."

Jace's gaze moves from Rym to me. "It got you out. Out of where?"

Another nervous laugh. "From here."

"You've been down here? They locked you up?" His nostrils flare with each shallow breath. He closes his eyes, takes a slow, deep breath, and then focuses on Rym again. "It got you out."

"Yes." I speak slowly and Jace's eyes find mine. "Rym is here to help."

He tenses his jaw and flexes his hand a few times. "Okay," he says curtly. "Let's go."

I sigh in relief, a matching one coming from Rym. "How do we get these restraints off?"

Rym edges forward. "A little piece of tech I like to call a key." He holds up a tiny silver key and points to the locks. "This should work." He places the key in my hand and then retreats to the wall, quietly observing.

The key fits perfectly and I have the chains unlocked and unwound in seconds. Jace waves off my attempts to help him into a sitting position and swings his legs over the side of the bed and pushes himself up with one arm. He wobbles for a moment, but quickly regains his balance. Eyeing Rym, he rubs at his wrists for a moment before turning his attention to me and putting his arms out. I fall into them, wrapping my arms around his waist as he runs one hand over my head.

His ribs poke me in the side and the hand on my back has a slight tremble. He is dirty and he smells horrible, but I just press closer to him. After everything I've gone through to get him back, this one hug from my weakened but still whole, still *living*, brother is more than I'd ever dared to hope for.

Twenty-eight

It takes time for Jace to gather enough strength to stand and take a few feeble steps around the room. He stumbles and Rym straightens off the wall, but puts his hands up and leans back when Jace glares at him and snarls, "I don't want your help."

Rym doesn't offer again and Jace spends most of the next twenty minutes stumbling around trying to get his body to cooperate.

Link with me. That's another thing—except for turning down his help, Jace refuses to address Rym directly and insists on talking to me only in our heads. *If you connect with me, we can share energy and this will go much quicker*, he says.

I don't know how. My gaze floats over to Rym and he shrugs. He has to know we're leaving him out of the conversation, but he doesn't look irritated about it.

Give me your hand and close your eyes. I comply with Jace's request and he gives my hand a squeeze. *Now just relax and focus on the connection between us.*

Easy for you to say.

Jace chuckles.

In the darkness of my mind I concentrate on the place Jace's voice comes from. *Say something.*

Something. It's amazing how sarcasm can even come across mentally.

I zero in on the bright spot illuminated with his words and trace their shape. A thin thread extends from the edge and I grab it, following it until I feel . . . separated from myself. To my surprise the glowing trail forks, one side red and one side green. The red is brighter, stronger, closer and it can only be Jace. The green . . . is flickering, fading, and, foolishly, I choose to follow that one.

I open my (his) eyes, run one hand over my (his) newly shorn head, and stare blankly at the stark white walls around me. I'm (he's) not restrained, but my (his) stomach rumbles with hunger and my (his) throat is parched by thirst. Pain radiates from one arm, bloody furrows around the *kitu* there. I (he) tried to rip it off. *Why?*

Jax? Lir's voice in my head.

Any thought I share with Lir could be used against me. Scrambling back, I pull away, skimming along the thread until I reach the fork and fly down the red side and crash into my brother's head.

He shakes me out so I'm just resting on the surface of his consciousness. *Whoa, sis. You don't need to be all the way in my head. That's just creepy.*

You're telling me. A fleeting sense of confusion. *Never mind. Sorry. Now what?*

Nothing. Just relax and let the connection do the work.

Jace's thread gradually glows brighter until he pulls back and I open my eyes. He looks a little steadier and there's more life in his eyes than before. That whole thing was kinda weird, but definitely handy.

We grin at each other and he pats my cheek. "Let's get the hell out of here."

Rym pulls away from the wall and gives me a stunned look. "What did you two do?"

"We—"

"Nothing," Jace says. "It was nothing." He pulls me out of the room and practically runs down the hall.

His speed is no match for Rym's, who quickly catches up to us. "All due respect and all, but do you even know where the hell you're going? This place is like a maze down here and I've got the map, so it might be best if I were the one choosing directions."

"Okay." Jace slows, but keeps a tight hold on my hand. "Lead the way then."

A few minutes later, we approach an elevator bay.

"Just take it up to the ground floor and turn left. It should bring you right out the back door," says Rym. He eyes Jace, presses his lips together, and then turns to me. "Jax, I've got to go get my cousin. I know it's a lot to ask, but . . ." His eyes go to Jace and back to me. "I could really use your help. I won't say anything if you'd rather just get on that elevator and get out of here, and I know you two didn't part well. *Really* not well, if earlier was any indication." He laughs to himself. "But Lir is—"

"Lir?" Jace breaks in, his gaze leveled at me. "Your friend. The E'rikon."

"Yes," I say.

"Forget it," says Jace, slamming one finger against the call button. "We're leaving. Let him take care of his own. You don't owe them anything."

If Rym is telling the truth, Lir had no idea how the bond could be used and he's down here because of me. "I can't just leave him here," I say, pleading with my eyes for Jace to understand.

"Your travel buddy? The one that brought you here and landed you down here?" Jace's brow furrows and he gestures erratically with his arms. "That's crazy. We're not going back." A hard look at Rym. "Let his people take care of him." He grabs my hand and pulls me toward the elevator, but my feet stay planted.

"No," I say. Whether it's the tenor of my voice or the confidence I exude, Jace looks at me like he's never seen me before. "I love you, Jace. You don't have to do this and I won't even ask you to, but I do. You can't protect me forever."

His eyes flit from me to the metal doors. "Jax . . ." He follows with a sigh when I simply walk away, heading back down the hallway in the direction that we came from. "Where to, navigator?"

"I have no idea," says Rym. "That's what I was hoping to get Jax's help with."

"How would . . ." His eyes widen. "He's the one, the one you connected with."

"Yeah."

"You're going to have a lot of explaining to do when we get home."

"Yeah." I close my eyes and pull up the green thread. Walking with my eyes closed is hazardous to my nose and I collide with a few walls before I get the idea to have Jace guide me while I point. The connection isn't blocked by walls, so it takes some wandering and some backtracking before we reach the door behind which I feel the end of the trail.

Rym opens the door with his *kitu* and motions for me to go in. "We'll wait out here."

Jace narrows his eyes, but doesn't disagree or follow me in.

The room is empty. I turn in confusion and Lir pulls away from the wall near the door. "You came back." His eyes search my face. What is he looking for? Whatever it is, he must find it, because he pulls me into his chest in a tight hug. "Thank you." He leans away from me, smiling, and cradles my chin in one of his hands. When he leans forward, his eyes slip closed and his lips inch toward mine.

Jace clears his throat from outside the doorway. Lir spins away from me and pulls me behind his body, crouching down slightly, ready to attack as my brother enters the room.

Jace just snorts. "Come on, Jax. We've got to get out of here."

Lir's eyes travel from me to Jace and comprehension dawns on his face. He straightens his shoulders and holds out a hand. "You must be Jace."

Jace narrows his eyes, glancing down at his outstretched hand. "Yeah," he says, hands still at his sides. "Let's go." He spins on his heel and marches out the door, not even looking back to see if I'm following.

I don't know whether to be mad or embarrassed about Jace's behavior, so I just shrug and incline my head toward the doorway. "We gotta go."

Lir follows us back to the elevator. I stand in front, closest to the door, and the boys stand behind me on my right, Jace slightly behind Lir and Rym. Once the four of us are on board I let out a sigh of relief. I'm getting out of here. My brother is safe. Everything might just turn out okay.

There's a loud noise from above and the light in the elevator flickers. A sick feeling curls in my stomach when the tiny car shakes in place a little. It still keeps moving, but I don't feel quite as home free anymore. I force myself to take a deep breath, and then another. I don't have time to lose it right now. My eyes slide closed as I concentrate on inhaling and exhaling.

One hand wraps around mine from behind me and I open my eyes. It's Lir giving my hand a gentle squeeze. Jace has moved even farther back in the elevator car until he is leaning against the wall with his arms crossed, glaring with narrowed eyes at our joined hands.

Jace doesn't understand. And I don't need him right now . . . When was the last time I didn't need my brother? I'm not ready to replace Jace and that's what it feels like I am doing. I drop Lir's hand, ignoring his confused look, and take a step back until I'm next to Jace, taking his hand instead. Jace throws his arm over my shoulder and pulls me in next to him with a subtle tilt to his lips. He's smiling at Lir, not at me, a small, triumphant smile. Lir rubs his lips together, blinks slowly, and nods once before turning away from us. I don't want to hurt him, but I can't hurt my brother.

The seconds drag by in silence until the elevator stops and the doors slide open. Lir and Rym step out first and Jace and I follow. Tension radiates from Jace. Is it the situation or Lir's presence?

Can he hear us like this? Jace's voice sounds in my head.

No, I say. *I don't think so, at least. It's not like this with him.*

Good. We have to get rid of him. It's done. He's out. You saved him, now let him be on his way. Scorn bleeds into his words. Is it for me or for Lir?

No. Jace stops walking and the tug of his hand brings me to a stop beside him.

Jax, what do you think this is? Do you honestly think we're going to get out of here and take him with us? We don't need him. His eyes drill into mine, conviction and anger swirling in their depths.

I look away and shake my head. *I need him.*

He's an alien. He's not one of us! I flinch away at the anger in his words, nearly screaming in my head.

This isn't how I wanted our reunion to go. What do I even say? I bring my eyes to his and put as much emotion into them as I can when I send him my response. *Don't you understand? No one is one of us, Jace. We're different. We have feet in two different worlds. Lir is part of mine.* Willing him to understand, I continue. *I came here for you. I've nearly died for you. I'm not who I was when you were taken. I'll always be your sister, but I can't sit back and let you . . . control me anymore.*

Jace's eyes widen and harden. I've said the wrong thing. His anger rolls off of him and into me, flames licking at my skin. *Control you! Don't you mean protect you? Don't you mean put aside my every happiness to get you through the day?* He steps into me and I back up until I hit the wall behind me. I've never seen Jace act like this. He has never cornered me like this and my body doesn't know what to do.

Is Jace safety or threat? A switch flips and my body chooses a response, an answer. One I can't handle. Ice shoots through my veins and my heart pounds in my ears. Short gasping breaths in through my nose are all that I can manage. My eyes can't blink; they just watch the twisted anger on my brother's face. When my arms start shaking, Jace steps back with his hand over his mouth, shaking his head. He reaches out a hand, but I flinch and his face falls. I can't reassure him. I can't do anything but stand there frozen and hope this passes soon. My eyes close, unable to watch the emotions trailing across Jace's face. Still anger, but mostly horror and shame. Tears trail down my cheeks and I don't know who they're for, me or Jace.

"Jax." My eyes shoot open and Lir is standing in front of me, his green eyes direct and honest. He reaches out a hand and I want to flinch away, save Jace this pain, but I can't. My body and my heart know Lir. To them he's safety and assurance. At some point he's filled the gaping hole left when my brother was taken and he can calm me. Gentle reassurance flows from him, quenching the fire and washing away the fear. When Lir's hand reaches my cheek, I lean into it and the choking gasp from Jace breaks my heart.

The panic fades and we start off again, Jace in front of me and Lir and Rym bringing up the rear. The whole exchange took no more than five minutes. Five minutes that have uprooted my life and everything I thought I knew. Five minutes that have destroyed Jace more than anything the E'rikon could have done to him and it's all my fault.

The silence, already uncomfortable before, is painful now, cutting into me like a knife and giving my brain free rein to replay Jace's horrified face over and over again. I reach out for him, but Jace pulls his hand away from me and angles his body away.

There's no going back from this. My chin falls to my chest in defeat. Lir's hand searches out mine and I grasp it like the lifeline it is. I'm selfish and I'm horrible, but I need that hand no matter how much it hurts Jace. I can't do this alone.

Twenty-nine

We end up in a large lobby area, a glass wall separating us from the street. Through the glass, it's clear that there is chaos outside. There's no fighting where I can see, but smoke or dust fills the air and another distant explosion rattles the glass and rumbles under our feet. Not distant enough.

"I need to find Trel and"—Rym presses his lips together and glances at me—"try to stop this."

Lir steps in front of him. "This is not your fault, cousin. There is no way we could have known."

Jace tilts his head to the side and looks back and forth between them with narrowed eyes. "What are—"

"So what now?" I ask.

"Now . . ." Lir's gaze goes from the window and back to me, a pained expression on his face. "You and your brother should wait here. There's—"

"Wait here?" Jace throws his arms up. "There are bombs going off out there. We need to get out of here."

Lir shakes his head. "This building will be safe. It's on the outskirts of the city and the humans have no reason to target it. No tactical value. It's only a research facility and—"

"Research? That's what you're calling it these days?" Jace steps forward and jams one finger into Lir's shoulder. "Back where I come from they call that torture, erk."

Lir whirls to face my brother, his posture vibrating with rage. "And where I come from we call the killing of helpless civilians murder. But you would know all about murder, wouldn't you?" Without taking his eyes from my brother, he points one finger toward the window. "I realize that you would not recognize our skyline, or rather, what is missing from it, but I do. The building that stands right there"—he jabs his finger against the glass—"is gone. My *family's* building. I pray for your sake they were not inside."

Jace snorts, but he won't meet Lir's eyes and his voice is strained. "Why? What are you going to do?"

Rym takes a small step backward.

Lir's eyes slide closed and he takes a deep breath, letting it out slowly. When he opens them again, nothing but coldness lingers in his gaze. The heat of his anger rolls through the link to me in contradiction with the icy stoicism he wears on his face. "What I must." He turns briskly. "Rym. Let's go."

"Lir." I step forward.

With a curt shake of his head, he steps out of my reach. "I cannot do this right now." His shoulders droop. "Please. You need to stay here, stay safe. I can't worry about you *and* them."

His face blurs behind the moisture building in my eyes. A single tear falls and tracks down my cheek. After a moment's hesitation, Lir moves forward, wipes it away with one finger, and then cups my cheek with his hand. "I will keep you safe however I can." He leans forward and gently presses his lips to mine.

I don't want gentle. I use both hands to pull him closer, pressing my lips so hard to his that it's almost painful. His mouth tilts and opens and I slide my tongue past his lips with a whimper. He groans and moves his other hand up until he has one on either side of my face. There's so much I need to say, but there's no time to say it. *I'm sorry. I need you. Thank you. Please don't leave me.*

I love you.

The hitch in his breath is the only clue I have that something changes in that moment. I open my eyes at the sound, my lips still pressed against his, and he looks back at me in surprise. The emerald-green orbs of his eyes glow with something I can't name. It's only there for a moment before he closes his eyes again and pulls away from me.

"Jax . . . ."

I don't want to hear this, so I cut him off. "It's okay. Go. We can talk later."

I fall back against the wall with a huff and watch him walk out the doors. Lir and Rym disappear around a corner in the distance and I close my eyes and take a deep breath, sliding down the wall until I'm sitting. I may never see him again.

Jace speaks up beside me. "Jax . . ."

"Just don't. I know what you're going to say and I will not defend him to you." I send a glare his way. "I shouldn't need to."

"You're right." He sighs. "But I can't help that my gut reaction is not to trust any of them."

"You don't have to, just trust me."

His hand moves across the floor and he twines his fingers with mine. "I do . . ." The next words come out in a whisper and his voice breaks. "I never thought I'd see you again. It kills me that I wasn't there to protect you."

"You've been the strong one for a while. It's my turn now."

Jace smiles at me and squeezes my hand. "Thanks, sis."

Then the world explodes around us.

The walls don't just rattle, they crack and shatter. Chunks of debris rain down from above and I'm thrown backward with the force of the explosion, skidding to a stop twenty feet away with a burning pain in my side, a five-inch shard of glass sticking out just below my ribs.

Coughing, I fumble at the glass, my fingertip fumbling for a grip against the blood that coats it. The feel of the skin parting registers before the pain as my right palm splits against the edge. I pull my hand back with a hiss, the blood welling around the cut and trailing down my wrist. The cut isn't too deep—my fingers still bend and I've got feeling in it, so no nerves or tendons were severed. Raising my hand above my head, I rip at the gown with my other hand, yanking on a torn edge until a swath of cloth pulls away. I wrap my palm as tightly as I can, then grit my teeth and use the padding my bandage provides to grab the glass and pull it out, a pained gasp erupting from my mouth.

My back hits the wall and I lean back and catalog the rest of my body. Sore and obviously bruised, but not critically injured. At least, I don't think so. I blink the dust out of my burning eyes and take in the room around me.

The ceiling has collapsed at least most of the way, and I've been forced to the back of the room, almost into the hallway. There will be no going out the front doors. They aren't even visible over the pile of debris in front of me. Thank goodness it appears the facility is mostly underground—a few more stories on top of me and I wouldn't be here.

But where the hell is Jace? I scan the room frantically before a groan calls my attention to a pile of rubble to my left. Jace lies there, one leg trapped under a large chunk of the collapsed ceiling. I run to him and fall to my knees next to him, ignoring the sharp agony that travels from my side and the blood soaking my gown. "Jace."

"It's okay, Jax," he says. He pats my arm. "You've got to go. Get out of here."

"No, I'm not leaving you." This building was supposed to be *safe*!

I grasp Jace's arms and pull, my feet scrabbling on the tile for purchase. He doesn't budge—even worse, he lets out an awful scream and his eyes roll back in his head. One foot slides out from under me and my butt slams to the ground. My brother's head ends up half in my lap and my other leg is twisted behind me.

Each breath brings another stinging pain up from my ribs and into my arm. More blood, too. The stupid gown is soaked on one side and it doesn't really show any sign of slowing. I need to stop the bleeding. It won't do anyone any good if I pass out, too. I'm alone and injured. Jace is hurt. The walls close in on me and my breaths come faster. Panic claws at my chest and I scramble up to my feet.

I wedge my fingers under the biggest piece of concrete holding Jace down and pull until my arms scream. One hand slips and I lose my grip, going back down to the floor. Up. Pull. Slip. Fall. Again. And again.

Tears blur my vision. The bandage on my palm is nearly shredded, the blood from the wound staining the rock holding my brother down. My fingers will barely curl around the rough-edged rubble anymore, scraped and bloody as they are, one fingernail ripped off. I haven't come this far just to lose him. I refuse to let this happen.

The floor beneath my feet shakes and I slam back down to the ground. My side is on fire and black spots swim through my vision. Too much blood, but I can't stop. *Get up! Try again!* I screech at myself until I stand up again on wobbly legs.

Did it move that time?

A panting whimper escapes my mouth as I rage against that rock. If it's moved, I can't tell. The room spins when I stand again and I don't even have time to batter my poor fingers again. It's just straight back down for me. My butt crashes against the floor. Scooting closer to Jace, I pull my knees into my chest and rest my head between them to let the dizziness pass.

I've lost a lot of blood and who knows the extent of Jace's injuries. Just look at us, the only hope for the survival of the E'rikon and human races. If what Lir said is true, Jace and I are somehow meant to unite them. And we're going to die in the crossfire between them without anyone the wiser. How stupidly ironic.

The sound of a rock skittering across the floor and a flash of movement to my left bring my head up. An instant, fiery anger licks at my blood when the white-coated form slinks around the corner with his hands up.

Not one I know, at least not one I remember, but he might have been one of Jace's tormentors. He won't be hurting my brother any more.

My lips pull back from my teeth in a snarl and I'm on my feet, a blend of hysteria and hot rage powering my movements. Quick, smooth, and purposeful, I grasp a shard of glass on my way up. Unbalanced and awkward, it won't make a good throwing weapon, but it's all I have.

He—no, this one with the white coat is an it—*it* moves one small step forward, a simple sliding of its feet moving it within feet of me. Slowly, cautiously, it takes another step.

"Stay back!" The makeshift bandage provides me with a perfect handle as I grip the shard in my fist.

Hands go up. Yellow eyes with a starburst of red in the center never leave my own. Something—*this* thing pushes against the link, gently but persistently.

A hiss from me. My other hand curls into a fist and I position myself between Jace and it, legs spread, knees slightly bent.

"I will not harm you." Of course not, it will be dead before it has a chance to do so. Another step.

I narrow my eyes. It's taller than me. Go for the throat? Quick and easy, won't require as much strength, but it will be expecting that. The leg, femoral artery. One good slice and it will be down. Hopefully before it can do me any damage.

"I am unarmed."

Good. A creeping, twisted smile pulls at my lips. Easier to dispatch.

"My name is Jastren Reva."

Does it think I care? I knew the names of the men at the cabin. I knew Zach's name. Didn't change the outcome. I crouch lower, shielding Jace from its view.

"He is injured. Let me help you." Another step. My eyes track every movement. "Let me link with you."

I snort. "Doesn't work. They've tried. By the looks of that coat, you should know that."

"But"—he sighs and lowers his hands—"familial links are different."

Familial? As in . . . He said his name was Reva. Cocking my head to the side and straightening, I study the alien in front of me. He's obviously on the older side of their age spectrum. There's no gray in his bright red hair, but there are subtle lines on his face and just something in his eyes . . . a tiredness? "Who are you?"

"My bondmate was part of one of the first teams to arrive. She was pregnant . . ." He takes in the details of my face as if he's looking for something or someone, a sad and almost defeated look on his face. "Our daughter was born here on Earth soon after my bondmate arrived. Following our traditions, she was named for her father's line, my line . . . Jaslyn."

The name—my mother's name—sends me back a step and my eyes widen. Jastren moves closer and my hand brings the glass shard up higher.

"Stay back." The command is softer this time.

"There is not much time. You need to get out of here. We—"

"How did you find us?" I step closer, brandishing the glass in front of me. "You're dressed like them . . . the ones that locked us up. The ones that . . . studied us. Why should I trust you?"

"Right now you have no other choice. I imagine at this point I am just as much of a target as you are, and I know another way out."

"Target? Why would you be a target?"

"Although I had nothing to do with what happened to you and your brother, I know too much. The same reason young Steliro was meant to be here when that bomb hit."

"But how would the humans even know—"

Jastren shakes his head. "Do you really think this was the humans' doing? This is an unmarked building well away from any potential targets, but that last one was almost on the doorstep. Vitrad is making his move and your arrival gave him the perfect scapegoat. Wipe out the Vestras and who would be left? Who would the people turn to for direction? Who will fuel the flames of their anger and incite this war with a few well-picked targets?"

"But why?"

"That is a story for another time, and right now we need to get you and your brother out of the city." He hesitates for a moment and then strides forward, glancing from my face to my hand.

Oh. I'm still clutching my improvised weapon. He's the only help I have, so I'm going to have to trust him. I lower my hand slowly. "How are we going to get Jace out?"

He doesn't answer, merely sifts through the rubble until he finds a long metal rod and then slides it underneath the concrete. Pushing down on one end of the lever, his face reddens and there's a small shift in the rock, enough that I'm able to slide Jace out from underneath.

After I pat his cheek a few times, Jace's eyes flutter open and focus on my face. He struggles to stand, but his leg is twisted in a direction it's not meant to go and his face goes pale before he can reach his feet. Leaning down, I pull him up and throw his arm over my shoulder. I'm not strong enough to hold him up, though, so Jastren steps up.

Jace furrows his brow and looks at me. "You sure seem adept at finding alien admirers. Although this one's a little old."

I chuckle and Jastren tries to conceal a smile. "Yeah, say hi to Grandpa."

Thirty

I scavenge for a change of clothes and a pair of boots as we navigate our way out of the building. There is only so much blood-covered fabric I can take, and the gown keeps sticking to my side one moment and ripping away the next. Not the most comfortable feeling in the world, plus it keeps the wound from clotting. Thankfully, I'm able to scrounge up one of those snazzy gray uniforms that everyone seems to wear around here and a pair of boots somewhat close to my size.

There's more to my change in wardrobe than temporary comfort, but not something that I'm willing to share with the guys yet. Jace will not approve and I'm not entirely sure what Jastren will say.

Once we stumble our way through a maze of back hallways and are outside, I can see the edge of the forest from where I stand. So close. Everything in me just wants to jog into the trees, leave all this behind, and go hide somewhere familiar and safe, but I can't leave without Lir.

And that's what is going to make for a very uncomfortable conversation with Jace right now.

"That outbuilding over there looks like it might be a good stopping place." I point to a small shed right inside the shimmering barrier that surrounds the city.

"Stopping place?" Jace leans forward from beside Jastren. "Why would we be stopping?"

Deep breath. "I'm going back for him."

"For . . ."

"For Lir."

I expect Jace's protest, but not Jastren's. "Steliro Vestra is not to be trusted. I do not know what your experience has been with him, but he is Vitrad's."

"Yeah, Vitrad's nephew. Why shouldn't I trust him? I thought you said he was a target, too."

"He is, but should he have survived that bombing, I am positive Vitrad will find another use for him. He—"

"Wait a second here," Jace breaks in. "This Lir guy is one of the Vestras and he's related to the Vitrad guy? The one that started all this? The one that wants to kill us all? Hell, no, Jax. You aren't going anywhere. It's bad enough you broke him out of lockup. You don't owe that guy anything."

"You don't understand."

"Damn right I don't. We're together. We're alive and mostly whole. Why would you want to risk yourself on a rescue mission for some alien that probably doesn't even need to be rescued?"

I stop walking and curl my fingers into my palms, digging in to prevent my temper from exploding. "You don't even know him."

"Yeah, but *he* does." He jerks his thumb at Jastren. "And even he thinks it's a bad idea."

"And you trust him, just like that? What happened to your whole 'aliens are the devil' spiel?"

They've pulled a few feet ahead of me and Jace finally stops to face me. "Verifying the family connection is pretty simple stuff. I checked him out as soon as he came over to help."

Pretty simple stuff? Maybe for him. Is it worse that Jace kept things from me or that he's so dismissive about my feelings and abilities? If he hadn't kept me in the dark for so long, none of this would be necessary. I clench my teeth and try to rein in my growing irritation.

"Fine, then. Go hang out with Gramps. I'll be back." I spin around and take off running. Jace calls out my name and the wound in my side screams, but I ignore both. I refuse to let them see me falter. Before I round the corner of the first building, I call back over my shoulder, "Why don't you get in touch with Flint while I'm gone? You know, arrange a ride or something. Should be pretty simple stuff for you, right?"

I don't wait for an answer.

§

The streets are deserted. Great news for me, but also a little disconcerting. Where is everyone? They're under attack, or at least they're supposed to think they are, so where are they?

My steps have slowed to a jog and each empty block I traverse just increases my desire to turn around. Each time my chest expands, my indecision increases. What am I thinking? I'm putting myself and my brother in more unnecessary danger for a guy I'm not entirely sure about. I'm basing everything on Rym's assertion that Lir didn't know, that Lir was a victim of Vitrad's manipulations, but what if he was lying? And even if he told me the truth, what was Lir doing out in the clearing that day? Jastren, Jace, and Vitrad planted the seeds of doubt and now the questions slink into my brain, taking root in my suspicion and confusion.

I round a corner and I've just made the decision to turn back when I nearly run into a blue-haired E'rikon standing at the edge of a large crowd that's gathered in front of a smoking pile of rubble. Stopping just in time, I avoid a collision and back up until I'm huddled in a recessed doorway, hopefully far enough away that I won't be seen. Not that anyone appears to be looking at anything other than the oversized hologram ahead, showing the elevated platform that holds a perfectly poised Trel beside another gorgeous E'rikon teen, a coldly smiling Vitrad, an ash-covered Lir, and three other bedraggled E'rikon.

Lir's face is carefully blank, but even at this distance I can feel the sorrow rolling off him. Shoulders pulled back and ramrod straight, only the tension in his jaw gives any hint of the anguish simmering under his features.

The platform is blocks away and a sea of bodies rests between me and it. Even if I made it up there, how would I get to Lir? This was a stupid idea. It's not like Lir couldn't find his own way out of the city and to me—if he wanted to—and I'm just asking to be caught by standing here. I risked everything to get Jace back and being here is just putting me in unnecessary danger. I'm turning to go when Vitrad's voice booms out over the crowd, freezing me in place.

"We have lost too many today. This is all that remains of our great Council." He gestures toward the three. "My dear daughter narrowly escaped with her life and that of her friend." Lir moves jerkily to put one arm around the friend's shoulders, pulling her close against him. "My son is still unaccounted for, and my nephew has lost his parents, my sister, our steadfast leaders . . ." Vitrad bows his head and shakes it sadly for a moment before raising his eyes slowly and sending a glare directly at the crowd. His next words are edged with a fervor that could easily be mistaken for anger, but that I recognize as triumph. "This will not stand.

"Now is the time to act," he continues. "We cannot stand idly aside anymore and we must adapt to these new and tragic circumstances. Steliro has declined to step into his father's place and has instead chosen to stand behind me as I unite our Council and our military into one unit for the betterment of our race . . ."

The rest of Vitrad's words fade into the background and all I can do is stare at Lir's face in horror. Standing behind him, supporting him, the man who locked me up, who locked him up, who . . . wants to kill us all? My hand flies up to cover my mouth and contain the wail that threatens to break free. The cold sense of betrayal seeps into my limbs, infiltrating my body until I almost shiver from it.

I take three slow, robotic steps back, shaking my head and fighting against tears. *This isn't happening. This can't be right.* My denial rings false even to me. Jastren was right. Lir *is* Vitrad's, his gofer, his follower, his lackey. And I am a fool.

I steel my nerves and feed the spark of anger brewing in my stomach until it's a raging inferno pushing away any more denials and overshadowing the icy betrayal twisting through me. My narrowed eyes go back to the holo, focusing on his face, willing him to look at me, to face me. And he does.

A barely perceptible widening of the eyes, the clenching of his teeth and one hand curling into a white-knuckled fist are the only outward signs of emotion from him. But the other emotions, the ones he can't—or won't—show, flow through the link and nearly knock me over. Anguish. Indecision. Regret. The eyes that meet mine are swirling green pain shot through with golden lightning. He opens his mouth, but quickly closes it again, pressing his lips together as if to hold the words inside. His eyes close and two words make their way into my head. *I'm sorry.*

It doesn't hurt when the bond snaps, when Lir breaks it, but I feel it all the same. A loss, like something I didn't even notice before is missing. Quick and painless, but it leaves me reeling backward with my arms wrapped tightly around my stomach to anchor me, to hold myself together in the face of this new fracture in my already broken world.

"Jax, it's not—" A hand lands on my back and sits for only a second before I whip away and whirl around to find Rym behind me. "Look—"

He has nothing that I want to hear. A mixture of loss and rage, that molten lava kind that's been simmering since they tortured me, bubbles up and . . . out. It overflows and heads straight at the golden-haired alien in front of me in a concentrated stream, smashing into him and bringing him to his knees with his hands pressed to his head and a silent scream on his face. There's no wound, not a single mark on him, but it's no less a weapon than a knife and infinitely worse. A cold, cruel part of me smiles at his pain, but then a single thought pulls me back and sends me sprinting away as Rym crumples to the ground, unconscious, with green blood leaking from his nose.

Is that what I looked like when they put the kiun *on me?*

My heart pounds along with my feet, each step taking me farther and farther away from the crowd, the holo, Lir, and Rym's very still body lying on asphalt. Tears drip down my cheeks and put a hazy film over the world in front of me. I don't even bother to wipe them away, just let them drip off my chin and hit the ground beneath me.

I keep expecting to hear the sound of boots behind me, chasing me, just itching to drag me back into that underground facility and run more experiments. I'm sure my newfound skill would be of interest to Vitrad. Is it something they all can do, the focused mental gutting? No, it can't be. If it were, they would have used it on me.

Now that I've used it, my anger feels like a living thing rattling at the cage of my body and anxious to get out. Its cry is convincing. *Let me out. You will find peace with me. Just like before.* It would be so easy to go back and just lay waste to their entire population, and some enraged, primal part of me practically salivates at the thought. The E'rikon have no clue that they created a monster, one that hates the darkness but also craves the serenity that would come with its embrace.

No! I refuse to be a weapon of destruction. I already know what it feels like to kill and I will not give in to it. I will find another way.

I stop, close my eyes, and just breathe. *In. Out. In. Out.* Each breath brings in a cooling calm that spreads through my body until I'm left sweaty and depleted, standing in the middle of the street. But at least I feel like myself again.

In my frantic dash, I've managed to stay mostly on track. After a short backtrack and a series of turns, I'm back to the research facility. Not much farther and I can spend the rest of my life just being thankful that I managed to get my brother back. He's really all I need, anyway. Just a little farther.

I've slowed to a walk and the wound in my side is back to making its presence known with every step. My legs wobble and spots form in my vision. Is my nose bleeding? A quick swipe below my left nostril confirms that is the case. *What?*

Then a solid rock of exhaustion slams into me. The world shifts around me and I crash to my knees on the asphalt, dizzy and shaken. My new weapon has a price that is just now catching up with me. Something titters in the back of my mind . . . *If you'd just given in, it wouldn't be like this.*

Blackness presses in around the edges of my vision, but I push it away and reach for my brother, finding the thread of our connection easily.

Jace? I think I'm going to need some help.

What's going on? Where are you? Are you okay? The frantic pulse of his words hammers against the pain in my head.

Not far. The research facility. Did you reach Flint?

Yeah, I'm sitting in the back of his truck right now.

And Jastren?

Up front. Says he's coming with us.

Send someone for me?

Are you okay? What's going on? Jax?

I release the connection and settle back onto the ground. They'll figure it out. I'm certainly not walking out of here.

Watching for animals in the clouds, I let my mind drift. There's so much that needs to be done. Exploring my abilities. Returning to Bridgelake to keep my promise to Emily. Preparing for a war I want no part of, in which there's a piece of me on either side and against *people* that shouldn't be my enemy. So very much to do.

My head lolls from side to side and I find myself tracking the flight of a large bird. I whistle, a simple call my father taught me, and reach my hand up. Surprisingly, the bird changes its course to head toward me, flying lower and lower . . . until a face blocks my view.

For a moment, with the sun behind him, his hair looks golden with bits of green and my traitor heart tries to leap, but my eyes adjust and show me blond hair instead, with bits of leaves scattered through it. Blue eyes, like the sky without clouds peer down at me.

"You're in deep trouble, aren't you? Me too, actually." I pat his cheek and giggle. "Did Jace give you the 'I can't believe you didn't listen to me' glare? Don't worry, I'm sure you boys will kiss and make up." I laugh, a ragged sound that evolves into a sob and then I'm crying again while Flint gathers me into his arms and picks me up off the ground.

He doesn't say anything, just plods along the street carrying me with my head resting on his shoulder. Not an unpleasant way to travel, certainly better than walking.

"I'm sorry," I whisper.

He pauses and tilts his head to the side so he can see my face. "For what? You didn't do anything wrong, Jax."

"I've done a lot of wrong . . ." My voice trails off and I shake my head softly, tallying up my wrongs. Jace's pain when I turned away from him. The blood leaking from Rym's nose. The thunk of a knife into Zach's neck. Me, battered, bruised, and bloody, knife in hand and two slit throats before me. "A lot."

His steps start up again, steady and even. "Nonsense. Anything you think you've done wrong can't possibly overshadow what you've done for Jace today."

I don't respond and we walk in silence. When the barrier is in view, I feel a tug at my mind. Not Jace—someone else, tugging gently on a broken green string.

No words come through and even the emotions are faint, but it's just enough that I know Lir is trying to get my attention. I squeeze my eyes shut, close the connection, and bury my face in Flint's chest. "Walk faster," I say.

Once we cross the barrier, I don't have to try so hard to shut out the intruder.

Flint places me in the back of the truck and I scoot up until I'm beside the cab. My brother looks at me with a combination of relief and exasperation and pulls me into a hug, then lies down with his head in my lap. I absently stroke his hair and stare into the distance, letting the warmth of our connection blot out everything else . . . for now.

The rumble of the truck starting jostles me. I watch the receding city until it's out of sight. The entire time Lir flutters around in my head, his attempts at contact getting weaker and weaker until they cease completely. Something squeezes my hand and I look down to find Jace's eyes studying me.

"It's going to be okay," he says.

But I know it's not. I don't know if anything is ever going to be okay again.

Epilogue

"Try again," says Jastren.

Closing my eyes with a huff, I try to focus on linking with him. Still no luck. Though my connection with Jace is as strong as ever, no matter what I do, I can't connect with Jastren. Or anyone else, for that matter. I've even attempted to follow Jace's connection to Flint, with no success.

"Concentrate on hearing my broadcast and—"

"Visualize the words and follow them through the link." I grit my teeth. "I know how to do it. I just can't. Repeating yourself isn't helping, Gramps." In fact, I wish he'd just shut up about the whole thing, but apparently he's not going to give it a rest.

"Jasmine . . ."

I roll my eyes. "It's Jax. Just because there's some alien tradition about names doesn't mean I'm changing mine." I shoot up and head toward the door. "This is a waste of time. I'm going to get some air."

Jace's voice calls out from one of the back bedrooms. "Why don't you split some more wood while you're out there? It's getting chilly in here."

"You're not helpless. Hobble on over and do it yourself," I yell back.

There's a thump and I hear the sound of Jace's crutches carrying him across the floor until he pokes his head out of the doorway. "Ha-ha, sis. You want me to break the other leg?"

"It would save me the trouble of breaking it for you," Flint says from the living room. "You don't make for a very agreeable patient . . ."

"Aw, come on, you're supposed to be on my side." Jace makes his way across the room and plops down on the couch beside Flint. Leaning backward over Flint's lap with his face up, he bats his eyelashes and sticks his lower lip out. "You know you love me."

Flint stares into his eyes for a moment with a soft smile. "I guess so," he says with an exaggerated sigh.

Jace grins and winks. "I knew it." He leans up and presses a kiss to Flint's cheek.

Flint blushes and rolls his eyes. "But if you ever do something so stupid as to get yourself abducted by aliens again, I'm gonna have to rethink that."

"You could always just send my sister in after me again." Jace straightens and sits back into the couch.

And here it comes . . . they've been needling at each other since we got here.

"What did you expect me to do? Sit there? Do nothing?" Flint tosses his hands in the air. "It's not like I forced her to go. I tried to stop her. She would have gone anyway. Isn't that right, Jax?"

I put my hands up and take a step back. "I'm not in this, guys. This is between you two."

Jace narrows his eyes and jerks his thumb at Flint. "*He* was supposed to protect you. Not let you wander off with some damn erk." A glance at Jastren. "Sorry, Grandfather."

"Well, how was I to know who he was? It's not like I had any long conversations with the . . . guy." Flint turns until he's facing my brother. "*You* shouldn't have—"

"Just stop it!" My yell brings both of their faces to me. "You're both safe. You're together. Why can't you just be grateful for that? I'm just so sick . . . Why don't you . . . ugh!" I throw my hands up and stomp out of the cabin. The crisp air clears my head and I head over to the woodpile. Splitting firewood actually sounds like a good way to blow off some steam.

Being back at Peter's cabin is hard. Being back here with the two bickering lovebirds and my disappointed grandfather is torture. Of all the people here, Peter's the only one who doesn't want anything from me. He doesn't ask me a bunch of questions. He isn't worried about the link. And he doesn't push me when I just want to be left alone. Peter's more than happy to chatter away at me and doesn't care much whether I respond or not, and I've found that I actually enjoy his company, more than anyone else's here. Even still, I've never felt more alone.

I'm happy for my brother, I really am. And Flint, too. Jastren . . . I guess he's family and he's been kind of helpful, at least for Jace, who can actually link with him. I just wish . . .

I squeeze my eyes shut to block out the thought and the burn of tears. *Nothing. I wish for nothing.*

So far we've learned from Jastren that some of our abilities are normal for the E'rikon—the telepathy, the emotional connection. Some are very rare, like the sharing of energy. And there is one that is solely our own—the manipulation of others' emotions. While the *dhama* will allow E'rikon to feel others' emotions, they can't push emotions at each other like Jace and—apparently—I can.

Good news—that means Lir never manipulated my emotions. Bad news—I almost wish he had. I may have picked up on his emotions and they may have had some sort of calming effect on me, especially once the bond was formed, but he couldn't have *made* me fall in love with him, couldn't have forced the bond to use it against me. So he didn't lie about that . . . just nearly everything else, according to Jastren. The thought that I managed to fall for Lir on my own eats at me. I never should have trusted him. How could I have been so blind?

It doesn't matter. He means nothing to me now.

No one knows about what I did to Rym—well, except Rym. If he survived. I don't know that that's the weapon Vitrad had in mind or if there's some other horrifying ability even farther down in the blackness from which I've now drawn twice. Either way, Jace and Jastren seem a little too excited to find a way to weaponize us, and I'm not entirely sure that's a good idea.

I came back from the blackness the first time with the help of my brother. Empathy brought me back the second time—just barely. What's left that could bring me back a third time? For that matter, what's to stop my brother from falling into that dark hatred himself if he were to unlock the ability?

I will never tell them.

Now that I know about the emotional control Jace has over me, I'm able to block it out. He wasn't too thrilled about that, but I told him I had to learn to control my own emotions. I can't afford to be dependent on someone else for my own sanity. Besides, I've had a little practice now, and each day it gets a little easier.

But it's been a slow process. When we first got back to Peter's cabin, Daniel was still here. He stepped a bit too close to me and I attacked. I nearly killed him before Flint managed to pull me off of him. Daniel and the other two soldiers left soon after that, heading to Bridgelake to report in to Dane. I suppose we'll eventually make it back there, too, but with Jace's leg broken and winter approaching, we probably won't be able to leave until spring.

Or until Vitrad wises up and starts looking for us.

After I've got a nice stack of firewood split, I drop the maul and sit on the ground with my back against the woodshed. It's early for it, but in the past couple days, the temperature has dropped rapidly, and with the sky as white as it is, I wouldn't be surprised if it snowed soon. Just what I need—another excuse for Jastren to keep me cooped up in the cabin trying to get the link to work.

I run a hand over my face and sigh. Might as well get a long walk in while I still can. As I reach the edge of the woods, Peter pokes his head out the front door.

"Just the person I was looking for. I see you're headed off on a walk. Would you mind horribly if I came along with you? I've just been in the house much too long and some air would be good for this old man. I'd invite the others, but I can't imagine Jace could get around on those crutches out here very well. And young Flint just won't leave his side. Reminds me a bit of your young man—" Peter actually manages to stop one of his own rambles. He swallows and gives me a weak smile. "So, do you mind some company?"

"It's fine," I say.

Leaves crunch under our feet as we make our way through the trees. Peter's quiet, whether it's because he feels guilty for slipping up earlier or he has picked up on the fact that I need the silence of the forest right now, I don't know. Either way, I'm thankful for it.

Twenty minutes later we reach a small clearing and stop to rest against a tree. The pause gives him an opening to start speaking.

"I think it is time we talked, my dear. I may not have had a congregation in a very long time, but I still know the look of someone who has lost their way and perhaps could use an ear to listen." He pauses and takes a deep breath in through his nose. "There is nothing you can say that will make me think any less of you. I am not here to judge you."

Jastren just wants my link to work. Jace is only worried about saying *I told you so*. Flint is too wrapped up in my brother to really care one way or the other. Not one of them has even bothered to ask me how I'm feeling, how I'm handling everything, and even though I don't really *want* to talk about him, not a single one of them has asked about Lir. But wanting to and needing to are very different things. I've kept it all locked carefully inside, a concrete rock holding back my pain, my guilt, and my loss. The simple splash of kindness and concern in Peter's eyes smashes that rock.

My eyes burn and a tear makes its way down my cheek. A sob catches in my throat, almost choking me, before escaping from my mouth in a low wail.

Peter's shoulder is a soggy mess and my eyes are red and puffy before I finally get done telling him everything. And I mean *everything*, even what I did to Rym. When I finally pull back and wipe my eyes with the edge of my shirt, he smiles softly and places his hands on my shoulders.

"You don't need to feel guilty for mourning your loss. Even though you believe Lir betrayed you, that does not negate your own feelings for him. Don't think that having those feelings makes you any less." He gives my shoulders a light squeeze. "And as for what happened to the other young man, do not hold on to guilt for that, either. From the way you've described it, you may have given in to the darkness at first, but you pushed it away. The first step to making peace with it is forgiving yourself." He clears his throat and lowers his voice. "And what happened to you before, with the men at your cabin. That was not your fault. Do not let it break you."

"Thank you," I whisper.

Peter pulls me into a tight hug. I don't flinch. I don't count my breaths. And my pulse stays steady. It wasn't just Lir's influence, then. I really am learning to overcome my fear on my own.

After a quick good-bye, I stay by the tree while Peter disappears back toward the cabin.

Eyes to the sky, I rub my mother's pendant between my fingers and watch the storm clouds roll in. A low screech to my right pulls my attention to the underbrush. It's a Harris's hawk and one of his feet is tangled in the vines. By the whitish streaking on his chest and on the undersides of his wings, I can tell he's a young one, likely less than a year old.

Drawing closer, I whisper to him, "Hey, pretty bird. Let me help you."

He does that jerky, rotating head tilt characteristic of birds and studies me as I approach. Surprisingly, he doesn't react when I reach my hand out toward his foot and slowly disentangle him. I lean back until I'm squatting almost right next to him. He still doesn't move.

"Well, go on then. You're free."

He just stands there, moving his head from side to side, never taking his deep brown eyes from my face. He hops forward and angles his wings out a bit, enough for me to see that one of them is damaged. Poor thing probably banged it against the ground or something trying to get free of the vines.

I eye the clouds above. I can't just leave him here. If he can't fly, he won't be able to seek shelter from the storm. Removing my jacket, I wrap it around my arm and hold it out to him. I let out a shrill two-beat whistle and he hops onto my extended arm. It's strange that he'd take to me so easily, but maybe he belongs to someone and he's just lost. He has to have had training of some sort.

I rise carefully until I'm standing with my arm bent out in front of me. The hawk shifts from foot to foot, but continues to stare at me. I reach out with my other hand and stroke the top of his head with one finger. He doesn't pull away.

I smile and run my finger over his feathers again. Looks like I've made a new friend.

And with what's coming, the interspecies war that's brewing, the promises I have to keep, the secrets that I have to hide . . . and a fractured heart that has to mend . . . I'll need all the friends I can get.

Acknowledgments

I think this is the toughest part of the book to write (and now I have to do it again!). There are so many people who have helped me and inspired me along the way and I don't want to leave a single one of them out.

Writing has been a lifelong dream of mine, so this book is the culmination of a lot of hard work and determination. I couldn't have done it without the early support of my family. From buying me the massive number of books I read when I was a kid to reading my young (and admittedly poor) attempts at crafting novels, my parents and the rest of my extended family have always encouraged me to follow this dream.

So I had the desire, but not the confidence or the motivation, and for many years I wrote nothing. Not. One. Single. Word. And then two seemingly random things happened that sparked my creativity again. One was that I discovered NaNoWriMo, the fifty-thousand-words-in-thirty-days challenge. It doesn't matter if those words are utter nonsense, just that they get written. The second thing was a question my pastor posed in one of his sermons: "What have you done with your God-given creative talent today?" My answer at the time was, "Nothing," and I didn't like it, so I picked up my laptop and started typing. That was almost two years ago.

I started out my writing journey simply with the idea that I wanted to put my book out there and hopefully some people (beyond my friends and family) would find it and enjoy it. I never expected the response I've gotten from you readers and I am extremely grateful for every single one of you. So thank you from the bottom of my heart to all of you that read, reviewed, shared, tweeted, and/or talked about *Broken Skies*. Without your support I never would have made it this far.

With the growing number of indie authors, I had plenty of inspiration and I'd especially like to thank those who took time out of their busy schedules to answer questions, cheer me on, or sometimes just chat: Elle Casey, Rachel Higginson, and Jason Brant.

I haven't been alone in this journey to publication, either. I had support, companionship, and sanity-saving late-night discussions about geography, book boyfriends, spoilers, TV shows, and everything else under the sun thanks to my writing group, the Rebel Writers. Elizabeth: This book is dedicated to you for a reason. Without you, I would have thrown it out the window long before it ever saw completion. Regan: TRW started with you and your enthusiasm. I just love you to pieces. Stormy: Oh, goodness, where to start, besides to say that you amaze me. Not only do you manage to juggle work and school and writing, you find time in between all that to be so awesomely supportive of everyone else. Caylie: My Netflix buddy and fellow Marshmallow, even though we're not always on the same team, we make a great one. Kat: From the moment I walked up to you at the MMH, I knew we'd get along so very well. From line dancing to stalking cover models, I can't wait to meet up with you again. Deanna: You're a quiet one, but that makes you no less essential to the group. I loved having the chance to meet you in person and can't wait to do so again. Briggs: The best unicorn I know. I'm looking forward to your first release. Jocelyn: Another quiet one and such a sweet, positive woman who uplifts everyone she comes across.

This story also wouldn't be what it is without my wonderful beta readers, Susannah, Kirsten, and superfan Lenore (you said you'd be my first fangirl, and you so are!).

Thanks also goes out to all the Reckless Rebels who took the time to read and review for me, as well as all the bloggers who helped spread the word: Becca, Ren, Paula, Shannon and Kelly, Brianna, Mikky, Barbara, Michelle, Amanda, Brenda, Aret, Sue, Kathryn, Emma, Bobbi Jo, Christy . . . Goodness, there are so many of you wonderful people! I know I'm leaving people out (sorry!), but just know that you guys have been essential to me in helping to get *Broken Skies* out there.

Another thanks to Margaret Rainforth for editing the indie version of this novel.

And since I can make pictures with words but otherwise have no visual creativity, thank you to Nicole Spence of Cover Shot Creations for taking my random ideas and my blurb and making me the perfect cover.

Last, but not least, thank you again to my family and also to my friends. And even though he'll probably never read this (I love you anyway, honey!), thank you to my husband, Chris, for letting me lock myself away with my laptop and my music and keeping the kids from burning the house down while I was doing it.

About the Author

Theresa Kay's love for writing manifested in her youth, when she found joy in working on middle school research papers that her fellow students considered pure drudgery. In addition to the novel *Broken Skies*, she is the author of the Bright Beyond novella series, as well as its short story prequel, *Dark Expanse*. A paralegal by day and a devoted member of the Rebel Writers critique group, she currently lives in central Virginia with her husband and two children.